More Than a Fantasy
A Fortuna, Texas Novel

Book 3

Rochelle Bradley

DEDICATION

For law enforcement officers everywhere: your service,
sacrifice, and dedication to your communities, small town
and big cities alike, are appreciated. Stay safe!

ACKNOWLEDGMENTS

For my writing group who keep me company throughout NaNoWriMo and the rest of the year: Thank you. Your energy charges and inspires me. Keep writing!

To author CJ Baty: Thank you for being my friend and putting up with my endless questions. Your encouragement helped push me through a dark time.

To my beta reader and friend Dawn: thank you for investing your time and finding things my tired brain has missed. Your peppy comments made it fun to edit.

CHAPTER 1

Kelly

SEX. IT HAD BEEN ON her mind way too much lately, as evidenced by the screams of her passengers, the one-finger salute of the passing sedan, and the flashing blue and red lights in the rearview mirror.

"Holy crap, Kelly!" Piper Dart yelled from the backseat. "You could've killed us." Then she laughed.

Kelly Jo Greene swallowed the bile in her throat, signaled, and turned into the parking lot of the Wertz grocery. She hated that feeling of seeing police lights behind her. She pulled into an end row as far from the store as possible and shifted into park. Pressing back into her seat, she closed her eyes, hoping no one she knew would drive by. She drew in a deep breath.

"Uh oh," Jessie Barnes said.

Kelly's lids popped open in time to see her parents' wide-eyed, nosy neighbor Rose Bush driving past and slip into a handicap parking slot. Kelly grimaced. Her mother would know as soon as Ms. Bush got to a phone. Ugh. She'd get a lecture from her father about insurance costs. She groaned and Jessie patted her arm.

Sometimes living in a small town sucked. Nobody could get away with anything. Most times, it was a good thing, but she was a twenty-seven-year-old woman and a full-time teacher, and she could take care of herself. A smile flitted across her lips but fell off again when she looked at the rearview mirror.

The officer in mirrored sunglasses made her heart gallop. She glanced away, hoping it wasn't anyone she knew. But in Fortuna, Texas, that was impossible, since her sister-in-law worked at the station and her father golfed with the chief, Colin Copper. And she had gone to school with most

1

of the younger guys.

The side mirror revealed the squad car door opening. The man approached her car. She tried to meld with the seat but couldn't vanish. He paused next to her door, and she swallowed, lowering the window.

"Howdy, Ben," Piper said from the backseat. She stuck her hand out Kelly's window and waved. Ever since the officer had helped Cole, Piper's husband, rescue her from the stalker who kidnapped her, the couple considered him a close friend.

"Good afternoon, ladies." Ben tipped his head so Kelly could see his dark eyes over the mirrored lenses. "Kelly, do you know why I stopped you?"

No, she didn't. Well, not really. It appeared daydreaming and driving don't mix. Kelly may have run a stop sign, almost hit someone, and nearly killed her friends. She opened her mouth to speak, but Piper answered for her. "Kelly's clueless. She's been thinking about sex."

"Again," Jessie mumbled.

Kelly jerked her head toward her friends. Her neck ached from whiplash. "What?" Her cheeks heated, and she knew her face was the same color as her cherry red car.

Ben pushed the glasses back and leaned forward. "Ladies?"

Jessie giggled, but Piper took command of the mystery. "She's had this brilliant smile for the last few days. It has to be a guy."

Kelly's face pulled tight into a high smile. She couldn't help it. She hadn't meant that night to happen, but it did. It had left its mark, though.

"Yes, she's been smiling for days. It started Wednesday." Jessie looked to Piper to confirm.

"No, that smile was there Wednesday morning. It had to have been Tuesday night, because Tuesday afternoon she wasn't in a good mood." Piper rolled down the back window, letting in the warm humid morning air. "Whatever happened, happened Tuesday night. It just has to be a guy."

"Not Sawyer, either," Jessie chimed in.

Kelly clamped her fingers around the wheel and clenched her teeth at the mention of her ex-boyfriend's name.

"See. Look at that frown. It's definitely not him." Jessie pointed to Kelly's face as Piper stuck her head between the headrests to see it.

"I saw Kelly Tuesday night," Ben offered.

Kelly sucked in a quick breath and glanced at him with her peripheral vision. His eyes were hidden, but one side of his lips quirked up in a smirk.

Both of her friends leaned so they could better see Ben's face, their eyes wide in expectation. "Well, it was at Hammered. I suppose she was hungry, because she sat down at the bar and ordered a burger. That was before she noticed Mona flirting with Sawyer."

He'd said Mona with a hint of hostility. They had gone on a couple of

2

dates before Mona decided Ben wasn't her type. Kelly never understood why Mona wasn't attracted to Ben.

Jessie groaned. "Not those two."

Kelly crossed her arms and held tight. Mona used to be one of her best friends, but now that Mona had set her sights on Sawyer, Kelly felt betrayed. She couldn't stand to be around them when they hung on each other.

"Mona came over to talk to me." Ben glanced behind him, as if he'd find her there. "Kelly told her to take a hike. Thanks for that." He nodded at Kelly and she shrugged.

"Mona retreated and must have boo-hooed to Sawyer because he came over next. He said some stupid things and made Kelly mad. She told him off, then got her food to go." Ben stopped talking and straightened.

"That's it?" Piper asked, blinking.

"I saw her leave the restaurant with her takeout." Ben shifted.

Kelly let out a long breath and relaxed her arms. Ben didn't say anything that her friends couldn't already have guessed. They didn't need to know what happened later. The smile returned.

"It's back," Jessie said, nudging Piper. Her brows crinkled as she inspected Kelly's face. "It happened later on Tuesday."

Kelly chanced a peek at the officer. His lips were pressed into a thin line, but there were creases beside his eyes indicating his amusement. Ben looked good in his uniform, his shirt pulled tight over muscled biceps. He'd graduated a few years before Kelly and Jessie. She swallowed. Her face and body grew hot even though the air was on full blast.

"There's only so many single guys in Fortuna," Jessie hummed, rubbing her hands together.

"Kelly said she'd had the best sex ever," Piper prodded.

She'd said no such thing but that hadn't stopped her friend from trying to get her to admit something. Kelly clamped her lips shut and sent a pleading look to Ben.

That was a mistake. His smile, now full-blown, shined like a beacon even though his own face had turned beet red. She wished she could see his eyes.

"Are you going to give me a ticket?" She hoped the swift subject change would divert the conversation away from her sex life. She thrust her license toward him.

Ben chuckled and took it. As he stared at the information he asked, "So are you going to see him again?"

Both Jessie and Piper giggled and reiterated the question. Kelly closed her eyes, and the smile came back. She couldn't help it. Piper had been right—it had been the best sex ever. Kelly could have ignited, as she remembered his body next to hers. She sighed as a wave of desire rolled over her.

"She has to," Jessie said.

"Call him, Kelly. Have him come over and make dinner for you naked," Piper giggled again. Kelly's eyes popped open, and she glanced at Ben. His mouth hung open.

Kelly leaned in his direction and rested her arm on the edge of the open window. "This is what happens when both your best friends are newlyweds; all they ever talk about is sex. Do you have this problem?"

Ben stared at her then shook his head. She knew he lived the bachelor life with another officer, Indigo Black. The man was just as good looking as Ben; she didn't understand why they both weren't married. They were dependable men with smoking hot bodies and better catches than Sawyer Hickey—that was for darn sure.

Ben cleared his throat. "You should call him."

Encouraged, her friends joined in. "Call him. Have him make dinner."

"Why should he make dinner?" Ben asked, leaning in to view her passengers and echoing her unaired question.

"It's every girl's fantasy to have a man cook for her," Jessie said in a whimsical voice.

"Naked is better," added Piper.

"Is this true?" Ben asked looking down at Kelly.

She smiled weakly and gave a one shoulder shrug. "It wouldn't be a bad thing." She wouldn't mind anyone cooking a meal for her, let alone a sexy naked man.

There were already people who'd done jail time for acting out scenes from one or two romance books, but those had been in public places. Indecent exposure, or almost, if not caught by the police in time. One incident had saved a marriage and made that couple the talk of the town. It wasn't long before other men were trying to please their women in a similar manner.

Ben stood straight again and handed back her license. Tingles shot up her arm from where his fingers touched hers. He put his hand on the door frame and removed his glasses as he looked in. His brown eyes were framed with long dark lashes. He grinned at Kelly and her heart jumped into her throat. "I think you should call him."

Jessie gasped and Piper giggled. Kelly watched his snug fitting pants as he walked back to the car. "He didn't give me a ticket," she realized.

"I guess he values the world's best sex," Piper teased.

Kelly rolled her eyes and put the car into drive. They needed to get to the new store Jessie had bought. She had scheduled a contractor to meet them there. Kelly zipped into the street, noticing Ben followed for a while. She parked and watched Ben slow as he passed. He gave her a salute and winked. The smile blossomed on her lips.

CHAPTER 2

Ben

BEN MOORE WAVED WHEN HE passed Kelly and her friends. He had been tempted to blow her a kiss to see her face bloom into that pretty blush again, but instead he drove to the station. Slamming the door, he made a beeline for the office and Kelly's sister-in-law Ivy Greene. The woman in question sat hunched over her desk, typing a report into the computer. Her hair had been pulled up into a severe bun, what she called "a poor man's face-lift."

Her brown eyes flicked up at him then once again focused on the screen. She had a round pleasant face. When she smiled she was anybody's friend, but when she got angry, she could be a hellcat. She was known as the station's mom even though Ben knew she had to be close to his age of thirty.

He shifted uneasily. Finally, she pushed back from the desk and shook out her arms. "Ben," she acknowledged. "What do you need?"

Ben grinned. "Now, Ivy, why do you assume I need anything?"

She chuckled. "Why else would you be standing here? Is something wrong with your hours?"

He crossed his arms and gave a small shake of his head. "No. I just pulled Kelly over."

"Oh?" Ivy raised her eyebrows.

"She seemed distracted." He shrugged.

Ivy leaned back and looked off as if remembering. "Yeah, she was like that last night too." She refocused on Ben. "Did you ticket her?"

"No. I didn't know Jessie and Piper were in the car with her."

"Distracted with those two in the car? That's understandable." Ivy

5

snickered.

Ben hesitated, not wanting to seem too eager. Maybe the world's greatest sex had preoccupied Kelly's thoughts then, too. "So, you said she was distracted last night. What happened?" He tried to look casual as he glanced around the room.

Ivy snorted and crossed her arms. "My daughter Jade is talking, and she pronounces a few words funny. I know she's only a year, but I thought she might have a speech problem and mentioned it to Kelly." Ivy shrugged and a faint smile tugged at her lips. "Kelly came over to assess Jade. They played, sung, and, talked but I don't think Kelly could stay focused on Jade. She kept staring off into space with a goofy grin."

"A smile, huh?" Ben tried to mask his own with a look of concern.

"When I asked Kelly about it, she blushed and said it's nothing." Ivy started waving her hands around excitedly. "You know what I think it is? A guy. I think she's seeing someone." Giggling, Ivy covered her mouth and nose. "That's the way Forrest acted when we dated. She's just like him. And God help Kelly when her mother finds out."

Ben shifted his weight and checked the clock on the wall. He had planned to meet Indigo for lunch at the Pink Taco Mexican restaurant. Settled in the heart of Fortuna, it got most of the small business lunch rush. He might even get to see Kelly and her friends again if he timed it right.

But he didn't want to miss out on any inside scoop on the Greene family either, especially if he was the reason for Kelly's smile. He glanced at the framed pictures on Ivy's desk, most held Jade and Forrest's visages but one family photo from Christmas held all three siblings. Big brother Forrest and the sisters. Both single, Kelly was the middle child and Olivia was still in college. "What happens if her mother finds out?"

Ivy smirked and chuckled low. "That poor girl is going to get dragged to get fitted for her wedding dress. No ifs, ands, or buts—unless it's that character Sawyer Hickey. Her parents never liked him."

"Maybe that's why she dated him." Ben said, remembering the sour expression on Kelly's face at the mention of her ex.

"Maybe, but whoever she's gaga for now is going to have his eyes opened, and quick, too, once Mama Greene gets his name and number." Ivy tilted her head and scanned his face.

Ben snapped his mouth shut. Suddenly hot, he didn't know how to respond and glanced again at the clock.

"Oh, Indigo asked me to let you know Walter Mellan called. Apparently, there's been more drag racing on Oak Street in front of his house and the elementary school again. Indigo is going to stop and speak with him before he meets you." She winked, knowing the men were going out for lunch.

"How did you…?"

"I know all." She laughed and waved him off, effectively dismissing him, then turned back to the screen.

Ben rubbed his chin as he walked back to his desk. He filed papers then checked a few items on the computer. After reviewing Mr. Mellan's complaint, he wondered if Kelly might have a few suggestions regarding the dangerous situation. Several instances of speeding, racing, and vandalism have been reported, mostly by Walter Mellan, but by others as well. Soon summer break would be over and the children would return to school. An incident could prove deadly. Some action needed to be taken, but what? He needed to talk with Colin about patrolling the area more often.

His phone vibrated. Indigo was done. Time to eat. He grabbed his keys with a grin.

★★★

The smells wafting from the open door of the Pink Taco made Ben's stomach sing with want. He loved Mexican food, the spicier the better. Indigo raised a hand in greeting. He sat at the bar, sipping sweet tea. Ben slid onto the stool next to him.

Tish Hughes, the waitress, pulled out a pad and scribbled down their orders. She set a sweet tea in front of Ben and refilled Indigo's.

"The Mellan place is on a corner lot," Indigo said, turning to face Ben. "He's got a view of both roads and the crosswalk. The other night a race happened and one car pushed the other off the road onto the property. It took down a couple of mail boxes and gouged deep ruts in the yards. Luckily, no one was out that time of night walking their dog or anything."

"It's getting worse," Ben shook his head, frustrated.

"I agree."

The door opened and five giggling women entered. Piper Dart, Jessie Barnes, Desire Hardmann, Gloria Sass, and the one Ben hoped to see— Kelly Greene. He tried to hide a grin.

"You aren't listening to me," Indigo grumbled.

"What?" Ben turned toward a frowning Indigo.

"You didn't hear a word I said." Indigo crossed his arms.

"Yes, I did."

"What did I say then?"

"Walter Mellan smells like wintergreen muscle rub."

Indigo's stoic features remained immobile at first but soon his lip twitched. "Not exactly." His gaze slid toward the noisy women taking a round six seater near the window. "Who are you watching?"

"No one in particular," Ben said knowing his friend sensed the lie. He took a long drink to counteract the heat on his face.

"It's not the newlyweds because you respect their men and know their friend Dakota could snipe you from Kansas." Indigo paused, studying the

7

ladies as they opened the menus.

Ben had met Dakota Redd, the Army Ranger, a few months back when Piper had been kidnapped. The retired ranger had befriended the couple and had been on hand when she'd been swiped from her engagement party. The man was dependable in a crunch. Ben didn't want to get on his bad side.

Ben wouldn't want to hurt his friends, Cole or Josiah, either. Neither Piper nor Jessie appealed to him. Sure, they were pretty, but there wasn't that certain zing.

"Not the old lady, even though she'd probably fancy the handcuffs." Indigo laughed quietly.

Ben gasped in shock. His friend didn't usually tease. But he hit it dead on. Desire Hardmann had been Jessie's grandmother's, Undine Love Davidson, best friend and cohort. She helped Undine stockpile a hoard of romance novels into one of the Double D Ranch's bedrooms. Those books were stacked floor to ceiling and poor Jessie had to get them out. Fortunately for her, she dared a man to read a few before donating them, then he had dared a few men and so on until the entire male population of town became addicted to reading the novels.

It had livened up his job, that was for sure. There'd been many incidents of indecent exposure when husbands were caught sneaking around their residences acting out a favorite hero. One couple was found at the park. He chuckled, remembering the man's face with the big spot light on it.

"Maybe it's Desire's receptionist?" Indigo fished. He grinned when he looked at Ben's sour expression. "Yeah, I didn't think so. That one has a chip on her shoulder the size of Texas. That leaves the petite, pretty Ms. Greene."

Now Ben frowned. Kelly was beautiful, and he didn't like Indigo noticing. He scrubbed his face. How could he be jealous? They weren't dating.

"She's a teacher at the elementary school, isn't she?" Indigo had turned serious.

Ben nodded, not fazed the other officer knew where Kelly worked. "Yeah, so?"

"So… you should talk to her about the danger the school will be in come this fall. See what she has to say. Maybe she and the other teachers have been talking it over. They might offer some solutions we haven't thought of."

"I could." Ben focused in on Kelly, and heat crept to his cheeks. Her lips glistened with dampness from her drink. Suddenly, he wanted to taste them. He swallowed and glanced at the other women. Piper stared at him with a suspecting smirk. She murmured something to Kelly sitting next to her and pointed in his direction. Ironically, the feeling you get when you see red and blue lights in the rearview mirror was the sensation he got as Kelly met his gaze.

He could tell by Indigo's smirk, the man loved Ben's unease. He wasn't going to hear the end of it.

Tish set the food down and the men began eating. Ben caught Kelly's eye a few times. She tried to be sly, but she blushed every time.

Ben and Indigo paid and started for the door. He scratched the back of his head, searching for something to say to Kelly as he passed but his brain stalled. Indigo stopped and Ben quickly halted behind him.

"Howdy, ladies," Indigo said, tipping his tan hat.

"Hello, tall, dark and handsome," Desire purred. At eighty-plus years she held the title of town flirt, even more so than Sawyer Hickey. She looked Indigo up and down and licked her lips. The other women, being used to her orneriness, ignored the comment.

"Hey, Indigo, what's up?" Jessie asked.

"Actually, Ben and I were talking," he started in a Texan drawl, "The community has an issue with speeders and drag racing near the Fortuna elementary school. Ben's in charge of looking into the occurrences, and we were wondering if you, Kelly, being a teacher there and all, would be willing to meet with him and add your insight?"

All eyes turned to Kelly. Her jaw dropped as she paled, and her large round eyes blinked. Apparently Ben wasn't the only one who couldn't find words. A smile crept to his face, and he winked at her. Her skin flushed and a huge smile bloomed. Piper elbowed Jessie and nodded in Ben's direction.

Oh, yeah. He'd put that smile there.

"So, Ben, pull over any more people for daydreaming about men?" Piper asked. Gloria's eyes narrowed, but Desire and Jessie snickered. Kelly gasped in shock.

"Sorry, Piper, only one today." He winked at Kelly again. She covered her face with her hands and groaned.

Desire patted her arm. "Honey, can I have his number?"

Kelly dropped her hands and squealed, "No way." Everyone laughed.

"Do you know anyone who'll cook for their woman naked?" Desire asked the officers.

Indigo raised an eyebrow as he looked to Ben for answers. Ben shrugged but offered, "It's supposed to be every woman's fantasy."

CHAPTER 3

Kelly

KELLY INSPECTED BEN'S CLINGING PANTS as he and Indigo walked toward their squad cars. At least she could excuse her drooling and blame the scrumptious food before her. Piper nudged Kelly with her elbow and raised her eyebrows repeatedly. "Ben's cute, huh?"

Yes, he most definitely is. Now that she had an intimate knowledge of all his muscles, Kelly could appreciate the way the clothes fit his hard body. She sighed and inspected the other officer, Indigo Black. He was a hottie, too. "Indigo sure is handsome, and look how those pants fit him." Kelly offered as a diversion and pointed out the window.

Piper's smile wavered and her brow knit into a frown.

Desire hopped on Kelly's comment like a vulture on roadkill. "Yes, that's one smokin' hot Indian."

"Native American," Kelly corrected.

"He looks like a tan version of Cole," Gloria murmured. At the mention of her husband, Piper turned her attention away from Kelly toward the men out the window.

"That's true," Jessie added, "Cole and Indigo are probably cousins."

The discussion turned to Piper's husband's wacky and twisted family tree. Cole's grandfather had impregnated many women spanning decades and had children scattered around the area. It was likely Cole's granddad and Indigo's were the same, since they looked so similar. But without a DNA test they couldn't be certain.

Kelly watched Ben and Indigo talk while she ate, responding to the group with an appropriate nod. When Ben climbed in his squad car and drove away, she sighed and returned her attention to the table.

After lunch, the women headed to the soon to be opened Double D Intimates shop. Kelly paused outside The Gift Spot and stared at the window display. Until recently, the first floor shop primarily sold novelties, including candles and cards. The owners had expanded the new book area and children's costume section. The store dedicated prime floor space for an expanding adult costume area with makeup and hats. They still had children's items, but the business had shifted, because of the romance book reading fad.

Kelly crossed her arms and frowned. Not once had her ex attempted to act out a plot from a book. "I'm better than any hero in those books," Sawyer had said. A real life boyfriend was fun to hold, but just once she would have liked to use her imagination. She understood his insecurity: book boyfriends are heroes and real men are flawed. He had voiced his fear that she might expect him to act out characters all the time. But his fear had been unfounded; she'd only wanted to play. Sawyer liked her to model sexy Double D Intimates lingerie, yet he wouldn't slip on angel wings for her. *Double standards suck.*

The bright colors of superhero costumes in the window attracted her eye at first, but a black suit caught her attention. Cat woman or Batgirl? The black ensemble appeared to be faux leather, and Ben's face flashed before her. She grinned as a wave of heat rolled over her.

"Hey, Kelly, you coming?" Jessie called over her shoulder, then she disappeared inside the doorway.

Kelly shook thoughts of men from her head and followed Jessie up a step into the square vestibule. The small space had a terracotta tiled floor. To her left, The Gift Spot's hours hung on the glass entry door.

Gloria held open one of the double doors leading to the second story space. As handles, the doors each had a sideways horseshoe. Ironically, when closed together the double door horseshoes resembled the back-to-back Ds logo of the Double D ranch.

Kelly trailed behind Desire as she held onto the rail, climbing the stairs. The only drawback to the second story store was the lack of elevator. The stairs opened into a large room.

"This is perfect," Desire claimed in a reverberating voice. With a wide grin, she clasped her hands and slowly spun.

"Uh huh." Gloria rolled her eyes and snapped her gum. She leaned against a dusty oak desk and pulled out her phone. The woman had been in the same class as Kelly and Jessie, but had dropped out of high school. Desire had given her a job as the receptionist at her salon Tease Me. While Gloria really wasn't Kelly's friend, she helped at Jessie's inaugural fashion show. Kelly shifted her weight, wishing she'd been there.

"How did you find this space?" Kelly asked.

Jessie walked into the center of the room. "Piper found it in the Fortuna Forum. The Gift Spot owners listed it for rent."

"I called them and got the details." Piper tapped her foot and crinkled her nose. "I'm just glad they didn't realize they could use this space for a book shop or a store dedicated to cosplay." Piper pointed to the back. "I'm going to check the plumbing." She disappeared into the backroom.

"Cosplay? I would have liked to seen that," Desire mumbled. "But I'm glad you got it, Jessie. Your grandma would be proud."

"It needs work, but mostly it will be a place to process the orders. Small sales floor here and a workroom in the back." She had to make changes to fit her small business needs, and various contractor appointments.

Kelly's footsteps echoed as she walked toward the oversize windows facing the street. Some individual panes had been replaced but most were old thick glass. The Gift Spot had used the space as a warehouse. The big windows let in sunlight, making the space bright and open. Dust motes floated in the air. Jessie walked over to her and bumped her shoulder.

"I can't believe how far you've come in a year," Kelly said, turning toward Jessie.

The smile on Jessie's face widened, and her eyes took on a dreamy cast. "I know. I wouldn't be here without your support and belief in me." She took Kelly's hand in hers and squeezed.

"I got to test your product. It's a fun job, I'll admit."

"Being a lingerie beta tester isn't always easy. Remember that thong that went wrong," Jessie snickered and covered her mouth.

Kelly shook her head and sighed. "Don't remind me. I had to sit through church without any underwear."

"That's a weekly occurrence for me," Desire said with a wink.

Piper returned to the room, groaned and spun in place, then hurried out again.

"This will be perfect." Jessie stared up at the high ceiling. The large room's dingy tan walls needed a new coat of paint in a refreshing color.

An electrician had met with Jessie that morning while Kelly and Piper swept the floors and cleaned up the bathroom. The plumber was due any moment. The existing bathroom might have started as a broom closet.

Footsteps resounded as someone climbed the staircase. "Excuse me, Ms. Davidson," a short balding man said. The women turned toward him. He blushed and his eyes widened. "Oh, I'm sorry. *Mrs. Barnes*, I forgot." He chuckled uneasily.

"It's okay." Jessie waved him in. "The room is back here."

Piper peeked into the room, glancing at Kelly who motioned it was safe.

"I haven't been here in ages. Did you know this building was once a livery? Originally, this building didn't have indoor plumbing." He offered, then they walked out of earshot into a hallway at the back of the showroom.

Desire whistled. "A livery. That was before my time, and that's saying something,"

Gloria actually giggled, causing Kelly to gasp. Gloria's behavior must have also struck Piper as unusual, because she met Kelly's gaze with raised eyebrows.

"Can you picture yourself working in here?" Kelly asked Piper.

Piper glanced and slowly circled in place. She pointed to the tin ceiling. "I think this place is cool; if it's done right it will be chic. Yeah, I could see a desk over there." She pointed near the entry. Downtown Fortuna was closer to the property Piper and Cole owned. Once the couple built their house, the store would be a shorter commute. "I can answer the phone anywhere, but packing the items for shipment is another thing."

Desire glanced at the vibrating phone in her hand then over at Gloria "Hmm, looks as if I need to go to the bank. Come on, hot shot, you can drive me."

"Do you want to visit the G Spot first?" Gloria asked without cracking a smile. Kelly bit her knuckles to keep from laughing.

"Oh, I'd love to stimulate the G Spot, but I'm afraid the Tease Me needs change. Another time."

Gloria followed Desire to the stairs, and the two ladies descended.

"Did you call him yet?" Piper asked Kelly.

Kelly turned away from her friend, toward the window again. A smile crept onto her face. The suspected secret had to be gnawing at Piper or else she wouldn't continue to hound her. "Of course not, I haven't had the time."

"I think you should. You deserve some happiness in the love department. If this guy makes you smile, then you should see him again."

"Piper," Jessie called. "We need your opinion. Come here a sec."

"Be back in a minute." Piper's footsteps echoed, sounding like an eerie drum.

Kelly watched her go. The room suddenly felt dark and empty, reminding her of her loveless life. She had tried to fill it with love, but Sawyer wouldn't commit.

She had fallen hard for the fun-loving man when he'd caught her eye with a kind gesture for an abused woman. It exposed a hidden depth within him, and it fascinated her. Their relationship had been steaming hot or freezing cold. She had thought he'd romanced her, but looking back, he might have wanted her only to scratch a hormonal itch.

Kelly chewed her lip and closed her eyes, forcing the tears away.

Sawyer didn't want her for more than a fun night out and a wild romp in the sack. At first she enjoyed the attention, but then her heart had begun to ache. She had a hole in her heart and tried to stuff Sawyer into it. He wouldn't fit. She sighed.

Then Ben happened.

Tuesday night had been a fluke. An accident. Kelly had driven to Hammered for dinner because she hated eating alone. She found her so-called friend Mona hanging on Sawyer. Kelly must have looked like a lovesick idiot standing frozen in the middle of the restaurant. Finally, she had locked eyes with Ben. He waved her over and tapped the seat next to him at the counter. She sat quietly, kneading the napkin in her lap while Ben tried to converse. Eventually her one-word replies got him out of his seat. He pulled her into his arms and hugged her, but it had been more than that—he held her in the middle of the restaurant with their exes not far from view. The small kindness helped to steady her. It kept the tears at bay.

Ben squeezed her hand when Mona kissed Sawyer after he'd won a pool game. Sawyer spun the obnoxious woman. Ben continued to hold on while she ordered her food even though Kelly's appetite had fled. But she had a right to be there too. She started to get mad when Sawyer and Mona's laughter kept leaking through the other noise. They flirted, touched, and continued to joke.

Turning to Ben, Kelly sought comfort, but found him frowning. He stared into space as if attempting to memorize the liquor bottles on the back wall. Touching his thigh was an act of solace. She hadn't meant for it to end in a one-night stand.

"You're smiling again."

Kelly jumped. She hadn't heard Piper come back. Piper crossed her arms and smirked.

Kelly's heart raced, and she touched her cheeks. Piper was right. The corners of her lips stretched into a wide smile. Whenever she thought of Ben, the smile magically appeared. Maybe she should call him. She tapped a finger to her lip, wondering if he'd be up for cooking without clothes. She giggled, not minding the idea.

"Call that man." Piper put a hand on her arm. "Or at least tell me what happened. Did you have dinner or coffee? Hot, steamy—dessert?" She wiggled her eyebrows.

As much as Kelly's fingers itched to call Ben, she couldn't. It had been a one-time deal. She wouldn't pester him. So she chickened out and changed the subject. "How's married life? Anything new on the house front?"

Piper smiled and started to talk happily about her and Cole's plans. "Well, Arlon's property is large. We had it surveyed. I think we've found the perfect place to build. Now we have to see if we can afford it."

The skinny old cowboy, Arlon, turned out to be Cole's uncle. The poor man died tragically before he revealed the genetic details to Cole. Cole and Arlon had worked together on the Big Deal ranch for years. Cole had confided in the older man when he'd been diagnosed with cancer. Arlon had been one of the few souls, other than his mother, able to see Cole during the chemotherapy. A tornado stole Arlon's life, but he left money and a parcel of paid-off land to Cole. Arlon's half-sister Morgan and Cole found out they were related when Arlon's will had been read. He'd lost an uncle but gained an aunt.

Piper and Cole wed a few days after her kidnapping rescue and had been happily planning their life together ever since. Kelly still occasionally stole Piper for a girls' night of karaoke and dancing.

"We're trying to decide between a log cabin and something more normal." Piper's eyes shined.

"Maybe you should plan lots of bedrooms for all those kids you're going to have," Kelly teased.

Piper blushed and hit her gently. "Maybe."

"Oh my God! Are you pregnant?" Kelly gasped.

Piper shook her head but smiled with unrestrained joy. "Not yet, but we're thinking about trying soon." She hummed happily and hugged her friend. "I want my kids to grow up with your kids."

Piper had thrown a metaphorical cold, wet blanket over Kelly. She sighed and tried to hide a frown. "Someday. Jessie and Josiah will have kids before I do."

Piper shook her head again. "They'll be focused on Double D Intimates and the ranch, working out the nuances of the business. Jessie loves creating; she feels it makes her closer to her grandma Undine. This business is her baby now." Piper trained her gaze on Kelly.

"Don't look at me like that. I might know what house I'd want to live in but I don't have a clue about a husband." Kelly put her hands on her hips. "That's pretty important."

"What house?"

"You know the one. I drove you by a few months ago. The big Victorian with the large wraparound porch." Kelly's voice softened as she pictured the spindle railing and gingerbread wood detailing. "It has an open staircase that sweeps up, curling around the walls of the entry with a chandelier hanging from the vaulted ceiling. On the front corner is a third story widow's walk with a pointed roof and balcony." Kelly guessed there had to be a secret passage somewhere inside.

As a child, she had visited Ms. Dungogh a handful of times. Kelly, Forrest, and Olivia would knock on her door for Halloween or to sell items. The house had been a stagecoach inn at some point in history, and Kelly thought it'd make a cute bed-and-breakfast. *If only…*

CHAPTER 4

Ben

BEN COULDN'T BELIEVE HIS LUCK. He had stumbled into a bunch of women who blatantly declared their fantasies. If extracting Kelly's most intimate desires was this simple, he'd be able to please her. He desired to bring her fantasies to life. He wanted her, not only physically, but all of her. Somehow, after one night, he knew she was the one. *The one.*

Ben slammed his hand over his heart, trying to keep it in his chest.

Closing his eyes, he took several deep breaths. He planned to do something he would probably regret for the rest of his life. Scrolling through his contact list, he found his brother's name: Leslie Moore. Sure, Ben had other choices, but in a small town the queries would feed the rumor mill. Hell, it could embarrass Kelly and get Mrs. Greene all fired up. The last thing he wanted to do was cause conflict between Kelly and her mother.

Sweat broke out on his forehead. Ben stole one more breath then pushed the button. He simultaneously wished the call would pass directly to voice mail and the other line would pick up.

The phone rang.

As a big visual reminder to obey the law, he had parked his squad car in Walter Mellan's driveway. He glanced down the street toward the elementary school entry.

His phone continued to ring. Ben wiped perspiration off his forehead.

Ben thought it safe to make a potentially long call. Then again, it might be the shortest call of the day.

"What do you want?"

"It's nice to hear your voice too, little brother."

A scratchy laugh met his ears. "Ah, never said it was nice."

Ben pinched his nose and prayed for patience. "Leslie, I need your advice." Silence. He pulled the phone from his ear, thinking the line dead but it was still connected.

"Excuse me?" Leslie breathed. "I don't think I heard you right. You need me? Well, hell must have just frozen over."

"It's about a girl." Admitting something so personal to his brother could backfire. He chanced being heckled for eternity, but maybe his brother would have pity on him. Les had always had luck with the ladies, something Ben failed at, especially in the kitchen.

"You're gay, why do you need advice about a woman?" Leslie's low chuckle brought heat to Ben's face. He closed his eyes, grateful no one had overheard.

"I found out one of her fantasies and I want to bring it to life," he admitted. "I plan to cook dinner for her."

Les laughed loud and long. Ben pulled the phone away from his ear and grimaced. "You, cook? That's hilarious," Les said.

"I'm serious. She's special."

Another pause and a large breath. "Why me? You could ask anyone."

Ben couldn't blow it or his brother would never speak to him again. "I've heard great things about your culinary talents. You have the skills, and you know my quirks. Besides microwave popcorn, I'm not any good in a kitchen, and I'd like to please her and not kill her. Are you willing to help me?"

"Yeah, bro. Dude, I feel honored and all that shit." His little brother chuckled again. Ben imagined Les's tattooed arms wrapped around his gut, doubled over in a belly laugh. "What kind of girly cooking advice do you need? They like chocolates."

"I want to fix a full meal. Start to finish. From scratch. Something that will make her place smell great so when she gets home her mouth will water. I know I'll need to keep it simple, but I don't mind making multiple things at once."

"Whoa, you've thought this out. Crazy." He paused. "What type of oven does she have? How many burners?"

"Um, a hot one. It's not built into the wall. She lives in an apartment, so nothing fancy."

"My brother is dating an apartment dweller, huh? Never thought there'd come a day."

"You can stop judging me now," Ben said in a dry tone.

"That's my line." Les chuckled and then mumbled something to someone else. "Okay, I'll put together a menu for you. When are you going shopping? Is this for the weekend?"

"Tonight."

"Shit." It sounded as if Les dropped the phone. "I'll create a menu and make a list of ingredients."

"Thank you." Gratitude welled in his heart, making a lump form in his throat so he cleared it. He couldn't go to pieces now. "I've got another hour then I can go to the store."

Ben smiled. He needed to clean up and pack an overnight bag, just in case.

In Wertz grocery he bumped into half the town of Fortuna. Ben greeted them with smiles and nods. He scanned his list and dutifully picked the food items. He hoped Kelly didn't have any food allergies.

At her apartment building, Ben sat in the car contemplating the illegal thing he was about to do. It ground against his training. He shook his head. He planned a surprise for a friend, a potential girlfriend. With a sigh, he pushed open the car door.

First things first. He needed to find a way into her apartment.

Wearing a T-shirt and shorts, he hoped to look like a normal guy and not a thief. Ben tried the door handle, but no luck. Glancing around the small entry cove and the other three doors, then the parking lot, he found no one watching. Kneeling, he lifted one corner of the welcome mat.

Tuesday night Kelly had revealed the key's location. "You shouldn't keep it under the mat where anyone could find it," he'd admonished her for the cliché hiding spot.

"It's there for the lady who cleans my house." Kelly had glanced around then leaned close and lowered her voice. "Her deadbeat husband doesn't give her enough money for food or clothes for their little girl. Mierda isn't the best cleaning lady, but I'm helping to feed her daughter, Cali."

Ben hadn't said another word about the key or what the husband might do if he found out Kelly had been empowering his wife. Ben swung his head around, wondering where the bastard lived. The apartment complex was home to the dysfunctional family, and the little girl attended Kelly's school.

The lock disengaged, and he twisted the knob. Stepping into the living room, he caught a whiff of vanilla.

Given the boring white walls, Kelly had tastefully decorated the apartment, adding splashes of color with framed wall art and decorative pillows on a tan sofa. The building was less than a year old and still smelled like new construction mixed with Kelly's favorite vanilla lotion.

Ben smiled and rubbed his hands together.

After carrying in the groceries, he preheated the oven. He glanced around the small galley kitchen. The counters were clean and the sink devoid of dishes. He pulled open drawer after drawer and opened the cabinets searching for the supplies he needed.

He paused to check his reflection in the hall mirror. The excited man gazed at him with a smile that matched the one Kelly wore when he had pulled her over. His short cropped brown hair stood up in front as expected. His face looked presentable, but his body was another thing. He'd gone for a run then showered. He sniffed under his arms, hoping he hadn't worked up a sweat grocery shopping. Satisfied, he shimmied out of his shorts then pulled off his T-shirt and flexed. Kelly had mentioned she liked his arms. He folded his clothes and set them on her bed.

Ben left his boxers on. He could strip them off later, but for now they stayed on as a last second defense against any hot wayward food.

On the counter, Ben had the measuring cups, cutting board, and bowls ready for use. He followed his brother's recipe and put the main dish into the oven. The timer was set for an hour. The aroma of dinner would fill the apartment by the time Kelly arrived.

"If she comes home to eat," he said to himself, rubbing his recently shaved chin. "What if she made plans with Piper and Jessie?" Ben picked up his phone. Time for a fishing expedition. "Hey there, Cole, how's it going? I was wondering if you have plans tonight."

"Not really. Just dinner with Piper. She's out with Jessie and Kelly, checking the new building and meeting with contractors. She called and said she'd be another hour. What's up?"

"I saw them at the Pink Taco this morning. It's great Jessie's business is growing." Ben paused. "I was just wanting to see if y'all were available for an early dinner, but it sounds like it will be too late. Are Jessie and Kelly going to dinner with you two?"

Cole chuckled. "No. Jessie and Josiah have plans. And Kelly..." he sighed, "she's probably tired of my wife's match-making schemes."

"What?" Ben sucked in a breath.

"Piper is determined to find Kelly a man." Cole chuckled again. "She wants to double date."

"Isn't it usually Kelly who is always trying to help others?" Ben chuckled.

"Not this time." Cole laughed too. "This time it's my wife. My wife." He sighed. "I don't think I'll ever get used to saying that."

"You're a lucky man, Cole."

"Don't I know it." Cole cleared his throat. "Don't think you are beyond Piper's match-making reach. She's mentioned you need to find a nice girl."

"Oh no."

"Yeah, like I said, she's lookin' to find a guy for Kelly and you're single."

"Uh oh."

"I'll, well, maybe I won't mention you called. Might as well not get her match-making juices going, especially after she's been with Kelly all day," Cole said.

"Thanks, man. Have a great night." Ben ended the call.

A pink, flowery apron hung on a peg. He slipped it over his head, turned music on his phone then peeled potatoes. His phone vibrated on the counter.

Les texted, "Do you know how to sauté onions?"

Ben smiled and replied, "Following your instructions." He couldn't believe the communication Kelly had started between him and his estranged brother. Adding butter and the minced onions, he stirred, keeping the heat low.

Les had been in and out of jail, mostly for drinking related issues. With enough tattoos to rival a biker and more piercings than a circus side-show, the man could cook his way into any restaurant, catering business, or woman's bed. If anyone knew recipes that would work on a lady's heart, it would be Les.

Ben added the diced potatoes and covered the lid. His stomach protested the wait.

Lights slid across the room as a car parked. He glanced at the pink apron then scrambled out of it, dropping it to the floor and kicking it to the corner. He swiped the counters with a paper towel. Then he waited.

The knob turned and the door silently opened. Ben wrung his hands.

CHAPTER 5

Kelly

KELLY GRIPPED THE STEERING WHEEL and watched light flicker through the Venetian blinds of her apartment's sliding glass door. She distinctly remembered making sure the lights were off before leaving.

It could be Mierda, but she rarely came in the evenings because she kept the cleaning job a secret from her husband, Ricardo.

After a few minutes with no movement, Kelly decided she must have been seeing things and suspected she had left the light on in the kitchen.

Kelly clutched her handbag to her side and climbed the steps. She bent and flipped the corner of the welcome mat. Gone! The hidden key was missing. She swallowed bile and sucked in a deep breath. Pressing her ear to the door she heard music and what sounded like drawers being ransacked.

Reaching into her purse, she found Reba, her handgun. She closed her eyes, trying to still her heart. A car with a loud exhaust startled her. She squared her shoulders. Kelly opened the door as quietly as possible then jumped into the room, facing the assailant.

"Ben?" she squeaked.

He raised his hands. "Surprise. Dinner is almost ready,"

"What the heck?"

"It's your fantasy," he said with a shrug, still reaching his hands up.

"What?"

"A naked man making dinner."

"Oh." Kelly's child-like voice refused to sound normal. Her eyes scanned his shirtless upper torso, the beautiful sculpted—counter top? The wretched half-wall blocked her view.

Had he taken Jessie and Piper seriously? She swallowed then realized she still pointed the gun at him. "Oh, sorry." She quickly lowered it, opened, and emptied the chamber then sat it aside. She rolled her shoulders, relief flooding her. No one robbed her apartment and a sexy cop stood guard.

Kelly glanced down at her scroungy clothes and grimy hands. After helping clean the Double D Intimates new space, she needed a hot shower. But Ben had other ideas for their evening. Her stomach rumbled as she registered the heavenly scents. "Mmm, what's cooking?"

Ben's lips lifted, and he shook his head. "It's a surprise." He glanced at the timer. "It still has fifteen minutes. That's enough time to take a shower."

She placed her hands on her hips and narrowed her eyes. "Are you a mind reader?"

"Would you like it if I say yes?" His gaze raked her body and the temperature of the room skyrocketed.

Neither of them moved. She bit her lip wanting to find out if he wore any clothes, but first she needed to bring something inside. "I'll be right back." She turned and jogged to her car. Her prize sat on the backseat. She plucked up the paper sack and returned to her apartment, taking care to lock the door behind her. Again, the aroma of delectables made her mouth water. She grinned, hoping dinner would last all night.

"Look what I have for us." Kelly displayed three books. Unable to resist any longer, she walked around the half-wall. Ben's red boxer briefs stretched before her eyes. "I think Piper and Jessie were right. This is a good fantasy."

Ben stepped back and his jaw dropped. He forgot the book in his hand. "What do you mean? This isn't your fantasy?"

"No, it was their suggestion, remember? But the idea is growing on me." She inspected him head to foot, her eyes focusing on the red in the middle.

"If it isn't your fantasy, then tell me some of yours." He flipped the book over to read the back but kept his eyes on her.

If he wouldn't have outright asked, she might have rattled off several. Nothing popped into her mind except Ben naked. "Let me think about it. What are yours?"

His eyes narrowed, and he touched her arm. "Having a teacher school me in bedroom etiquette."

She tried to keep her face neutral and ignore the heat coursing through her blood. She wanted to educate him right then and, glanced toward the bedroom. "I think I can handle that."

His brows rose, and he leaned toward her. A faint hint of his cologne tantalized her. "Do you have any denim jumpers?"

He couldn't be serious, but his boxers looked ready to explode. It tickled her funny bone that one of those typical teacher dresses turned him on and she chuckled. Fortunately for Ben, she had one she wore in the winter with different turtlenecks. If she could find it she'd wear it.

"Give me a few minutes. I'll see what I can do." She leaned and kissed his lips, lingering. The tip of his tongue darted out, but she jumped out of his reach. If they started now, they would never eat.

After a quick shower, she dried off and searched her closet finding the sleeveless denim jumper hidden in the back. Buttons lined the front. The dress had started dark blue but now it appeared stonewashed. Twirling her damp hair up into a bun, she put on glasses and walked barefoot into the kitchen. Ignoring Ben the best she could, she pulled open a drawer. She shifted the pens, matches and other momentarily useless items until she found the yellow ruler. Kelly lifted it to show Ben.

His smoldering gaze raked her body, lingering on the pronounced V neck without an undershirt and the low armholes exposing the sides of her breasts.

"Ben, lift me onto the counter." She patted the empty space next to the sink. He put his warm hands on her waist and lifted her with ease. She kissed his neck; he moaned as she wrapped her legs around him. The timer rang, so she let him go. As he checked all the food, she picked up one book.

"I found these today. I wanted to read up on your little quirk and get ideas." One eyebrow raised in challenge.

His tanned skin was smooth but the corded muscles beneath firm. She wanted to touch his body, longing for him to drop the spoon. "You thought about me? I like that."

"I'm glad." Kelly took a big breath. She liked Ben and felt at ease talking to him even though the topic was hard, only made easier by the fact it was his preference not hers. His cheeks turned pink when she continued to stare. He was a beautiful man, and tonight he was hers. A longing to make it permanent hit her. That surprised her, especially when she swore off relationships after Sawyer Hickey.

Tuesday night after making love to Ben the second time, he had admitted he liked being bossed around in the bedroom. Kelly had never tried anything like it before, but it turned him on which turned her on.

"I'm going to read to you while you finish." She picked up the three books and tried to choose one. "Rumors about the mayor's office were right. Guess what? All the BDSM books and kinky stuff is there. They had a whole section of femdom. I took the tamest looking."

"That one." Ben pointed to a book with a dark cover. A woman stood over a pleading man on his knees. Kelly glanced at Ben, noting his sheepish grin.

"*She's the Boss?*" Kelly held up the book, and he nodded. "All right. *She's the Boss* it is."

She flipped open to the beginning and began reading. "When it came to men, Marla had always felt empty." She read on. Marla met the hero and the sexual tension was intense.

Marla liked to use leather bonds and even brought out a crop.

Kelly kept her voice in narrative mode with proper inflections throughout. She leaned back against the higher bar top and occasionally swung her leg, catching his attention. She continued reading while he set her table and dished out the food.

Ben offered her a hand down and held the book's place with his thumb. "It's pretty kinky."

"Yeah, I've never used my crop for anybody but a horse before," she teased.

He pulled out the chair. After she sat, he scooted it in then joined her at the table. "You found these at the mayor's office?"

She leaned forward with a sly grin. "The bookcase was in City Hall's lobby and it was filled to the brim. There are so many books that people have been stacking the books they're returning on the floor and on top."

"I'd heard the rumors, but I had always dismissed them." Ben rubbed his chin. "I would never have guessed Jasen Delay was into kinky stuff."

The food looked too pretty to eat, but it smelled delicious. The cheesy diced potatoes tasted divine, and the roast melted in her mouth. "This is awesome, Ben. Where did you learn to cook?"

He gave a half smile and blushed. "Funny story actually." He sat his fork down. "My brother."

Her eyes widened, and she leaned back. "Really? Oh, I'd forgotten he had gone to culinary school. Is he back in town?" Kelly remembered Les had left Fortuna as soon as he could.

"No. I called him. I wanted to give you some great food for your fantasy."

"You mean, besides the eye candy." She moved the fork around on her plate but studied his muscled chest, wishing she could taste it. Her eyes dipped lower through the table's glass-top.

Kelly had inherited the table and chairs from her brother, whose contemporary stint ended prematurely when he married Ivy. Kelly liked the chrome with black fabric seats. The glass-top offered a view of Ben's toned legs and tight boxer briefs. It was hard to keep her eyes on his face when those taut boxers revealed such a large, throbbing bulge.

Ben scratched his chest, then he leaned in with narrowed eyes. "I have dessert, too."

Kelly leaned forward, accepting the challenge. "You better."

CHAPTER 6

Ben

NOISE ASSAULTED BEN AS HE pulled open the door to Under the Table. In the neighboring town of Nockerville, the pub offered a great selection of artisan brews and wing sauces. Cole Dart and Dakota Redd sat at the high top table waiting for him. Cole lifted a hand in greeting.

Ben joined them and ordered. He rubbed his hands together, remembering his first visit to the tavern for Cole and Piper's engagement party. While parking, Ben had spied Cole next to his truck. Before the men entered the building, Cole received a text from Piper. Her stalker Justin Sane had kidnapped her out under from everyone's noses. Justin thought he'd knocked her out but the clever girl had played possum. Ben had launched an immediate search and rescue.

Eventually, Piper found the courage to escape then take on Justin. She was quite a lady.

But she wasn't Kelly. Ben's lips lifted in a grin which he tried to hide with a sip of amber ale.

Mostly hidden under his furrowed brow, Cole's deep blue eyes narrowed. He set his beer on the table. "What's up with you, Ben?"

Ben's booted foot tapped a nervous beat as he hoped to appear normal, shelling peanuts. He glanced at Dakota, who wore a "you better tell him" expression. Ben sighed again; he needed to keep Kelly's identity hidden. "I've met someone." Time for the interrogation to begin.

"That's great." Dakota smiled and raised his beer in salute.

Cole wasn't as easily fooled. "But?"

"She's great. We've had two dates, but she wants to keep it a secret." Ben lifted the bottle to his lips and took a long pull. Relief flooded him. His friends knew. Even if he kept Kelly's name out of the conversation, it was nice to talk about her.

"Is she married?" Dakota asked with a frown.

"No, of course not." Ben chuckled.

"What's the issue then?" Cole's piercing gaze pinned Ben down.

"I don't know if I should continue to see her." Ben shrugged at the blatant lie. Abandoning the relationship in its fledgling stage was the furthest thing from his mind. He'd already contemplated ways to make it permanent.

Dakota whistled. "Man, that's tough."

"She has her reasons."

"It's not Mona, is it?" Cole asked.

At the mention of Mona's name, Ben frowned and stared over at two guys playing darts. "Nah, apparently I'm not her type."

"More like she's not your type." Cole slapped him on the back. "You'll find your one and only and, believe me, she'll be worth the wait."

Ben nodded and couldn't help the smile that instantly appeared at the thought of Kelly

"So these two dates. What happened?" Dakota grinned and winked at Ben.

Ben's face heated. He couldn't slip too many details for fear he would give Kelly away. "They both revolved around food. One night we had dinner out." *Then we got carry-out and had mind-blowing sex before remembering our dinner.* "The other I made dinner." *More mind-blowing sex.*

"Dessert?" Cole asked, the tips of his ears turning red. Dakota and Ben both chuckled.

"Give me some credit." Ben rolled his eyes. And knowing Cole hadn't meant food, he continued, "Caramel cheesecake. It was pretty rich, but we both ate two pieces." *One after dinner and one around two a.m. after more sexual Olympics.* "So, how are the plans for your new home coming along?" Ben asked Cole.

The usually impassive Cole's eyes lit up, and he waved his hands as he discussed floor plans and building materials. "I want a garage for the vehicles and a tractor. I'd put my tools and equipment in it, and I could do with a workroom so I don't bring the mess into the house." He laughed, fingering his bottle. "Piper says we should build a barn and live in it."

Expounding about the property, Cole spoke in an animated fashion, like a conductor leading an orchestra. A couple times Ben and Dakota shared a glance and a smirk.

"You've got the girl of your dreams to make it all worth it," Dakota said with a wistful smile. He raised his bottle in a toast and Ben clinked it with his. Dakota's eyes seemed empty, as if he forced the happiness. At one time Dakota had set his sights on Piper, but when she had arrived in Texas, an instant attraction sparked for cowboy Cole. Poor Dakota hadn't stood a chance. Piper had even pushed Dakota in Kelly's direction. Ben witnessed them dancing a few times, but that was when things had been rocky between Kelly and Hickey. Thankfully Kelly hadn't liked Dakota for more than a dance partner.

Ben's mind wandered, and he envisioned his own dream house. He saw Kelly smiling at him and his heart raced.

After dinner Thursday night, Kelly had opened up to him about her fantasies. Ben never expected the ideas she divulged or the level of her excitement. Warmth started in his chest as he brainstormed ways to fulfill her desires. His elbow on the table, he rested his chin in his hand and covered his lips. Again a smile grew until his cheeks hurt.

"My biggest fantasy, ever since I was a little girl, is to own the Dungogh house." Kelly closed her eyes and grinned, snuggling back into the pillow and rubbing her rear against Ben's groin. He had wrapped his arm around her waist and pulled her against his hard-on, letting her know how much he wanted her. His heart raced, and his longing to please her swelled like his manhood. He ached to fulfill her heart's desire.

Ben whispered against her neck and she shivered. "I meant sexual fantasy. Although, if I could arrange it, we would make love in each room of the house."

She turned to face him with big eyes and a sweet smile. Her nipples grazed his chest, making his breath catch. "Normal naughty fantasies, like the mile high club?" Her fingers played with his chest hair, trailing toward his belly button, then continued downward. "I'd always thought about making love someplace public." She paused and her fingers stopped moving. "Not out where everyone could see, but where you might get caught. Outside somewhere at night. In a hot tub, maybe."

He lay on his back, pulling her on top of him, and touched her lips. Those love-swollen lips had kissed him everywhere. She pushed up, again grazing him with her pert breasts. He moaned. She leaned and kissed his chin.

"I'll have you know you've already fulfilled two of my fantasies." Kelly laid her head on his shoulder. Her breath grazed his neck. Running his hands up and down her back, he tried to coax the information out of her. He found it odd she'd suddenly become shy after everything they had done to each other's bodies.

She inhaled deeply and whispered, "The wall." Kelly giggled then claimed his neck with her lips and teeth.

"You liked that?" he chuckled low and grabbed her bottom in a firm but gentle squeeze.

Tuesday night, after various pieces of clothing had fallen to the living room floor, he suggested taking it to the bedroom. Kelly commanded,

"Right here, right now." So he had sheathed himself, she wrapped her legs around him, then he took her against the living room wall. It had been the hottest spontaneous sex of his life.

"I did like it. So did you."

"What was the other?" Ben kissed her forehead.

She sighed and snuggled against him. "Waking up to find you still here."

He stymied a gasp. Hickey hadn't stayed the night with her. Why the hell not? What man could make love to Kelly and not want more? He couldn't fathom it. If Ben had his way, Kelly would never wake up alone again.

CHAPTER 7

Kelly

DURING KELLY AND BEN'S LOVE sessions her long hair had become a nuisance. It would get in the way and they'd lay on it, so she usually braided it or put it into a ponytail. He loved to run his fingers through it, but he couldn't do it if it was up. She decided it was time for a cut.

As Kelly entered the Tease Me salon, chemical odors from dyes and perms stung her nose. She threw a smile toward Gloria Sass sitting at the receptionist's desk. The woman barely acknowledged her with a glance before going back to painting her nails. Her reaction was typical and didn't bother Kelly.

Derry Yare, Kelly's long time stylist, called her name and waved. "It'll be another five, Kelly."

Kelly nodded and closed her eyes to envision Ben's naked body and what she could do to it on a hammock in the back garden of the Dungogh House.

A firm hand gently shook her shoulder. Derry grinned down at her. "Oh, whoever he was, I hope it was a good daydream." Kelly blushed, nodded, and tugged at her long braids.

Walking Kelly to the styling chair, Derry asked, "What are we doing today?"

"I think my hair is long enough to donate," Kelly said. She sat and let Derry put a pink smock around her neck.

Derry took out the braids and brushed Kelly's brown locks. "Your hair grows so fast. Goodness me, it's midway down your back already. You have such a pretty natural shade and when the light hits it, I can see both red and blond highlights." She lifted strands of hair and let them sift through her

29

fingers. "I love the slight wave, too. People pay money for that, you know."

Together they decided on a length and then Derry cut it right above a ponytail holder. "I'll put this with the others." She walked to a hallway and out of sight, taking Kelly's hair donation.

Kelly glanced at the other chairs filled with chatting women. She recognized one of Bunny Hopkins' teen daughters. She lifted a hand to Lily White, one of Fortuna's notorious first-pew church ladies. The women, mostly widows and spinsters, fueled the town rumor mill.

Through Tease Me's large picture windows, a police car caught Kelly's eye. She strained to see the driver. Disappointment flooded her when she realized it was Colin, Ben's boss.

Derry returned and after a quick wash, she snipped and shaped Kelly's hair into a work of art. "Any plans tonight?" Derry wiggled her eyebrows and giggled.

Kelly shrugged her shoulders, making bits of hair slide off the smock. "I'm going to a bridal shower for one of my cousins."

"That will be fun."

"I guess." Kelly frowned into the mirror. If her mother started her match-making schemes, it would be torture. Her sister and Ivy would be there to help, but then Kelly would have to hear her mother brag about Olivia and Forrest to all her distant relatives.

"You don't sound convinced," Derry said, pausing and lifting a brow.

"My mom wants me married—yesterday. I'm next in line even though I'm not ready." Kelly crossed her arms under the cape. In the past, her mother had gone to great lengths to get a ride from a friend's single son in order to introduce him to Kelly.

She would also have to endure the nagging and the boasting. Her stomach rumbled, and she rubbed it, hoping she wouldn't get an ulcer.

Luckily, her cousin June would get off her mom's blind date list.

"Moms worry about their kids, and that's all I'm going to say." Derry zipped her lips.

"Well, at least I look respectable. I don't have to worry about Mom telling me my hair is too long or styled like a little girl." Kelly turned her head, making her hair flare out and spring back. "It's so cute, I love it! I'll never get it to look the same. Do you want to come home with me?"

Derry giggled and removed the cape. "You can come in anytime." She swept up the hair from under the chair.

"Kelly Jo," Desire said from behind Derry. Kelly turned and greeted the older woman with a hug. "I have a question for you. Come back to my office once you're finished, all right?"

Gloria stared as if Kelly had been busted and had to go to the principal's office. Gloria snapped her gum and sneered as Kelly paid. She canted her head, examining poor Gloria, remembering a few kind acts. She helped

Desire without complaint and Gloria had helped Jessie by modeling for the Double D Intimates inaugural fashion show. Even with the scoffing, she never gossiped. The young woman's profile was regal until she threw the mean mask back in place. Gloria handed back change and Kelly offered a genuine smile. "Thank you and have a great day, Gloria."

The receptionist sputtered but finally got out, "You too."

Desire's office door was open and the old woman sat in the desk chair. She glanced up when Kelly entered. "Have a seat." Kelly sat in the small oak wood chair and crossed her ankles, then smoothed her skirt.

"Thanks for stopping by, I know you have someplace to be. Derry's done good. You look real pretty." Desire smiled and folded her hands. "Now, Kelly, we didn't have a chance to speak about this the other day and I didn't want to say anything in front of Jessie, Piper, or Gloria." She stood up and closed the door, leaving them alone in the dark-paneled room.

Kelly swallowed and picked a fingernail. She watched Desire reclaim her seat. She couldn't read the old woman's face, but her eyes held a hint of mirth.

"On Thursday, you almost sideswiped me with your car, young lady. What do you have to say for yourself?" Her wrinkled brow pinched into a V.

"I'm sorry, Ms. Hardmann." She wrung her hands, and her face grew hot.

"Jessie said I might excuse you from this mishap if I knew what you were thinking. Is this true?"

Horrified, Kelly tried to keep her expression neutral. "I don't know, ma'am."

"I don't know either, but I'd like to find out. Will you tell me what was all consuming that put my life, your life, and the lives of your friends in jeopardy?" She smiled and leaned forward. "Don't worry, dear. Consider this Confession; nothing goes any further than this desk."

Kelly took a deep breath for fortitude and let it out. "Sex." The silence stretched, and she tried to steady her heart by slowing her breathing.

After what seemed like an eternity, Desire pushed back with a smile. "Well, hot damn, Jessie was right."

A nervous twitter escaped Kelly's lips.

"Tell me about him…"

"Well…" Kelly's face lit up in a smile, making her cheeks ache. "It started with a one-night stand. I'd never done that before. We didn't plan it. We've known each other since high school but we've never gone out or anything and the other night we ended up consoling each other. One thing led to another and," she shrugged, "best sex of my life."

Desire hummed and looked impressed. "Best sex? And you almost hit me the morning after."

"Days later." Kelly grinned and blushed. "He's super sweet and made dinner for me." Kelly glanced down at the tiled floor, hoping Desire wouldn't ask if he had cooked naked. Kelly sighed, fanning herself. She needed to stop thinking of Ben without clothes or she might need to go home and change her panties.

"Sounds a little more serious than a one-night stand." Desire reached across the desk and Kelly clasped her hand. "How do you feel?"

Kelly took a deep breath and smiled. "Wonderful. Happy. Wanted. Sexy. Beautiful."

Desire squeezed her hand. "He sounds like a keeper."

★ ★ ★

Kelly arrived at the Tea Shack and stared up at the gaudy sign branding the lot in the strip mall. It wasn't a house or a shack but a long generic space. As she parked, she noticed other cars slowing and passengers pointing toward the vet clinic. A large white banner with black letters hung in the window. "Please spay and neuter your animals," it read. Someone made an addendum in red, "and weird friends and relatives."

Her thoughts shifted from the town prankster to the bridal shower as she followed a hostess through the dining area toward a large community room at the back. Covered in lace, the tables held small vases of fresh flowers. Black and white photos in ornate gilded frames hung on the walls reminding her of Grandma Myrtle's parlor. Next to the entry was a table with gifts. Kelly added her gift bag hoping the young newlyweds would appreciate the saucy dress up goodies.

Several family members had already arrived. Her cousin June waved. Kelly's mother and her aunts surrounded poor June in the corner. The older women appeared as if they had dressed for church. Kelly looked down at her sundress and hoped her mother wouldn't point it out as being too casual.

"Kelly," a soft voice called from somewhere to her right. Turning, she found Olivia, also in a sundress, staring at the crowd like a nervous horse. It'd been a while since she'd seen her younger sister. Olivia had stayed in Austin over the summer to work. She pulled Olivia into her arms and hugged her.

"Oh thank God, you're here. Now maybe Mom will shut up about how wonderful you and your job are," Olivia said.

"Right, like Mom brags about me. It's me who never hears the end of 'your sister is on the honor roll and she works. Why didn't you work through school?'" Kelly put one hand on her hip and thrust her chin out, mimicking her mother and Olivia giggled.

"You got your hair cut. Wow, I can't believe how short it is." Olivia reached out and touched it.

"Do you like it?" Kelly asked, turning her head to make her waves bounce.

"Yes, it's super-cute." Olivia nodded then whispered, "Let's go rescue June."

Kelly and Olivia greeted their cousin and pulled her away from the corner. "Did you see the sign?" Kelly asked.

"Yes, of all days for the prankster to strike," June giggled. "I'll always remember it."

"I know a couple weird relatives we can neuter," Olivia said, and the girls laughed.

Kelly made the rounds with her sister by her side. Her mother left her alone until they sat for cake. Kelly had made a mistake of sitting between her mother and Martha Maddox, her aunt's best friend. There was a gleam in her mother's eye as she leaned close and asked, "Kelly dear, you remember Martha's boy, Mathias?"

Here we go. Kelly searched for her sister. Olivia was talking with the sister of the groom and was oblivious to Kelly's plight.

"Of course, I remember Mathias." He'd been an awkward teen the last time they had encountered each other. "He must be happily married with lots of kids by now." She crossed her fingers under the table.

"I wish," Martha said with a frown. "He's an executive at a company out of Dallas. And, Fern, he'll be working remotely this summer so he can help me move. He's a good boy." She straightened and sighed.

Also a momma's boy. "That's nice of him."

"Kelly needs a good man," her mother started.

Kelly took a deep breath and murmured, "Don't we all."

"Martha, you know, Forrest and Ivy have one child, Jade. A lovely little girl, but she needs a playmate." She shoved a picture of Jade over Kelly's cake plate. Martha took the photo and gushed. Her mother continued as if Kelly wasn't there. "I hoped Kelly would have married and had a child by now so the cousins could grow up together."

The conversation focused on Kelly's singleness throughout the remainder of the shower. Her head throbbed and her poor tongue had holes where she bit it to keep from lashing out. Her sister had wisely chosen to sit on the other side of the room to avoid becoming someone's arranged bride.

"Martha, do you think Mathias would mind visiting with Kelly while he's in town? She broke up with that showoff she had been dating." She glanced at Kelly.

"I don't see why not," Martha gleefully said.

Kelly fumed, her arms pulled tight over her chest.

"Mathias and Kelly would make beautiful children. Don't you think?"

"Why yes," the other woman agreed.

Kelly reached her breaking point and slapped her palms on the table.

"Well, Mother if you want me to have a child so badly, I just need sex." Kelly shifted to face her mother's crony. "Martha, do you think Mathias would have sex with me so I can provide a beautiful grandchild for my mother to hold? Or I could ask him." Her voice rose as she pointed to the table busser. "It doesn't matter—all I need is a penis."

Every woman turned and gawked at her.

"Kelly Jo!" her mother gasped.

Furious, Kelly slumped in her chair. Heat radiated from her face. She took a gulp of water and stared at the table cloth. Tears gathered. Her chest clenched, and she found it hard to breathe. She pushed the chair back and stood.

Her mother placed a hand on Kelly's arm.

Kelly winced and yanked her arm away. In a hoarse voice she said, "I know my marital status isn't what you want. I know I'm a failure in your eyes, Mom, but my relationships are mine. They aren't yours." She turned and fled the party, hitting her hip on a table in the dining room. She pushed open the front door and left.

The sun warmed her skin, and she inhaled. The sunlight blinded her already blurry vision, but it didn't slow her. She blinked, trying to clear her eyes as she stepped off the sidewalk onto the blacktop.

A screech and a honk. Kelly fell, grasping at the air, but hit something hard, knocking the air out of her lungs. Her heart threatened to pound itself out of her chest. In shock, she opened her eyes to Ben Moore's dark gaze studying her. His hands gripped her elbows where he'd caught her. They stood in the middle of the street.

"Kelly, you were nearly hit by a truck. Why did you run into the road?" He scanned her face then stepped back and assessed the rest of her. "You okay?"

She nodded, unable to speak.

"There are a few ladies exiting the Tea Shack, do you want to talk to them?" he asked. She shook her head. "It's okay, Kelly-bean. I got you." His tender words touched her and the floodgates opened. He pulled her into his arms and held her. She didn't want to leave tear stains on his shirt, but she needed him. Encased in his embrace, she felt at home. After not feeling accepted for who she was, she felt cherished by this man.

Ben walked her away from the onlookers and over to her car. When he glanced back at the crowd, his face transformed into a serious, almost grim expression. He opened the door then started her car. She caught her breath and answered a few questions. Once seated, he leaned in and smiled. "I'll stop by your place tonight." He caressed her cheek. "I love your hair." He winked and returned to his squad car.

Kelly relaxed back, swiped the tears away, and cranked the air conditioner. She didn't know when his shift ended, but she couldn't wait.

CHAPTER 8

Ben

MONDAY, BEN HOPPED UP THE front steps to Fortuna elementary. The large red brick building with fluted pillars had three sets of four steps to enter the front doors.

When he opened the door, the smell took him back to Mrs. Hart's third grade class. He paused, reminiscing. Number lines, ABCs, history, and posters encouraging reminders to think of others first.

He entered the office and announced himself to the secretary. "Mrs. Horne, I'm here for a tour of the building with Herb Utzmeld."

"Yes, Ben," Ima Horne said, pushing her glasses up her nose. She glanced over the computer screen without pausing her typing. "Principal Utzmeld is expecting you." Her attention snapped back to the screen. With pursed lips, her fingers kept clacking. Ima had been the secretary when Ben attended Fortuna elementary school. She wore her gray hair the same way, pulled into a high bun on the crown of her head.

Ben lowered himself into a chair. The itchy brown fabric reminded him of burlap. His knee bumped up and down as he glanced around the room. A round clock hung on one of the pale yellow painted cinderblock walls. Every time the second hand passed twelve, the minute hand clicked into place.

The door with an engraved "World's Best Principal" plaque opened and Herb emerged with a broad grin.

"Welcome, Officer Moore," Herb said. Ben rose and took Herb's offered hand.

"Thanks. It's Ben, please," he smiled.

Herb nodded. "I'm grateful Colin has assigned you as the school liaison.

We need to keep abreast of any potentially disastrous situations." He motioned for Ben to follow. "Should we start with a tour of the building?" They turned right and headed toward the fourth and fifth grade rooms.

"That's fine," Ben said, shadowing the principal.

Even though school wasn't in session yet, Herb wore a brown suit and yellow tie as if to blend in with his surroundings. He walked with his hands clasped behind his back and tilted his head when Ben asked questions. "Do you have any security cameras?"

Herb pointed to the end of the hall to the double door emergency exit. "Yes. There are cameras at the end of each hallway, at the outside doors, and inside the office."

As they approached the end of the hallway Ben studied the small wall mounted camera then peered out the glass doors into the side yard. He pointed toward a mound of sand ten feet from the doorway. "You have fire ants."

"What?" Herb pressed in close fogging the glass. "That won't do." He pulled a walkie-talkie from his pocket, pushed a button, and uttered, "Mrs. Horne."

A static voice replied, "Go ahead, Principal Utzmeld."

"There's a fire ant colony outside Mrs. Barnes room."

"Oh dear! I'll call the exterminator."

"ASAP. Thank you." Herb depressed the button and shoved the walkie-talkie into his front pocket.

The men backtracked to another hallway where the younger grades veered left. Ben scanned the names at each classroom, searching for Kelly's. He observed many teachers in the building putting the finishing touches on their rooms.

"How serious is this problem?" Herb asked, smoothing down his comb-over.

Ben slowed, spotting Ms. Greene's room. "Until we figure out who's behind the racing, it's dangerous."

He peered into Kelly's room. Her mouth formed a perfect O. He waved then continued down the hall.

"Will Ms. Greene be on the safety committee?" Ben asked, glancing into the next room.

"Let's ask her. She would be a valuable asset." Herb nodded. Their footsteps resounded in the vacant corridor.

They rounded the end of the hallway and turned back. Kelly stuck her head out of her room.

Herb raised his hand. "A minute, Ms. Greene. This is Officer Moore. We're starting a safety committee, and Officer Moore is the liaison between Fortuna police and the school."

Her cheeks blossomed pink as she took Ben's outstretched hand.

"Hello. It's a pleasure, Officer Moore."

"The pleasure is mine, Ms. Greene. I hope you're interested in joining the committee but I'll warn you now, you will have to work with me." He threw the challenge out there and the subtle movement of one of her slender brows piqued his curiosity.

"I don't have an issue working with Fortuna's finest." Her gaze raked his body and Ben found it hard to breathe in the stuffy hall.

With a nod, he and Principal Utzmeld moved on. When he glanced back toward her room, she stood mesmerized by his rear. He wiggled it for her, and she crossed her arms and grinned, but didn't leave the doorway.

★ ★ ★

After the meeting, he sat in his squad car watching the traffic in front of the school and listing ideas. He noted a few cars and took down license numbers. They didn't break the law, but he was curious if they lived in the area or were only cutting through. Once Kelly visited her car and retrieved a box. She had effortlessly carried it into the building. Though tempted to help her, he hadn't wanted to draw unnecessary attention to their relationship.

Over the past two weeks, he had stayed at Kelly's apartment five nights. Each time they had sex. Sometimes they would savor each touch, loving each other slowly, and other nights spurred a fevered frenzy. Like Saturday, after the shower. Kelly had hopped on him the moment he walked in the door. He shifted in his seat and turned the AC down a notch. They worked together to achieve new positions and climax. She turned him on like no other woman.

A vehicle slammed on its brakes when the driver noticed his car. It looked and sounded familiar. Ben scribbled down the number and put a star next to it. He scrubbed his face, knowing he'd seen the white Honda before. It had a wide purple stripe and sounded like it needed a new exhaust.

Driving around the school building, he found the windows of Kelly's classroom. Ben parked two spaces away from her red sedan and penned a note on a napkin. He studied the trickle of traffic through the lot. Blowing a long breath, he unbuckled his seatbelt and placed the napkin under Kelly's windshield wiper.

Circling the high school before making his way back to the station, he daydreamed about her response to his note. As he pulled into the station lot, he received a text acknowledging his request. He whistled, practically skipping into the building.

"Ben," Ivy called. "About Kelly."

His whistle fizzled into a sputter. "Excuse me?"

She glanced away. "She was crying, wasn't she?" Ben's face remained passive. "It was a family get together and Kelly's mother can get a little…"

"Overwhelming?" Ben sat on the edge of Ivy's desk.

She nodded. "Over the last few years, I've learned Fern means well, but she comes across as pushy. All the kids think she favors the others more. It's terrible. This time Kelly happened to be sitting between Fern and her good friend who has an unmarried son. Kelly had to endure match-making attempts and jibes about her taste in men because of Sawyer. Poor Kelly snapped. Thank you for catching her. She could have really been hurt if she fell." Ivy reached over and patted his arm.

"I'm glad I was there at the right time," he said in a gravelly voice. Not liking emotion the in his quiet tone, he sprang to his feet, making a quick escape to his small workspace. He rubbed his eyes and leaned back, releasing a pent up breath.

Would Kelly's picky mother approve of an officer for her little girl? Would her father? He pushed the thoughts away. First things first, he'd have to convince Kelly they were more than friends with benefits. It proved hard to do when she wanted to keep the relationship in the closet.

He shook his head and rubbed the ache in his chest.

The computer hummed to life with his touch and he searched the license database. Nothing conclusive other than a wide variety of people traveled the road. Two lived in the neighborhood, one on the other side of Nockerville, and the rest near the high school.

"Ah ha!" The striped Honda lived in Kelly's apartment complex.

★★★

Tuesday mid-morning, Ben carried a manila envelope up the steps through the Fortuna elementary doors, nodding to Ima Horne. Instead of his uniform, he wore a squad T-shirt and shorts. His athletic shoes squeaked as he strode down the tan tiled hallway. He chuckled, trying to step without making any noise on the polished flooring.

Ben wiped damp hands on his shorts, nervous about his mission to fulfill one of Kelly's fantasies. If he was honest with himself, one of his, too. He swallowed and slowed. Looking down, his black basketball shorts had become a tent. He shifted uncomfortably and paused outside her classroom.

Kelly knelt on the floor, stocking a short bookcase with thin paperback books. Her skirt fanned out around her making him grin, wondering if she'd heeded his request.

Only one way to find out. Ben stepped into the room and cleared his throat.

Kelly turned and smiled at him. "About time you got here. I was wondering if you'd show." She stood, dusting her palms on her navy skirt.

Her knees flared the bandanna print hem as she stalked toward him. The feminine sway of her hips hypnotized him, freezing him in place. She touched his face, a gentle caress, snapping him out of the daze. He caught her hand and brought it to his lips. Then he tugged her into an embrace and she sighed against him. "It's nice to have a break. Thanks for giving me an opportunity,"

"Anytime." He placed a kiss on top of her head, breathing in her citrusy scented shampoo. "I need to show you something. Let's go over to the desk." He shook the envelope and handed it to her. She started toward her desk in the corner. Opening the flap, she peeked inside.

Ben scanned the hallway, straining his hearing. The minute hand snapped into place. He dragged the heavy steel door shut and locked it. He tugged on it, making sure it wouldn't open.

Kelly watched with an alluring smile and raised eyebrows. Her eyes dropped to his shorts, and she covered her smile. A blush bloomed on her face and she leaned against the desk. Ben strode to her with confidence and claimed her mouth. Her tongue responded with fervor.

Pulling away, with a raspy voice, he asked, "Did you do it?" His forehead rested against hers.

"You'll have to see," she replied, equally winded.

"First I need to clear the desk." He took her hand and tugged her next to the swivel desk chair. Ben removed a planner, a water bottle, a stapler, and a desktop calendar. He made a pile on the floor where it wouldn't be stepped on.

"What's going on?" Kelly asked with her hands on her hips, the envelope sticking out to the side.

If he was lucky, and he meant to get lucky, Kelly would be okay with an amorous dalliance.

"Check out the envelope." He pointed to her hands. "Now you can dump the contents on the desk."

"Okay," she said, turning the envelope upside down. The paper slid out.

Ben pressed behind her, pinning her to the desk, the photo of the white Honda fluttering to the floor and slipping under the desk. "I'm going to check and see if you followed directions." He placed a string of kisses down her neck, and she shuddered.

"Ben," she breathed, turning slightly. Her lips tipped into a teasing grin. "I didn't do exactly as you asked, but I hope you like it better."

He gasped. Better? Christ. He had asked her to wear a thong. His hands ventured under her skirt, skimming her toned thighs, then traveled up to her buttocks. She moaned as he caressed in circles. His fingers searched for an undergarment, one that might have been created at Double D Intimates, but there was nothing. *Nothing.* He had to see; lifting her skirt, he exposed the flawless round warmth that fit his palms with perfection. His fingers dipped lower, between her legs. She arched her back, inviting. One finger slid into the moist cavity, making her moan his name. He loved the sound, and possessiveness overtook him. He longed to please her. Ben continued to rub and stroke until her breaths came in short pants.

"Ben. I'm close."

He pulled out and turned her around. She pouted. "Don't worry, Kelly-bean. We're only getting started." He lifted her, sat her on the desk, and pulled her against his tent. She latched her arms around his neck and her legs around his back. With only the thin material to separate their hot spots, they groaned. He tipped her head back and plundered her lips. She surrendered with a sigh. Even while their tongues wrestled, he shifted her onto the edge of the desk. He massaged her shoulders. "Lay back on your elbows."

She opened her legs in surrender, wanting to be conquered. Longing threatened to consume Ben, but Kelly's fantasy came first. With a wry grin, he fell to his knees before her and plunged a finger into her core once more. She whimpered when he tasted her nectar. His love nibbles had her mewling, and she rammed her fingers through his hair. She threw her head back, moaning his name as her body shuddered in ecstasy.

He stood, hastily dropping his pants and tried to put a condom on with shaking fingers. Kelly watched through languid eyes, a grin on her swollen lips. "Need help?" she asked, her eyes sparkling with mischief.

Ben didn't want to end it with one thrust, but the heat of her gaze coupled with her touch turned his blood into fire. He glanced over her head. He'd forgotten anyone could see inside. But the side yard remained a ghost town, the bright sun and tinted glass offering protection.

Kelly shifted, drawing his attention once more. "Did you like your surprise?" She chewed on her bottom lip.

"Hell, yes." Ben leaned over her and clutched her hips, pulling them in alignment. She watched his eyes as he buried himself. He pulled out slowly, hanging on by a thread. He repeated the controlled movement.

Frustration apparent, she commanded, "Ben, hard and fast. Now!" Her legs locked around his waist, pulling him in deep. He leaned over her to grab the edge of the desk on either side of her head.

"Yes, ma'am." He pistoned fast and hard, breaking into a sweat. Her hands slid under his shirt against his skin. Together they crescendoed.

He tucked her rag doll-like form against him. Her beautiful, sated body fit his. He pressed his forehead to hers and closed his eyes, trying to stymie the sudden wave of emotion. He had poured himself into her, not only physically, but he'd given Kelly his soul. He breathed in her tropical scent, the fragrance of their love, and tried to ride the euphoria he felt.

Kelly took shallow, rapid breaths. "Wow." Eventually her senses returned, and she slid her arms upward until her hands cupped his face.

"You are amazing."

Ben's eyes snapped open, and her gaze bore into his. He recognized the tenderness mirrored there. Her expression softened as her tears welled, and she placed a whispered kiss against his lips.

He figured it was only a matter of time until she made their relationship public. Until that time he would wait and take what she gave him. His soul mate, his love.

CHAPTER 9

Kelly

MIERDA MOPPED THE BATHROOM WHILE Kelly packed a bag. "It smells good," Kelly said.

"Yes, this new cleaning solution smells better than the old one. Not so strong and chemically, more homey." Mierda's disembodied voice floated down the hall where Kelly was digging in the closet for a beach towel. She wanted the biggest one she owned. The yellow towel with fuchsia hibiscus flowers was her favorite and easy to spot in a crowded area.

Under her white tank top and gauzy skirt she wore a red bikini. She wanted to work on her tan one more time. Since school had started, she hadn't been outside much. She preferred to stay in with Ben, but she needed to head out with her friends before they came knocking on her door, catching the two of them smeared with chocolate syrup and whipped cream. With her bag packed, including an extra set of clothes, she pulled a bottled water out of the refrigerator. She sat at the table and read waiting until Mierda finished.

Mierda came in, her dainty hands clad in green rubber gloves. She wiped her forehead. "Whew. You're all clean. Thank you, Ms. Greene."

"I'm Kelly." She smiled and offered her a bottle of water.

Mierda returned the smile and took it. "When I'm working for you, you're the boss, Ms. Greene."

Kelly giggled. Mierda wasn't much older than her and they could be better friends if her husband would let her out of the house more. He didn't know about the cleaning job and it allowed Mierda money she used to buy groceries and feminine hygiene products. It also bought basics for her daughter, like underwear.

Kelly collected hand-me-down clothes for Mierda's daughter. "Melinda has another bag of clothes her daughter has out grown. Take a peek and see if there's anything Cali would like. I know Melinda gets hand-me-downs from her sisters' kids. I don't know the condition; some might be too worn."

Mierda gave a small shrug, pretending it didn't matter. "I'll look."

Usually she took most under the guise of "we'll see how it fits" and then Cali would wear it to school that week. The seven-year-old wasn't in Kelly's class this year, which was good because of the father. She didn't want Cali to mention her name too much lest he became suspicious of Mierda's side job and the money. Mierda pulled out the contents of the brown paper bag and wiped away a tear. "These are all her size, and I know she'd love this dress."

"Oh no. It has a hole in the back," Kelly said, pointing.

Mierda flipped the garment. A pink uni-kitten with a rainbow horn smiled at Kelly. Mierda brought the fabric closer, her forehead lined in thought. "This is one thing I can fix."

She lowered the favored garment and with a sniffle she admitted, "But Ricardo won't like it. He doesn't like Cali to wear used clothing." Staring at the floor, she quickly swiped a tear away.

"Does he want her to go to school naked?" Kelly grumbled.

Mierda snorted a hiccuping laugh then started to sob. Kelly took the desolate woman into her arms. Ricardo never gave her any money then complained when she didn't have food on the table. The poor little girl had a rat nest for hair because Ricardo had broken the brush while beating his wife, then accused Mierda of breaking it. Kelly couldn't change Mierda's mind or her fear, but she could encourage her friend and continue to gather clothes.

Kelly sent a prayer heavenward thanking God for a good man like Ben.

"You can keep them here if you'd like. You can add one or two a week to Cali's wardrobe. Ricardo won't be the wiser."

Mierda shook her head then slowly she nodded. The buzzer on the dryer sounded. The women folded Mierda's pitiful load of clothes. The tiny shirt with kittens and princesses sent a pang to Kelly's heart. It was a whole other sort of love to be a mother. Suddenly she felt guilty for the way she treated her mother. She rubbed her arm and squeezed her eyes closed. Pushing thoughts of her mother from her head, she folded a size four shirt.

After Mierda left, Kelly locked up then headed to the Double D ranch. The large busted anime woman with D shaped bikini cups on the side of the large steel barn always cracked her up. The crazy town prankster had graffitied the barn, but it turned into publicity and a tourist attraction. Jessie's grandparents had passed, leaving her land, two barns, a house and one sexy ranch hand. Once Josiah convinced Jessie she couldn't live without him, they had gotten married. Everyone could see that the couple had been crazy about each other way before they admitted it.

Kelly parked and wondered if she should go to the barn or the house, but the front door opened. Jessie came out, waving a bright piece of cloth.

"Kelly, look at this." Jessie's excited smile and wide green eyes made Kelly grin. Jessie waved a garment, possibly something sexy from Double D Intimates for Kelly to test. The yellow fabric shimmered like molten gold, every angle a slightly different shade and sheen.

"Gorgeous, I love it. What's it for?"

Jessie giggled, pulling Kelly's attention to her face. "Look again."

Kelly took the golden mass by the thin straps; spilling like a waterfall, it unfolded. "A night gown. Oh, it's a work of art, Jess." Kelly held the nearly floor-length gown against her and swayed back and forth.

"It's for you. I want you to wear it. Try it out. I took the side in here." Jessie pointed to the seam. "See if it's comfortable. I've given one to Piper too and both of you need to sleep in it."

Kelly felt heat rise, and she nodded. She set the gown on the passenger seat and imagined wearing it for Ben.

"Kelly, get your butt inside," Piper hollered from the door. Jessie slipped past Piper into the house.

Kelly skipped to the door and hugged her friend. In her hand, she held her beach bag. "Where are Cole and Josiah?"

"They went ahead to meet a friend. We will meet them there." Piper led the way to Jessie's kitchen where Jessie poured her husband's famous lemonade. Chewing her bottom lip, Jessie handed her a glass.

"Uh oh, you aren't trying to fix me up with someone, are you?" Her hand on her hips, Kelly glanced from one friend to the other.

Jessie examined the floor, and Piper fished a seed out of her glass.

"Mm hmm. Does this friend know what he's in for?" Kelly asked.

Piper had the decency to blush. "We didn't want you to feel like a third wheel. You know him and we trust him."

"Yeah, it's not a date or anything. Just evening up of numbers." Jessie shrugged and placed the paper plates and other items in to a large bag,

Kelly crossed her arms. "You mean when you're off sucking face, or whatever, with your husbands you won't feel guilty leaving me because I'll have someone to talk to." Dakota Redd's face crossed her mind. She sighed and turned to stare out the window. "You know, I don't need you to fix me up. I'm not broken."

"We didn't mean to imply you are," Jessie said, placing a hand on Kelly's shoulder.

"Yeah. Just ignore us. You're perfect." Piper gave her a hug. "Come on, let's load up."

They packed Jessie's truck. Piper took the front passenger seat next to

Jessie and stretched her long legs. Her blond bob swished as she turned to asked Kelly, "How's work?"

"I have eighteen kids this year." She launched into the antics of the first two weeks. "Snotty noses to homesickness. You name it, it happened."

"What about what's his name, your favorite student's dad from last year?" Jessie's eyes in the rearview mirror met Kelly's, and she grinned. "Oh my God, you've seen him, haven't you?"

Piper's head whipped around so fast Kelly thought it might pop off. "Do tell."

"There's nothing to say. Howie popped in to say hi the first day, then the night of the open house his dad stopped by. Since it was an open house they mulled around a while but I needed to focus on the parents of my new students. Andy understood and said he'd see me later."

"Somebody has a crush on you," Jessie teased. "That's great. You deserve a nice guy like that."

Kelly shrugged and leaned back against the seat. "He's good-looking and sweet, but there's no—"

"Sizzle?" offered Piper.

"Exactly. He doesn't do it for me. I love his son to death, though, and wish them well."

"You need sparks between you both," Jessie said.

Kelly crossed her arms and glanced out the window. "To hell with sparks, I want electricity."

CHAPTER 10

Ben

BEN SPIED COLE'S TRUCK IN the Dixon Springs parking lot and pulled into an empty spot next to it. He met Cole and Josiah at the tailgate and helped them unload two oversized coolers. "Holy hell, how much crap are you going to grill today?"

Josiah jumped down from the bed and smiled. "One cooler for the grub and—"

"Another for the beer," finished Cole with a grin.

They hefted the coolers to a shelter with tables, unloaded and set up the folding chairs. Josiah disappeared down the path toward the bathhouse to change into a swimsuit. Ben had seldom seen him out of jeans and a cowboy hat, with church being the only exception.

Ready to swim, Cole had come in a suit like Ben.

Dixon Springs was a summer mecca for the residents of Fortuna and Nockerville. With the school year started and a craft fair going on, the Barnes' had hoped the crowd wouldn't be as large. Most families with small children hung out at the public beach where the water was shallow and warmer. When Ben had driven by, he found the beach already packed.

Nestled under the shade of trees, the shelter was away from the main thoroughfare but near a trailhead. The path wound its way to the source of the spring in a protected grotto.

After Josiah returned and slathered sunscreen over his shoulders, he handed each of them a beer. They relaxed in folding chairs while drinking and talking. A group of giggling girls in bikinis walked toward the trail, casting glances toward them. Ben didn't notice except the noise. He sat up. "Where are your wives?"

Cole and Josiah exchanged a look. "They were waiting on Kelly, and we wanted to snag this primo spot," Josiah answered.

Ben sipped his beer and closed his eyes. The sun warmed his skin but visualizing Kelly's glimmering green eyes melted his heart.

Cole's phone chimed. He pulled it out and tapped the screen. "The girls are on the way," he informed them then scrolled and continued reading. "Piper isn't driving. Jessie is and—oh." He turned red to the tips of his ears and his lips twisted into a crooked smile.

Josiah leaned over, reading the message before Cole could jerk the phone out of eyesight. "Ah, she loves you and wants to kiss your pee-pee later." Josiah laughed.

Shaking his head, Cole covered his crimson face with both hands.

Ben smiled. "Lucky man."

"So I hear there's some unrest on the street near Fortuna Elementary?" Josiah asked.

Ben felt his smile fade and weariness settle upon his shoulders. "The citizens who live on the road went to town hall and demanded the city do something about racing and yard vandalism."

"That sounds serious. What's going on, Ben?" Cole leaned forward, his lips turned down.

Ben scrubbed his face. Would it be bad to get drunk on his day off? "It started with drag racing. Once school was out for the summer the races began. At first they were at night at odd times. The neighbors compared notes and complaints. Several cars have gone off the road into yards, knocking over mailboxes, causing ruts and damaging shrubbery. We're keeping a watch on the high schoolers. They cut through the neighborhood to get to school and football practice."

"Shit." Cole's brow furrowed. "My nephew goes to that school."

"I know. Nothing has happened during the day, and if we sit there all night nothing happens. It's like they know somehow."

"Maybe a racer or a friend lives on the street," Josiah suggested.

Or someone in the force warned them. Ben didn't want to delve there.

Josiah glanced away toward the parking lot. His face transformed into pure joy. "The girls are here." He left the men without a thought, jogging over to his wife. He kissed her like he hadn't seen her in days.

Cole wasn't as fast yet; he stalked his bride as if she were prey. Ben shoved his hands into his pockets, feeling like a stalker as he witnessed his friends' happiness.

Then Ben noticed a leg. Like a red flag to a bull, it stuck out of Jessie's truck door. He recognized Kelly's lithe body. He tried to swallow, his mouth suddenly dry. As she emerged, her skirt rode up, exposing her creamy thighs.

Ben stood, breathing deeply, hoping to relieve the pressure building in his chest. He attempted to portray the non-relationship she wanted and pivoted away. He needed to depict the guy invited along as a third wheel, or sixth in this case.

Unable to ignore her completely, Ben watched her smooth her gauzy skirt. From the corner of his eye he caught her bending into the truck. The skirt rode up again and finally she pulled out a large cloth bag with looping handles.

Kelly hadn't seen him, and she helped Jessie wrangle another bag. Their laughter rung and Ben grinned. She glided carefree between her friends, smiling and laughing. Her countenance was relaxed and happy compared to what he had seen at the bridal shower.

Cole took two bags and Josiah grabbed a pile of colorful towels, and they returned to the picnic shelter. Ben leaned against the wooden support with arms crossed over his blue T-shirt. The men deposited the items on the table.

Kelly still hadn't noticed him, although Piper had and winked. She was one smart cookie. Kelly and Jessie kicked off their sandals and started for the water's edge.

"Come on," Jessie shouted without looking back.

"Watch out for sharks," Ben called.

God, he wished he had a camera for the look of surprise on both women's faces. Kelly's mouth hung open and her gaze raked him from toe to crown.

Jessie squealed "Ben!" and came running, giving him a squeeze.

As he hugged Jessie, Ben met Kelly's eyes. She took a small hesitant step in his direction.

Ben struggled with pretending their relationship didn't exist. He wanted to yell "to hell with it," run to her, pick her up and swing her around. Embracing him tight, she would giggle. Then he'd kiss her and make her forget her name. His lips quirked into a half smile.

"Piper." Ben nodded in greeting. "Kelly."

Kelly raised her small hand and wiggled her fingers. "Hi, Ben." A faint blush feathered her cheeks.

"Are we going swimming?" Josiah asked as he kicked off his shoes. The youngest of the men at twenty-five, he had fine light chest hair that matched his wavy light-brown hair.

Close to Ben's age, Cole had a dark stripe of chest hair. Ben scratched the stubble on his abdomen, suddenly wondering if anyone would notice it. He and Indigo rented a house together and worked out regularly. Indigo's genes worked in his favor, making him mostly hairless, but Ben had shaved his chest. The hair was growing back and was short and prickly. It tickled when Kelly rubbed him.

Kelly stepped out of her skirt and pulled her shirt over her head. Her bikini's skimpy bottoms were red and white striped and the top—oh man. Small triangular scraps of fabric covered her breasts, patriotic navy blue with white stars and red and white stripes.

The men followed the women down toward the beach area. They walked out onto a narrow dock. Several people sat dangling their feet over the edge, and others jumped off the end into the deep water.

Further down, children played happily along the shore on the sandy beach. The sound of laughter met his ears. A little boy with water-wings stretched and batted a beach ball to his sister. A balmy breeze fanned him as he breathed in the fresh air. It was hard to believe nature had hidden the springs smack dab in the middle of the Texas prairie.

"No, Cole." Piper held her hands up. Her firm tone lost its ferocity when coupled with her smile. "It's too flipping cold. I'm not hot enough yet."

"No excuses, Pipes." Cole took a step toward her. She stepped back. "We came here to swim."

"Cole," she warned again.

Jessie snatched Josiah's hand; she covered her mouth to hide her smile. Cole turned around and Piper's shoulders dropped as she relaxed. Cole spun back and picked up his squealing wife and tossed her in. She popped above the water, sputtering, her blond hair now dark. She glared at him. Unfazed, he jumped, forming a cannon ball, and landing next to her, doused her. Piper slugged his arm, and they wrestled for a minute before the kissing began.

Ben clapped his hands once. "So what do you want to do?"

"Let's join them," Kelly answered. Yelling "cowabunga," she ran off the edge toward Piper.

"Hey!" Piper squeaked, wiping water from her face.

Jessie and Josiah shared a look, smiled, and shrugged then jumped together. That left Ben grinning and waiting for the right space. Jessie waded behind Josiah and held him. That opened a spot near Kelly.

"What are you waiting for, Ben?" Cole hollered.

"Your attention, of course." Ben bowed, then leapt off the dock, doing a flip. He drenched the group. When he popped his head above water, Cole splashed him.

"Man, you're a showoff," Cole laughed.

The friends swam and relaxed until Josiah mentioned lunch. He excused himself to grill the food. After a while, Ben and Cole joined him.

As they filled their plates, Kelly took a seat across from Jessie. They laughed while they ate and drank.

Piper opened a second beer and Cole teased. "Darlin', you're nearing kryptonite level."

"You sir, are a gentleman." Piper clinked his bottle.

Kelly leaned forward, glancing past Cole to her friend. "Piper, maybe he wants you at kryptonite level. You know how you get."

Across from Piper, Ben turned and asked Kelly, "Are you saying she's easy when she's drunk?"

Kelly looked down at her plate with a blush blooming on her cheeks. She drew a deep breath and straightened her shoulders before meeting his gaze. "I'm suggesting. Cole likes it."

"Nah," Ben said with a wave of his hand. "There isn't a challenge. We like a challenge."

Jessie snorted then tried to cover it by coughing. Jessie and Kelly shared a glance and giggled. They exchanged words, but uttered them too low for him to hear.

Piper cleared her throat. "What did you say?"

"Jess said that men sometimes like the hunt but they'll take easy. Especially if they are horny." Kelly's red face deepened in color.

"And they're always horny." Jessie poked Josiah in the side.

"Yep, that's the truth." He agreed and leaned back like he was full, his chest expanding.

"It's not just men," Ben offered. Kelly dropped her plastic fork to her plate with an inaudible gasp.

"That's true," Josiah once again agreed.

"Women want it just like guys do, sometimes even more." Ben took a long pull from his bottle to hide his grin and help defuse the heat on his face. *Let Kelly's panties get wet thinking about the wild thing.*

★★★

"Let's go jump off the cliff," Piper said. She swung her head around the table.

"You've never done it before?" Ben asked.

"Not yet," Piper said grinning. She gathered her and Cole's trash and tossed them in a nearby bin.

Ben turned, following her with his gaze. "You realize the cliff is more like a giant boulder." He hadn't jumped off in years.

Piper rubbed her hands together. "I know. I can't wait."

Ben glanced toward Kelly. She seemed to shrink as she rubbed her arm.

After cleaning up the picnic area, the group followed a trail worn smooth in the brown rock leading to the swimming hole.

The day had been sunny, but lazy clouds rolled in. Kelly walked beside Jessie; they'd giggle every so often.

On the banks of the water, people gathered, waiting for their friends or loved ones to climb and jump. Three young women ran off together, screeching all the way to the water. After they cleared the pool, a man dove.

The deep water was green, not a swampy, stagnant color but the color of life.

A rock outcropping yawned over the pathway near the base and around the swimming hole. It reminded Ben of a sinkhole, a giant drain in the earth. Hidden in the shadows, the temperature dropped a few degrees. Moss, lichen, and ferns speckled the brown stone with hues of green.

A man squealed like a wounded pterodactyl as he fell and hit the water's surface with a tooth-rattling smack. Every eyewitness cringed. The small man with a short crop of hair swam to another nearby rock and climbed up. He adjusted his trunks and goggles. A few bare-chested cowboys in cutoffs, cheered him. His stomach and legs tinged pink, he raised his fist in triumph, earning catcalls and whistles. Somebody threw him a towel.

Ben's group passed him as a couple jumped off holding hands. The girl's high pitch scream echoed off the walls. Suddenly Kelly and Jessie were laughing and all he heard was "Speedo." He caught Josiah's gaze, and they pressed closer to listen.

"Remember all those swim meets we sat through?" Jessie elbowed Kelly. "You had the biggest crush on Ben and that other guy. What's his name, Craig?"

Ben could not help himself—he reached out and pulled Kelly to a stop. "Hold up. You had a crush on me?"

Kelly's eyes widened but Jessie beat her to the answer. "Don't get all excited, Ben. We were sophomores, and you were a senior. You wouldn't have noticed her." They continued forward.

"Plus, you had a girlfriend, not that she came to any meets, though," Kelly mumbled.

"We were there mostly for the Speedos, anyway." Jessie giggled and elbowed Kelly.

"Who wants to go first?" Piper asked as they crested the plateau and looked over the rim. She gave Cole a nervous but excited smile. Two teens yelled and ran off the edge together. Kelly took a step backward, bumping into Ben.

"Sorry," she muttered, but she stayed close. He placed a palm on her back and her shoulders relaxed.

Jessie pulled Josiah behind the line of three waiting their turn. "Clear," one said then a girl ran and jumped, disappearing from sight. After a splash, occasional shouts resounded up the rock walls. The words swallowed by the space reflected the tone of good times and fun.

Ben had enjoyed going to Dixon Springs as a teen. Though his alcoholic mother had never taken him or his brother, Ben had always joined friends. Even as a kid, he believed the concave half-dome shape shading the pathway and the towering boulders gave a brave explorer a true cave-like experience.

Climbing to the pinnacle and gazing out over the pristine, spring-formed waterway, tall trees lining the sides, the divers would take a deep breath then plunge off the high peak into the cold, clear water below. Looking upward, the sky had turned gray and become crowded with clouds.

When Jessie's turn came she didn't hesitate, she ran and leaped off the side without fear. Josiah followed, diving like a frog with his legs in a V shape. Piper and Cole ran off together. One of them yelled the whole way.

Kelly peered over the edge again with a pasted-on smile and waved to Jessie. Her face had paled. Ben worried she would pass out and hit the rock surface on the way down.

The rock plateau remained empty except for them. "I don't think I can do this," she whispered, staring down into the murky pool.

Another group arrived, and she studied their feet as they jumped into the air. She gasped as they flayed their arms and hit the water. When they emerged, she let out a deep breath.

"You've done it before," Ben encouraged. He'd been there one time to see it.

"A long time ago," she breathed.

Her brittle tone made his heart ache to protect her. He tugged the string of her bikini top. She clutched it to her chest. "Ben!"

He led her away from the edge so she couldn't see the water. Stopping near the top of the pathway, he faced her. "I'm sorry. I wanted to distract you from the drop."

She nodded and spun. Lifting her hair, she said, "Fix it, please."

Ben tied the strings tight. He wanted to make sure her top stayed on when she hit the water.

Two tween kids pulled their dad up the trail. "Good luck, man." Ben said as the father passed.

Kelly's fists knotted and her foot tapped. He'd never seen her so nervous. He took her hands in his and tried to get her to focus on him. She looked back over toward the flying family. "Don't worry. Your friends can't see us." With one finger, he caressed her face, and she blinked. He stepped closer and kissed her cheek.

"I can't jump. Ben, I'm too afraid."

"How d'you do it before?" Ben cocked her chin so she gazed into his eyes.

A dry laugh escaped her lips. "Liquid courage."

"Well, I could offer encouragement of another sort." He took the hand he was holding and put it on the front of his bathing suit. Her warm palm cradled his dick, and it jerked. As his erection grew, her fingers curled around him and she raised a brow. A hint of a true smile bloomed.

"Do you want to see it?" he asked.

"Right now?" She tilted her head.

He messed with the trunk's tie, first untying it then retying it. Mesmerized by his hands, she frowned when he stopped. "You can't see it unless you jump with me."

Emotions scrolled over her face; first her brow dipped in annoyance, then her gaze rolled to the edge. Kelly sucked in her bottom lip but finally she squared her shoulders, pressing her lips into a grim line of determination. She stomped back up the trail.

He watched her scantily-clad rear wiggle as he tried to stymie a laugh. Who knew his dick had such power? He would have to follow through later. His heart kicked up a notch.

"You coming?" she asked, offering her hand.

He stalked up to her and hugged her then walked over to the ledge. Jessie and Piper had their heads tipped together while staring up. Ben waved.

Jessie cupped her hands to her mouth and yelled, "Help her down."

He saluted then squeezed Kelly's hand. "Together on three. Take a few deep breaths. Ready?"

Kelly nodded, her breasts rising as she inhaled.

Side by side they ran and plummeted over the edge, falling together and going underwater. She clawed the darkness. He reached for her and pulled her against him. "Hold on, Kelly-bean. I've got you."

CHAPTER 11

Kelly

HER HEART BEATING OVERTIME, KELLY quit squiggling and snuggled against Ben, forgetful of their touching boycott. He steadied her on the sandy, shallow creek bed then helped her out. He seemed reluctant to let her go.

"You okay?" Piper held out a towel.

"I'd forgotten how heights paralyzed her." Jessie frowned as she explained to Ben.

"She'll be fine. She just needed to work through the fear," he said, winking at Kelly.

Kelly's face heated at the fuss and she shifted the towel around her shoulders. "I'm okay, Jess."

Piper and Jessie whisked her off to the picnic area and sat her down with a cold beer. Kelly finally felt her heart slow. The whole experience seemed surreal. Her friends doted on her like an invalid. It annoyed her, but she let them.

The men waded far enough away to be out of earshot. Ben kept glancing over at her, keeping tabs.

Kelly couldn't help but watch him move. He was an extraordinary man, well-muscled and with a chiseled jaw that sported a sexy five o'clock shadow. Josiah and Ben started to wrestle, and the definition in Ben's biceps intrigued her.

Piper cleared her throat. *Uh, oh.* They'd spotted her drooling over Ben. She swallowed, feeling the heat on her face. "Ben saved you, Kelly." Piper glanced toward him and a stab of jealousy hit Kelly. He had saved Piper, too.

Kelly tried to keep her cool. "That's his job."

"Sure, he helps people, but he's a good man, Kelly." Jessie touched her arm. "You should ask him out."

Kelly opened her mouth to protest but Piper blurted. "I dare you to ask him out." She stood with hands on her hips, a look of challenge on her face. "Not dinner, but to coffee or something." Piper took Kelly by the hand and pulled her to her feet.

"Go talk to him." Jessie gave her a little push. "You should thank him, anyway."

Kelly glanced over at the men huddled in a group, and it looked as if Josiah and Cole were ganging up on Ben. She sighed then faced Piper. "What do I get if I accept your dare?" She poked Piper in the shoulder.

"Well, I—"

"A gift card to A Hole in One," Jessie blurted and gave Piper a wink.

"Sure, that's good," Piper agreed with a nod. "Go ask him."

Kelly did an about-face and stared at Ben. Sensing something, he straightened and met her gaze. She took a small step toward him then hesitated. Piper pushed her and Ben smirked. Kelly rolled her eyes, earning a large smile from him. Her stride steady, she headed forward.

Cole elbowed Ben and pointed toward Kelly. His only response to whatever Cole said was a nod. Ben's eyes remained fixed on Kelly's approach.

A horn honked, momentarily distracting her. She heard a familiar child's voice holler, "Ms. Greene," and she froze.

Kelly glanced over to Ben, who frowned and started toward her. She took a deep breath, reluctant to pull her gaze away.

Hurried footsteps drew near but stopped a few feet behind her. "Ms. Greene?" the voice said timidly.

Kelly turned and glanced down at Howie. He had grown since he'd been in her class last year.

A lanky man with a sheepish grin followed the sandy-haired youth.

"Hi, Ms. Greene. Have you been swimming? Daddy and I have. It was real fun but now it's gonna rain. Daddy says we need to get home before it thunders. I'm hungry. I think we should stop for food." The words tumbled out as one.

Both father and son had changed since Howie began second grade. Being raised by a single father, one who doesn't see things like personal grooming, he had disadvantages. Kelly had to meet with Andy and gently inform him that his son's odor had attracted the other kids' attention. Overwhelmed, Andy worked and parented full time while dealing with his ex-wife. His son's mother had been in and out of jail for drug addiction and at one point tried to sell Howie for drugs.

While Andy was a nice guy, and handsome to boot, there wasn't that spark. Like his son, Andy had the clearest blue eyes. Father and son wore damp trunks and Star Wars T-shirts. While Howie prattled on about swimming, Andy's gaze raked her bikini-clad body. She crossed her arms over her chest and hoped they'd move on soon.

"Daddy, can Ms. Greene come to dinner with us?" Howie looked up at his dad with puppy dog eyes.

"I don't see why not. Kelly?" Andy said, grinning.

Ben touched Kelly's elbow, and she relaxed. "Sorry, sport, we've got other plans," Ben said to Howie.

"Ah," Howie said his nose crinkling.

"Another time," Andy said, lowering his head.

"Thanks for asking," Kelly smiled. "Have a good dinner." She waved as she and Ben walked away. "Thanks again, you're a lifesaver. I could kiss you."

He chuckled. "Dare you."

Kelly gasped then laughed. "I was coming to talk to you because of a dare." Ben arched a brow. Kelly gave a sideways glance to inspect her friends. Heads together and eagle-eyed, Jessie and Piper watched her interaction with Ben. "Piper dared me to ask you out, you know, for saving my life and all."

"I'm detaching from the conversation," he said, staring toward the parking lot as he crossed his arms and widened his stance.

Kelly covered her mouth to hide her smile.

Ben shook his head, and she giggled. Over Ben's shoulder, Cole and Josiah watched as intently as Piper and Jessie. In fact, Josiah hastily texted someone on his phone. "Does Jessie have her phone out?" Kelly asked

Ben inspected Jessie. "Yeah, why?"

"Josiah must be texting her. I bet she's telling him about the dare."

"Are you going to ask me out?" Ben asked with a smirk.

"No. I'm too shy this time. I'm holding out for a gift card for a restaurant. A Hole in One isn't a good place for a first date."

Ben tilted his head, scratching the back of his neck.

"If I ask you out, I would get a gift card for coffee."

"I see." Ben nodded, rubbing his chin. "Maybe I can get the guys to up the ante. Cole mentioned something about Piper being in match-maker mode."

"I dare you." She winked. Then Kelly stepped close, reaching for his hand and squeezed it. "Thank you for distracting me up there. I couldn't move."

"No problem. All you needed was the proper motivation." Wiggling his brows, he pulled his hand away.

"You don't offer that motivation to all the girls you help, do you?" A sudden pang of worry washed over her. She didn't want to share.

Ben leaned in, a whisper of a smile on his lips, his dark eyes pools of liquid longing. "Only for you, Kelly-bean."

With a stiff nod she said, "Good." Her heart ached as she stepped away from him. "I've got to deliver the bad news."

"Okay. I'll stare at your ass the entire walk back and give them something to goad you with."

★ ★ ★

The windshield wipers groaned as Kelly relaxed in the passenger seat of Jessie's pickup, staring out the side window. "Thanks for riding with me," Jessie said.

"Of course," Kelly straightened. "I wouldn't have minded riding with Ben if you and Josiah wanted to be alone." Her face pulled into the familiar smile when she thought of Ben.

"It's fine. We see each other every day," Jessie said with a giggle. "Anyway, I didn't want it to be awkward for you. I can't believe this rain." Jessie hit her signal and then turned. "It cut short our outing."

Kelly glanced in the side mirror, spotting the caravan of Cole's and Ben's vehicles. "I enjoyed the sun while it lasted. But I don't care what I do as long as I'm with friends. Thanks for opening up your home."

"No problem. I think Cole and Ben were happy when Josiah invited them back to the Double D."

Kelly nodded. "I saw that. Both their faces lit up like they'd just won a million dollars."

"Who knew my grandma's books would create such a fuss?" Jessie giggled again.

"Don't forget your dare to read them," Kelly pointed out. "What are you working on now?"

The scenery flashed by as Jessie droned on about materials, cut of fabrics and types of straps. With Ben's offer fresh in her mind, Kelly had a hard time focusing on Jessie.

Kelly bolted upright, making her seatbelt lock. "Turn here!"

Jessie jerked the wheel, taking an alternate route. Her lips pressed in a firm line. "God, Kelly, you scared the bejesus out of me."

"Sorry, Jess, I wanted to see it. It's for sale again, you know."

Jessie's expression softened, and she glanced into the rearview mirror. The others had followed them on the detour. The rain turned from sprinkles to a steady drizzle. Jessie slowed and stopped next to a Victorian house with a for sale sign.

"So it's true." Kelly whispered then giggled, bouncing in the seat. "I've got to get the information from the info tube. Be right back."

Kelly pushed open the door and jogged through the yard to the sign.

She twisted the tube open and pulled out the paper. Five bedrooms, three and a half baths, cellar, remodeled master bath. She sighed and stared at the Victorian house. The grand home had fueled many of her dreams.

A car honked, but despite the drizzle, she continued to inspect the front porch. Weeds had grown up, and the paint peeled as if it was shedding skin. Kelly didn't know if she could afford the house, let alone the repairs. She could only hope. A smile broke out.

Kelly returned to the sidewalk reading the details, now soggy from the rain. When she looked up, the only car waiting was Ben's.

"The others went on," he informed.

As if she didn't know. Water dripped down her face. She futilely wiped at it. He reached back between the seats and grabbed his towel. "Here you go."

"Thanks."

Ben shifted into drive and started for the ranch. "That's your house?"

Kelly sighed and closed her eyes. "Yes. I've always loved that house. Back when I was a kid, I visited Mrs. Dungogh and helped my mom weed her garden. It's an English garden with roses and paths. We'd sit on the patio or porch and drink sweet tea. Honestly, I don't think she liked children much, but she loved my mother." Kelly set the paper aside and dried off.

The couple arrived last at the ranch and all eyes swiveled to them when they entered the kitchen. Kelly, in soggy clothes and damp hair, felt like a drowned rat.

"You can hop in the shower if you need to," Jessie offered. She pointed to the hall with the bath the cowboys used.

Piper frowned and waved her finger back and forth. "I wouldn't do it if I were you." Her voice lowered, but everyone still heard, "She locked Cole in the bathroom with me when I was in the shower."

"You didn't complain," Cole said nudging her.

"Well, you were smoking hot and protected me from Justin that day." Piper leaned close and kissed Cole on the cheek.

Ben clutched the top rung of the ladder-back chair. "That was the day Justin came but didn't leave?"

"Yes, sir." Piper shivered and Cole put an arm around her.

"What smells good?" Kelly asked, changing the topic to something that wouldn't upset Piper. Plus, she'd been with Sawyer when she had learned the stalker had arrived. The heavenly scent seemed an easy diversion.

"That's a new candle. Let's hang out in the living room," Josiah suggested and led the way. Piper and Cole shadowed Josiah and Jessie through the doorway.

Ben held out a hand, "Ladies first." Kelly's face heated at the simple gesture and when she'd passed, he playfully tapped her bottom.

CHAPTER 12

Ben

BEN RELAXED BACK INTO THE brown leather chair across from Kelly. She appeared childlike with her ankles crossed, swinging and her feet too short to touch the floor.

Sewing magazines and a dog-eared romance novel lay on the coffee table.

"Is it any good?" Cole asked, motioning toward the book.

Josiah shrugged. "It's not bad, but I've read better." He picked it up and tossed it to Cole who snatched it like a frog grabs a fly. He flipped it over and studied the blurb.

The air conditioning kicked on and a cool breeze fanned Ben's skin. Goosebumps rose on Kelly's arms. The hairs weren't the only thing standing erect; her nipples pressed through her damp white tank. He shifted uneasily. If he had noticed, then Cole and Josiah had too, and he wasn't okay with that. His gaze skittered around the living room searching for an excuse to cover Kelly properly. Thankfully, Jessie provided one.

"I'm going to get snacks." Jessie hopped up and exited the room.

"I'll help," Ben offered, following her out.

Jessie smiled when he entered the kitchen. She threw a bag of chips at him which he caught and opened. He poured them into a bowl she set on the counter.

Ben scratched the back of his head, wondering how to word his request.

Jessie faced him with hands on her hips. "Just say it, Ben; you look like Tippy has your tongue." At hearing her name, the orange three-legged tabby cat jumped down from a kitchen chair, stretched, then wove between his legs.

Ben patted the kitty then took a deep breath and rambled. "I think we need to find another shirt for Kelly." The sentence turned into one long word and Jessie just stood and grinned. He felt heat to the tips of his ears. He pointed his index fingers and placed them next to his chest. "Her headlights are on."

Jessie batted his arm. "Geez, Ben. I'm sure she'd appreciate you noticing." The sarcasm dripped from her tone.

Ben cleared his throat. "I'm a guy and I notice things like that. I'm also not the only guy in the room."

"Oh." Jessie's grin slid off her face. "Hmm, maybe you're right. Could you get Kelly and meet me in the laundry room? Back there." She pointed down a dim hallway leading off the kitchen toward the back of the home.

"Sure." Ben poked his head around the corner.

Kelly had crossed her arms, hugging herself. Ben grinned. She must have discovered the perkiness. "Hey, Kelly—" He caught himself before he said "Kelly-bean." "Jessie needs you."

Even though she eyed him warily, she followed him into the laundry room. Jessie had a selection of shirts. "All these are men's clothes. Either Josiah's or Matt's. I'd thought you might want to put on a dry shirt." Jessie stuck her hand back into the basket.

"Actually, I probably should get out of my wet bathing suit. My bag is in my car." Kelly stepped toward the door.

"I can run out and get it for you," Ben offered.

"But it's raining and I'm already wet."

Both women watched as he pulled off his shirt and threw it at Kelly. He loved the way Kelly's eyes raked his naked torso. God, he longed for her hands to touch him. Jessie cleared her throat, alerting him they were being observed. His lips twisted up into a smirk. "Is your bag in your car or one of the others?"

"Mine." Kelly smiled sweetly and his heart sped up. "Thanks, Ben."

"It's my pleasure."

With Jessie behind her, the tip of Kelly's tongue darted out and licked the corner of her lips. Damn, he needed to escape before he pulled Kelly into his arms and kissed her breathless.

In the hall out of eyesight, he drew in a deep breath. He paused, hearing Jessie tease, "He likes you. Have you asked him out yet?"

Kelly chuckled nervously. "I haven't had a chance."

"What about in the car? Or did you talk his ear off about that house? You did, didn't you?" Jessie sighed. "You're going to scare that man away before he gets to know you."

"Nothing wrong with him knowing my hopes and dreams." Ben envisioned her wide green eyes practically glowing with excitement like they did when she told him about the house.

"That's a big dream," Jessie said.

"Yeah, so is starting a new lingerie business," Kelly mumbled.

Ben recognized the hurt in Kelly's tone. And he agreed with her. Why couldn't she dream of starting a bed-and-breakfast in the awesome old house?

He hustled to Kelly's red sedan. The cool raindrops peppered his skin, relieving the balmy heat. On the passenger seat he found a purple bag with clothes and saw something shimmer. He touched the golden fabric and immediately dropped the bag on the car's floor. With both hands he gently picked up the silken material. It slid open, its length gathering in the seat like a puddle of sunshine. The striking feminine negligee with spaghetti straps was a Double D Intimates work of art. A lopsided grin formed, knowing Kelly would wear it.

Ben picked up the bag again and returned to the house.

He found Kelly alone in the bathroom working a comb through her hair. She wore his Fortuna squad tee that claimed her as his. "My shirt looks good on you."

She started and faced him. "As if I had a choice."

"I didn't want you to wear those other guys' things."

She raised a delicate brow. "Jessie was looking for one of her shirts. She hadn't dug one out of the clean laundry yet."

"Oh." Ben's face heated, and he shifted, remembering the bag. "Here."

She sat it down and turned lifting her hair. "Can you get this knot out?"

The bikini tie was visible on her neck as was the large knot he made before their jump. He tried to work the knot loose, but the damp material held. The strap left a red line, an imprint, in her skin. "I'm sorry it's so tight. Why didn't you say something?"

"I wasn't thinking correctly at the moment, remember?"

Frustrated he couldn't loosen the knot, he blew out a breath and slid his hands under her shirt to the other tie. This one pulled loose. He tugged the neck tie up and over her head. She continued to coax it out of her shirt then dropped it on the floor. He massaged the angry skin on her neck then kissed it.

In the mirror, Ben caught her hungry gaze staring at his lips. He pressed forward, his arms encircling her, and she leaned back against him. With a devilish smirk, he skimmed his hands up under the front of the T-shirt, caressing her once again pert nipples.

Kelly threw her head back on his shoulder and moaned. The sound went straight to his groin. Ben spun her around and placed a passion-laced kiss on her open mouth. Their tongues dueled for supremacy. He'd let her win every time. She locked her leg around his and tugged him closer.

Ben bit back a groan. He needed to rein it in or he'd take her against the wall like that first night.

A knock at the door startled them, and they broke apart with sheepish grins.

"Everything okay in there?" Jessie asked. Her sing-song voice spoke volumes.

Kelly picked up her bikini top and handed it to him, then opened the door and pushed him out. "I had a knot problem," she said to Jessie.

"I can dry those," Jessie said taking the top.

"Okay. Hold on." Kelly closed the door. Then the door opened a crack, and she handed out the bikini bottoms.

Jessie motioned for Ben to follow. They returned to the laundry room, and she pointed to a pile of folded shirts. "Pick a shirt, Ben."

Kelly stepped out of the bathroom clothed in a jean skirt and his squad tee. That look made him hot.

"You're wearing something else," Kelly said to Ben.

He pulled the gray Hammered shirt away from his stomach and rolled his shoulders. "It's Josiah's," and a little tight around the biceps.

When the three reappeared in the living room, the men glanced at Ben with crinkled eyes and smirks. "Nice shirt," Josiah said.

"Shut up." Ben laughed. "I think the guy who wore it has to be a shrimp."

"You've got that right," Cole teased.

Kelly's shoulders relaxed as the men's banter revolved around Ben.

"Nice of you to give a lady the shirt off your back, Ben. But Jess, couldn't you have given him one of Matt's shirts?" Josiah asked.

Without glancing up from her discussion with the women, Jessie replied, "that is one of Matt's shirts."

"It is?"

"No."

A round of laughter broke out. The Barnes' living room felt cozy when surrounded by friends.

Ben settled back into the leather chair, observing the group. He could get used to hanging out with the Barnes and Darts as a couple.

We could raise babies together. Ben sucked in a breath and started to cough. His thoughts were once again rebelling against his bachelorhood.

CHAPTER 13

Kelly

THE WORK WEEK SEEMED TO fly by during the day, yet for Kelly the evenings lagged. Ben had to work the night shift. They'd had dinner at her apartment a few nights. No sex, just conversation and a kiss when he left. Normalizing their relationship was nice, but she missed waking with him.

Friday the safety committee met after school to discuss options for keeping the kids safe. Kelly entered the conference room with a cold bottle of water, a pad of paper, and a blue ink pen.

Talking with Ben, Principal Utzmeld stood at the far end near the large dry erase board. He would run his fingers through his comb over as if the remaining hairs would jump ship. Herb's bright Buzz Lightyear tie caught her attention. His ties were fun cartoon characters or bright objects the kids liked.

Kelly sat her notepad down and smoothed her denim jumper. She anticipated his reaction when he realized she was wearing his fantasy dress. She grinned, studying the way his tight navy police polo and dress pants hugged his toned body.

"Wowza," Mia Hancock said as she fanned herself. The long-haired blonde second grade teacher had volunteered for the safety committee. She batted long eyelashes at Ben, trying to catch his attention. "Nobody said we'd get a hottie policeman here. It totally makes staying after school and listening to a boring meeting worth it."

Kelly barely kept from rolling her eyes. "I thought keeping the kids safe would be the best motivation."

"That too." Mia tutted then pushed past Kelly, whispering, "Eye candy is always nice." She crinkled her nose in a flirty smile, walked straight to

Ben, and stuck out her hand. Kelly's stomach gurgled, and she found it hard to breathe, as if someone had punched her.

Herb introduced Mia to Ben, and they talked. Ben's gaze circled the room until it fell on Kelly and his eyes widened. His gaze raked her dress, and he shifted his weight. He swallowed and had to clear his throat before continuing.

Mia followed his gaze and frowned then stepped in his line of sight.

When Ben excused himself to talk with an older teacher, Kelly bit her knuckles in relief. Harry Fawker was planning to retire at the end of the school year, opening a position for a fifth grade teacher. He had been teaching for over thirty years and loved the kids.

Prairie Barnes strolled into the room with a smile. "Sorry I'm late. I had a parent stop in." She took a vacant seat beside Kelly.

Herb called the meeting to order. "Thank you all for agreeing to be a part of this committee. You are all vital to its success and we value your ideas and time. As you know, we are partnering with the Fortuna Police department to help stem the wave of dangerous drivers that have been plaguing this neighborhood. Officer Moore is our liaison to the police department. He's here with some updates on the increased patrols. Officer Moore…"

"Thank you, Herb. I'd like to offer my appreciation for investing your time for the safety of Fortuna's legacy." Ben paused, meeting her eyes. His tender gaze made her stomach flip-flop. Kelly sipped her water. His face reddened, and he cleared his throat again.

Ben continued, "I recognize that your time is precious, and I won't keep you longer than necessary." He picked up a stack of papers and gave them to Herb who took one and passed them around. "We've been patrolling more and have given citations, but haven't caught the man whom the witness saw tearing up yards and drag racing." He glanced at his list. "The county has agreed to change the caution yellow school signs to florescent yellow. I hope it will make more of an impact, at least during school hours."

Kelly watched Ben's lips form words and his Adam's apple bob as he spoke. From the passion in his voice, she understood he enjoyed his job. Warmth nagged her heart, blossoming into full-blown pride.

Kelly took advantage of the time to memorize Ben's features. The color of his intelligent brown eyes reminded her of chocolate, and the movement of his sinfully long lashes fascinated her.

Herb took notes and occasionally peered around then returned to his chicken scratch.

"Does anyone have any ideas they'd like to add?" Ben asked, opening the floor to discussion.

Prairie raised her hand. "How about a neighborhood watch?"

Ben nodded and smiled. "Good idea. Mr. Mellan, the gentleman who lives on the corner of Oak Street, has started one, and he is petitioning to get a permanent program set up. He's been to see Mayor Delay."

Ben went into further detail regarding reported incidents to curb the rash of questions about victims and the violence.

"How about a night time stake out?" Mia asked brazenly. Elbows on the table, she rested her chin on her palms and smiled seductively.

"We have tried it. Nothing happens," Ben said.

Even though he answered Mia's questions with respect and patience, Kelly hoped from his clipped speech that Mia had annoyed him. Kelly rubbed her stomach.

"That's unfortunate," Harry remarked.

"It's odd. Any time a car sits overnight there isn't any activity," Ben said, rubbing his chin.

"Like they're being warned," Herb mused, tapping the notepad.

After a short silence Kelly asked, "What about speed bumps?"

"Ugh. I hate those things," Mia grimaced.

Kelly ignored Mia and focused on Ben. "Not the little ones, those big ones."

"Speed humps." He raised a brow and his lips parted slightly before he looked pointedly down at the paper before him. "That's an excellent idea."

"The residents won't like it," Harry said.

"The kids' safety is paramount, and they won't mind if it keeps the vandals from driving in their yards," Prairie reasoned.

After the meeting, Ben and Kelly strode side by side through the corridor lit by florescent lights. They remained quiet.

Kelly wiped her damp palms on the denim, unable to bring up Mia's name. Kelly's attraction to Ben had grown into affection and it complicated her plans. The ache that had started when Mia flirted with Ben hadn't eased.

Kelly stole a shy sideways glance, finding him looking forward with a furrowed brow and lips pressed together. He appeared to have a mission in mind and it involved her desk. She wanted more than the friends with benefits that had developed between them.

She tripped and caught herself. Dang, she could be clumsy if she became distracted.

"You okay?" Ben asked, taking her elbow.

She nodded and pushed her hair behind her ear. Just the touch of his hand sent a quiver to her core. They paused outside her door, and she smiled up into his dark chocolate eyes.

A rhythmic click-clack against the linoleum tiles caught their attention. Mia Hancock walked deliberately toward them, her blonde hair swishing in time to her steps. Her hips swayed a hypnotic trance to most men but Ben whispered into Kelly's ear, "That one's a floozy, isn't she?"

"Mia sees something she wants and goes after it." Kelly faced him. Her gaze held his. "You've got to admire that kind of determination." She rubbed her lips together.

"Oh, Kelly, thank you for detaining Ben for me," Mia said, stretching a slender arm out reaching for him.

White hot anger erupted and Kelly stepped between Mia and Ben. Balling her fists, Kelly said, "I did no such thing, Mia."

"Tsk, Kelly. You knew I needed to speak with him." Mia stepped around Kelly, her eyes blinking as if dust irritated them.

Kelly put her hands on her hips and took a step forward. "What do you want with my boyfriend?" she growled, sounding feral.

Mia paled and stepped back. "Oh. I didn't know," she stammered. "Why didn't you say?"

Kelly laughed and shook her head. "You were too busy trying to get close to the hottie." She inched toward Mia and thumbed over her shoulder at the dumbfounded man wearing a cheesy grin. "This hottie is mine. Keep your grubby mitts away from him."

Mia turned around and disappeared into her classroom, leaving Kelly to realize what she'd said. She blushed and glanced down at her cowgirl boots.

Ben tilted her chin up and his gaze caressed her lips, then met her eyes. "Do you mean it, Kelly-bean?" Ben's voice, low and gruff, touched a primeval part of her and she was suddenly hyperaware of the heat radiating off his body.

"Yes," Kelly breathed. The ache was now replaced with a fluttering of excitement and longing.

Ben gave her a quick kiss then turned around, thrusting his hand in the air. "All right!"

Kelly leaned against the cool wall, giggling and watching her man. *My man.* He took her hands and swung them, joining in her laughter.

"Let's celebrate."

"That's what I had in mind." Kelly placed a palm on his chest, the rapid beat of his heart stealing her breath. She knew of a good way to burn off the extra energy.

Ben chuckled and pulled her into a tight hug, then slid his hands to her backside and squeezed. "How about dinner first? A real date."

"Food. Yes, that's doable."

"Good, need to sustain my energy. Then we'll put into practice what you have in mind." Ben kissed her nose. "Would you like me to stay the night?"

"Yes, please, I've missed you." Kelly nuzzled her face against his chest, smelling his cologne and soap.

"Good, I was going to anyway." Ben squeezed her again then let her go. She pulled him into the classroom to get her purse. "First I need to go home and get a bag, then I can pick you up or meet you there."

"There." After they agreed on a time, he escorted her to her car and she drove home to change.

★ ★ ★

Whistling and hopping up the steps to the apartment, Kelly didn't realize the door was unlocked until she stood inside. She paused and studied the dark living space. A noise startled her, and she reached in her handbag for her gun, grateful her district allowed licensed carriers.

It sounded like sniffles. "Who's there?" her heart dropped.

"Kel-ley," Mierda snorted.

Kelly turned on the table lamp. The soft light cast a warm glow on her visitors.

"I'm sorry." Mierda wiped her face. Her voice barely a whisper. "I had nowhere else to go."

The poor woman's dirty clothes were torn at the shoulder. Mierda's face was red and swollen, but it could have been from crying. She sat on the sofa with Cali asleep in her lap, stroking the girl's long hair in a soothing manner. Cali's pink leggings had a hole in the knee.

"I'm glad you came. You know you are welcome here, especially in an emergency. Do you need to stay the night?" Kelly asked, sitting quietly.

Mierda's eyes widened. "Oh no. That will make it worse." She took a deep shuddering breath. She expertly maneuvered Cali off her lap and onto the sofa. She went to the bathroom to splash water on her face. Kelly handed her a small towel. "Did he hurt you?"

Mierda shrugged, frowning into the image in the mirror. She soothed a lump of hair down. "Nothing that hasn't happened before," she uttered in a flat tone.

"You can't go back, not until he gets help." Kelly touched her arm.

"I can't leave Ricardo. I have nothing. Nowhere to go." Mierda closed her eyes, and a tear escaped. "He'd find me and take Cali. What would happen to her if I wasn't there? He'd starve her or worse."

"Think what would happen to her if Ricardo kills you. She would have no one left to care for her. If she didn't behave, he'd threaten Cali, and she'd end up like you." Kelly seethed with anger. Who could do this to anyone, let alone the person they'd pledged to honor and love?

Mierda hugged herself and shook her head. "I can't leave. There's no way. It's easier to just go along with it."

"What's it teaching Cali? That it's okay to be with a man who hits you? Do you want this for her?"

Mierda's eyes turned hard. Her color remained red, but she trembled with festering anger. She could turn on Ricardo one of these days and kill him. Then Cali would have no parents.

68

Kelly took a deep breath. She couldn't have Ben over if she played hostess to Mierda and Cali. She crossed her arms and leaned against the doorjamb. "You both are welcome here anytime even in the middle of the night."

The fire left Mierda's eyes and her shoulders drooped; she seemed to shrink before Kelly's eyes. A timid mouse of a woman, nothing but a shell, remained. Poor Cali; she'd never get to see her mother strong, but always weak.

"I need to go." Mierda swept past Kelly and returned to the living room. She gazed down at her sleeping daughter.

"Please, reconsider." Kelly put a hand on her arm. "Mierda, we can get you help. I know a great social worker. She could find you housing, a job."

"Ricardo would still be out there." Mierda stared at the wall when she spoke. "I can't leave, not yet." With a groan, she sat next to Cali and rubbed her head again.

"At least rest here a while. I've got a frozen pizza and a bottle of wine," Kelly suggested.

Mierda's head came up, her eyes full of tears. "Sounds great."

As silently as she could, Kelly preheated the oven and poured glasses of wine. She brought Mierda her glass then returned to the kitchen. After a hasty text to Ben, canceling their first real date, she put the pizza in the oven.

Around eleven, Kelly unlatched the lock and watched Mierda holding Cali disappear down the sidewalk and around the corner. Kelly rubbed her arms, standing a moment in the breeze. The Texas autumn was warm, bordering on hot, but she felt as if she was being watched. She shivered.

She stepped backward a few steps up to the apartment door and scanned the area. Finding nothing suspicious, she entered the apartment and locked the door, remembering her boyfriend was a cop.

CHAPTER 14

Kelly

KELLY REFUSED TO LOOK ACROSS the table at her best friends, Jessie and Piper. Instead, she stared over at the cashier as the teen rang up a customer. Saturday morning buzzed at A Hole In One donut shop. Several families munched on fresh donuts while sipping coffee, juice, or Kelly's favorite, the chocolate mocha. Jessie drummed her fingers on the table.

Kelly sighed and fingered her mug.

"So…" Piper started. "What's up with you and Ben?"

"Nothing." Kelly lifted the mocha to her lips.

"That's bullshit, and I know bullshit since I live in a ranching town," Piper said, pointing at Kelly.

"That sounds familiar." Jessie tapped her chin, her eyes narrowing on Kelly. "Where have I heard it before?"

"Kelly used it on me when I was first attracted to Cole."

"The night you lost one of Jessie's bras to him," Kelly chuckled.

Jessie frowned at Piper. "I got it back, Jess." Piper crossed her arms over her breasts and shivered.

"Kelly used the bullshit thing on me too when she suspected Josiah and I had a thing," Jessie admitted.

"I was right." Kelly grinned and waved her hand.

Jessie narrowed her eyes again. "Now what's this about you and Ben?"

Kelly tried to guard her reaction to Ben's name, because every time they mentioned him, her heart fluttered and she felt heat creep to her face. "What's what?" she asked, glancing at the cashier again.

Piper coughed, "Bullshit."

They all laughed.

Jessie and Piper shared a look. Jessie played with the corner of her napkin and chewed her lip. Piper narrowed her eyes and hummed. "There's something going on with you two."

Kelly relaxed, confident, they hadn't figured anything out. This meeting was a fishing expedition. She reached for a donut hole and popped it into her mouth. She grinned, enjoying the chocolaty flavor.

"Have you asked Ben out yet?" Jessie asked.

Kelly took another sip of her mocha. "Mmm. That's good."

Exasperated, Piper pleaded, "Kelly, come on."

Kelly shifted on the hard booth. "I haven't asked him out."

"Why not?" Jessie picked up her mug. "I know you think he's cute."

"And we saw how he looked at you," Piper added. "His gaze was so intense it could have—"

"Ignited my underwear. I know. It's just..." Kelly shrugged and sighed again. "Sawyer made me cautious."

Jessie nodded but frowned. "Sawyer wasn't right for you. And I get being careful, but one date to see if you're compatible won't kill you."

"Yeah, it's not a marriage proposal," Piper said. She pulled the box close and chose a chocolate donut hole. "Oh my God, this is good," she moaned.

"That's what she said," Desire said as she slipped into the booth next to Kelly.

Jessie snorted, Kelly giggled, and Piper coughed on the donut hole.

Desire rubbed her hands. "What are we discussing?"

Kelly leaned back and crossed her arms. "My love life. They dared me to ask a guy out but I haven't done it."

"Why not?" Desire asked raising a penciled brow. "Don't you like him?"

"She likes him," Piper answered.

"Sh," Desire said to Piper. "Is he married?"

Kelly laughed. "No, of course not."

Desire tilted her head and inspected Kelly. "Do you like his—" She grabbed the air as if she squeezed something.

"Butt?" Kelly guessed.

"Not what I meant, but that works." Desire winked.

"Sure. He's cute."

"And he's into her," Piper added.

"Well, if he's not married, and you are attracted to each other, then what's the holdup?" Desire asked, folding her hands on the tabletop.

Kelly sipped her drink and contemplated telling her friends about her relationship with Ben. They wouldn't judge her, but something held her back. She sighed again.

"I'm afraid. In my last serious relationship, my boyfriend thought commitment was a dirty word. I don't want to get involved and fall head over heels again only to have my heart ripped out, stomped on then shoved down my throat." Kelly washed an imaginary bad taste away with her mocha.

Desire patted her hand and nodded sympathetically. Kelly leaned closer to Desire and continued, "Piper and Jessie bet me a gift card to this place. I'm holding out for a restaurant."

Desire cackled at Jessie and Piper's stunned expressions. "Honey, if you call him right now, I will give you forty dollars so you can take that man out to dinner."

Kelly pressed back against the seat. She tapped her chin then set her phone on the table. Ben's number had been the last number she dialed, but she didn't want to own that information. She picked it up and scrolled through the numbers stopping at Ivy's work extension. She dialed and held it to her ear.

Jessie's mouth made a perfect O while Piper grinned.

"Fortuna Police. How may I help you?" Ivy answered.

"Hi, Ivy. Is Ben Moore in?" Kelly asked.

"Um, sure. Let me put you through."

"Thanks. Have a great day." A moment later Ben picked up the line. Kelly sucked in a deep breath. "Hello, Ben. I have a question for you."

"Okay. Shoot."

"Remember the other day when I froze at the spring? I wanted to say thank you again. You didn't have to do what you did and I appreciate it."

"What's going on?" Ben asked.

"And with Howie and his dad. I should probably buy you a coffee at A Hole In One." She annunciated the donut shop's name.

"I bet you would," he chuckled. "Are you alone?"

She giggled. "No. How about dinner?"

"Awesome. Score!"

"That's later." Kelly's gaze snapped to Piper's. *Had they heard?* Kelly licked her lips then rattled off her number. After hanging up, she covered her hot face. Desire patted her back.

"Is this the one who made you smile?" Desire asked.

Kelly gasped but kept her hands hiding her face.

The door's bell chimed and Desire hummed. Piper turned and frowned. "Oh, no."

Kelly glanced up as her lanky ex entered the building.

Sawyer Hickey sauntered up to the table and tipped his hat. His sandy hair curled around his ears and neck. "Howdy, ladies."

Kelly crossed her arms and glowered at him.

"Hello, handsome," Desire said, eying the man candy as if addicted to sugar.

Sawyer blushed and replied, "Ma'am."

"How's life at the Big Deal?" Jessie asked.

"Your dad's working me hard." He tilted his head and smiled. "Maybe it's only hard since I've never worked on a ranch before. Either way, he's been good to me. I like the work. It keeps my mind occupied." His brow crinkled for a fleeting moment.

Desire slid to the edge of the booth and slapped his butt. "I know of something that will keep you busy if you need occupying."

"Why thank you for the offer," he paused and met Kelly's stare. "But it's something I need to work on alone. Now if you'll excuse me." He left them and ordered a big box of donuts before leaving.

"Is it me or did Sawyer seem down?" Jessie asked, watching him drive away.

"Subdued," Piper agreed.

Kelly tried not to care but her friends were right; he wasn't his usual "flirts with anyone with a vagina" self. She shrugged and sipped her drink.

"Maybe I could give him a little therapy," Desire said with a wink and a smirk. "I know something that will *lift* him up."

"Ms. Desire," Jessie giggled.

"What? It's just a sex-pression." Desire cackled like a witch and slapped the table. Once she sobered she leaned forward conspiringly, her gaze shifting around the room as she said, "Have you heard what the town prankster did?"

Jessie covered her face and groaned.

"What is it, Ms. Hardmann?" Kelly asked.

Desire waved her hand in the air as if it wasn't a big deal. "Just another funny sign with switched letters." She paused, tilting her head. "You know, I believe it's an entirely new message."

Kelly met Jessie's gaze. Piper leaned over the table. "Ms. Hardmann, spill!"

Desire chuckled and nodded. "The sidewalk sign for the G Spot has those removable letters. Anyway, it read: Dear Autocorrect, no one is trying to say ducking."

Piper gasped then shook her head. Jessie giggled, snorting as she buried her face in her hands. Kelly bumped Desire's shoulder as she laughed.

Kelly's heart warmed. She had made a date with Ben and the world hadn't screeched to a halt. Her cheeks hurt from smiling.

Desire stood up to leave. Kelly slid out of the booth and hugged her, whispering, "Thank you. I'm excited about my date. Don't tell the girls, but he's the one."

The older woman glanced into her eyes and squeezed Kelly's hands. After Desire left, Kelly looked down. In her hands were two folded twenty-dollar bills

CHAPTER 15

Ben

BEN WAITED IN HIS BLUE charger for Kelly to arrive at Hammered. She had texted when she left her apartment. His fingers drummed the steering wheel, cataloging which residents of Fortuna patronized the restaurant. He recognized the Barnes', the Fords and, oh joy, Hickey's vehicle.

After Kelly had canceled the previous night's date, when she called wanting to reschedule he'd jumped at the opportunity to have dinner. Ben had scrapped his workout plans with Indigo, grabbed his duffel, and abandoned his roommate.

Glancing in the rearview mirror, Ben adjusted it to study his dark, short cropped hair. He ran his fingers through it, blowing out a breath. He wanted tonight to be perfect, because it was their first official public dinner.

When Kelly arrived, he jumped to meet her at her car door. Keeping his hands stuffed in his back pockets, he refrained from pulling her into his arms and kissing her. She leaned into the passenger side, reaching for her satchel.

"Evenin', Kelly-bean." Ben grinned until she glanced up at him with red-rimmed eyes and a blotchy face. Unsettled, his stomach churned like a stormy sea. God, he hoped she didn't want to breakup. His heart thumped a fast tune.

"What's wrong?" Ben asked, offering her a hand.

She blinked and fell into his arms. "It's Mierda." Kelly relayed the continuing saga of her neighbor in the abusive relationship.

"Is she okay?" Ben asked.

Kelly shook her head and pressed her palms against her lids. "No. She crashed at my apartment again. I found her there when I came home from the grocery," Kelly explained. "Makeup didn't cover the bruises, Ben. I feel so helpless."

Tears welled in her eyes. He took her elbow and escorted her into Hammered. They located an empty booth, and he slid in across from her. Sharon Dix took their order.

"Why doesn't she leave him? She's crazy, putting Cali into harm's way. Who is going to stop Ricardo from hitting Cali next? Mierda can't." Kelly dabbed at her eyes with a napkin.

"You're a good friend, Kelly. You can't make her change. She needs to come to that conclusion on her own." Ben tried to keep his face masked with empathy but he worried Kelly could become a target in the middle of this volatile relationship. The husband could take issue with Kelly enabling the wife.

Kelly placed her elbows on the table and slumped forward, resting her chin in her hands. She sighed and drawled, "I know. It's just sad. Mierda deserves better." Kelly studied Ben with dark emerald eyes. "She needs a man like you."

Ben found it hard to talk with his heart in his throat. He stretched an arm across the table to take her hand. Her fingertips brushed his, sending a jolt up his arm. He cleared his throat. "There's only one of me." His fingers curled over hers and he squeezed.

"I said like you. I'm not getting rid of you for nothing." Kelly blotted her face again.

Her piercing gaze trapped him. Unable to tear his eyes away, he fell more deeply entranced. Ben's heart swelled. *Love.* His chest tightened, and he found it hard to breathe. Reaching over the table, he took her other hand in his.

Sensing eyes on him, the cop in Ben prompted him to act. He glanced around the restaurant. Jessie and Josiah sat at the bar with heads together. Every now and again the cowboy looked in Ben and Kelly's direction and then nudged his wife. The glow of Jessie's phone silhouetted her face.

Sharon placed plates of steaming food on the table. "Can I get you two anything else?" She smiled down at them.

"Maybe another beer in a few," Ben suggested.

"Will do. I'll keep a lookout." She nodded and wiped her hands on her apron. "You might want to steer clear of the pool area today." The older woman headed for another table and chatted with the Fords.

Sawyer Hickey, Gimme Malone, and Cole and Piper Dart stood around the furthest pool table. Malone, along with Hickey, worked on Brad Davidson's longhorn cattle ranch with Cole. Ben wasn't surprised to find the men socializing but suspected Piper and Jessie had come to spy on Kelly's date.

"Your friends are watching us," Ben said, tipping his head toward the

Darts.

Kelly shifted in time to witness Piper hastily type on her phone then glance toward Jessie. "Oh, God. Yeah, I might have let the details of our date slip." She straightened and picked up a fry. "Sorry about that."

"They're verifying you made good on your dare, I suppose," Ben teased.

"Or making sure Sawyer behaves," she said, tossing a glance over toward her ex.

They continued to eat in silence. Jealousy nagged at Ben, setting heavy in his gut. He inhaled deeply, trying to shake the sensation. Kelly was his girlfriend, not Hickey's.

He met Hickey's glare. Ben couldn't resist wiggling his fingers then relaxing back against the booth, watching the red-faced man miss a shot. Ben stretched his long legs and tapped Kelly's boot with his shoe. She acknowledged him with a nudge.

An angry outburst from the pool table had everyone in the restaurant staring. "What did you say?" Hickey held Malone at the neck by his shirt. The wide-eyed kid clutched Hickey's fist, dangling, the tips of his toes scraping the floor.

Kelly gasped and began shredding her napkin into tiny bits.

Ben straightened and slid to the end of the booth. He had broken up bar fights. He stood but Kelly grabbed his hand, shaking her head. Her pleading gaze made him hesitate.

Luckily, Cole intervened between Hickey and Malone. Whatever voice of reason Cole interjected made Malone nod in agreement. In a huff, Hickey released Malone with a shove. The kid stumbled backward and landed against the pool table, scattering the balls. A couple clattered to the floor.

"Not my balls!" the owner, Holden Dix hollered, hurrying from behind the bar.

Hickey skulked to a barstool and tipped a beer to his lips. He chugged it in two swallows. Scowling, he crossed his arms and stared at the flat screen on the wall.

Kelly's brow crinkled and Ben recognized her "I wish I could help" look. He doubted there was anything but time that would comfort Hickey. Neither Kelly nor Ben could help, since he suspected they were the reason for Hickey's piss-poor attitude.

"Kelly, would you like to leave?" Ben's feelings were conflicted. He would prefer to put Hickey in his place, but he was determined to keep his cool and not admit that Kelly's continued reaction to the other man bothered him.

Kelly had broken up with Hickey because he chose not to give her what she wanted: commitment. Ben was devoted but worried how Kelly would compare him and her ex. Hickey played the flirty bad boy while Ben followed rules. *Will she grow bored with me?*

Ben's phone vibrated in his pocket. He tapped the screen and laughed. Kelly raised a brow.

"Did you score?" Les asked. His brother checking on him was a new phenomenon.

"My brother wants to know how things are going. What should I tell him?" Ben leaned forward, pushing the device toward her.

She glanced at the message, then pushed it back, giggling. "I'd say you scored. Tell him that I'm glad he hadn't advised you before and that now you have a girlfriend."

Ben typed the short text then tucked the phone away. He studied Kelly's luminous green eyes. "I like having a girlfriend."

"Hmm, what do you like about it?" Kelly's lids slid partway closed, and she leaned over the table, chin in her hand again.

"Her lips, with the bottom slightly plumper, calling me to suck on it."

Kelly rubbed her lips together, as if checking her lip gloss, then bit the lower one.

"Caressing her soft skin, especially her belly and..." Ben inched closer.

"Oh?" Kelly squirmed in her seat.

"She has the sweetest taste." Ben hummed, waggling his brows.

Kelly's eyes popped open wide when his tongue darted out, tracing his lips. She swallowed and tugged on a braid.

Her gaze shifted to the bar. She sucked in a breath then shoved back from the table, shaking her head. She buried her face in her hands.

Josiah and Jessie watched them. Shit. So much for their first date facade.

★★★

In a fevered rush, Kelly thrust him backward through the bedroom doorway. Ben grinned as she nudged him toward the bed.

"Sit," she ordered. The command shot straight to his groin.

Kelly pulled something golden and shimmery off the dresser slowly, making the fabric lengthen like taffy.

He remembered the Double D Intimates piece. Knowing he would be the only man to see Kelly wear the exquisite gown made him throb with desire.

"I'm going to change, and I want you in nothing but your boxers and sitting on the bed." Kelly slid her finger along his jawline. Drawing near, she whispered, "I have plans for your body." Her tongue trailed down his neck until it met his shirt then she bit him. He moaned and reached for her.

"Not yet." She backed away, wearing a mischievous smirk, all tease in her eyes. "Boxers only."

"Yes, ma'am."

She vanished into the bathroom and he hastily undressed, stepping out of his tight boxer briefs too. Glancing down, he said, "We'll take the punishment, won't we?" Perched on the bed's edge, he drummed his fingers on his thighs.

A Roman empress exited the bathroom and ignored him. She held her head high with hair swept up—what she called sex hair.

Ben shifted his weight, the suspense making him ache.

Kelly dumped her clothes in the hamper then turned to him, zeroing in between his legs. She licked her lips. He groaned and a flirty grin flashed across her face.

"Ben, you've been a bad listener." She glided to his side. "I wanted to coax it out to play and ride it hard, but now…" She bit her lip.

He swallowed. The temperature of the room rose.

"You need to be punished." Kelly canted her head, staring at the wall. Her pensive eyes slowly closed, he hoped envisioning some sweet torture. A wicked smile erupted, and she lifted her arm and pointed to the bed. "Scoot back to the pillows. Make sure there are two or more behind your head. I want you propped so you can see. Bend your knees up. Legs together. That's it. Hands under the pillow."

Every time she bossed him around he swore he got harder. "Close your eyes." The tone of her commands had him breathing heavy.

The bed shook as Kelly shifted next to him, her warm hands skimming his ankles. She moved his heels until they touched his bum. She ignored the place that ached the most for her touch. Then she lifted his head and fluffed the pillows.

"Touch me," he rasped. "Please."

Her hair brushed his face. Then it swept his torso, the tingling sensations like the whispered touch of an angel's wing. He gasped when she seized his shaft. Her warmth cocooning him ended too soon when she tucked his boner between his legs.

"Ben, in a minute you can open your eyes but you can't move. Do you understand?" The fabric scraped across his chest as she stepped over him, then settled on the other side.

"Yes, ma'am. I won't move."

Sensations exploded around his left nipple as her tongue swirled along the edge, then she sucked it into her mouth, biting the tip. He moaned and angled his head toward her, begging for her kiss.

"You like that?" She flicked her tongue back and forth. He fought the urge to break his stillness. "Just wait," she threatened.

Ben's chest heaved like a marathon runner.

The pressure released from the bed. He heard drawers opening before the bed dipped again. The silky material slid over his skin, tickling and tingling.

"I'm going to sit on you," she said, straddling him.

"No panties," Ben moaned, feeling damp warmth slide over his abdomen.

"That's right." Kelly shifted again, kissing his nose. "Remember the only thing you can move is your eyes."

"I promise."

"Open them."

Ben snapped his lids wide, finding Kelly holding handfuls of the golden gown, a wily smile on glossy lips. Slowly she twisted the negligee, the slit perfectly dividing the material on either side of his body and revealing her sweet spot rubbing against him. He swallowed. Then she leaned back against his legs and opened for him to see.

"Oh shit." He couldn't touch. Ben fisted the pillowcase.

She reached for a large sparkly lavender sex toy and his eyes widened. It looked like a unicorn wanker. She touched the uni-dong to his lips. "Open up."

Ben's jaw dropped to—what? Question or protest?—but she stuck the thing in his mouth. He couldn't help but wonder if it produced rainbow orgasms. He found it impossible to smile while being molested by the glittery uni-dong.

"Make it wet. That's a good boy." A satisfied grin spread as Kelly moved the purple latex coated object in and out while twisting it. "It should be wet and warm now." She removed the toy, leaned back and slowly slid it into her.

Kelly touched herself. Heat flowed through his veins and threatened to make him spontaneously combust. Ben had never been jealous of a sex toy before.

As she worked to climax, her cheeks flushed and her forehead became dewy. He loved her in that state. She extended her legs, panting.

"Show me the rainbows, Kelly-bean." Ben said as she tossed her head back and her body spasmed. He felt her buttocks clench against his skin.

He never wished to have hard fast sex like he wanted to pound Kelly. But this, non-participatory sex, had him so worked up that if his legs moved, he'd probably come.

Kelly said nothing as she climbed off, taking the toy to the bathroom. The toilet flushed, and the water ran. Washing the toy or her hands, he didn't know, but he would be ready when she finished. He pulled his red boxer briefs over his erection.

When Kelly exited the bathroom, she paused and laughed. He sat on the edge of the bed again. This time with his boxers on.

"Somebody learned his lesson."

"You're an excellent teacher, Ms. Greene."

She approached him, hips swaying. He couldn't find the words. Tipping his chin up, she leaned to kiss his nose. "Close your eyes, Ben."

He obeyed, and a breeze fanned him. He reached for her but found nothing. To his left the scraping sound of a drawer opening made him turn. "Magical toy drawer?" he asked.

"Did you peek?" Her voice sounded closer.

"Just wishful thinking." He would have to get her to open that drawer more often.

She straddled his lap again, this time wrapping her legs around his back. He clutched her petite body, nuzzling her hair, breathing in her citrusy scent. Her hands kneaded his back.

"Ben, you can open your eyes." Kelly pulled back, her emerald eyes seeking his. "The scene is finished. I want you to be you now."

He rocked forward and tenderly kissed her lips. "My punishment is done?" He kissed her neck under her ear then took her earlobe in his teeth and nibbled.

She moaned, "Yes."

"That's a shame. I thought we could play with the unicorn dong—"

"Unicorn what?"

"The sparkling sex toy. It looks like a schlong from a mythological creature." Ben caressed her shoulders. "Anyway, I put my boxers back on for you. Kelly, you don't need to coax Woody out. He's more than willing to come out and play." He squeezed her butt, and she giggled.

"Good," she breathed, and drew his face to hers.

He hungrily kissed her wanton lips. When they took a breath, he mumbled, "I like Jessie's creation, but it's got to go now."

"Wait." Kelly felt along the side of the gown, then her fingers slipped inside a pocket. She nodded and raised her hands. He gathered the long gown and pulled it over her head. It flashed a static charge when he dropped it to the floor.

Kelly lay back on the bed and he crawled next to her. A blush blossomed across her cheeks. "You fulfilled another fantasy." She glanced away, the red deepening.

"I did?" Ben held his breath.

Hooded green eyes met his. "I've always wondered what it would be like to have someone watch." With a sheepish grin, she shrugged. "Now I know."

"It was hot." Ben closed his eyes, recalling how her muscles contracted on his abs and the dewy glow of her sated visage. "As far as I'm concerned, we can pencil it in on our weekly schedule. I propose Tuesdays. Can someone second the motion?" He glanced toward his manhood.

"He's waving," Kelly pointed.

"Woody seconds the motion. All in favor say 'aye.' Aye. Woody?" His boner bobbed again.

Kelly giggled and handed him a condom.

He rolled onto his back, sheathing himself. As she watched him roll the condom down his length, he almost lost control. The room seemed to lack oxygen. His lungs refused to fill. "It won't take long," he admitted.

"We've got all night to have fun." She opened her arms to him, an offering Ben would never refuse.

CHAPTER 16

Kelly

KELLY SMILED LIKE SHE KNEW a secret. She did. She was banging the hottest guy in town. Sex with Ben was beyond wondrous. He was an enthusiastic lover, but he could be gentle. She missed him when he worked and longed for his touch.

Rubbing her hands on her skirt, Kelly worried for the hundredth time if dropping off cookies for Ben at the police station was a good idea. Today, she ventured into the unknown, crossing a new bridge. Her sister-in-law would find out about her and Ben dating. It could make things weird between Ivy and Ben.

Kelly shrugged and opened the car door. She straightened the pale blue short gauzy skirt and glanced at her cream-colored blouse. "Crap," she said, trying to brush away cookie crumbs but smeared chocolate instead.

"Double crap."

She sighed and picked up the plate of homemade cookies. Even though she and Ben hadn't seen each other for a few hours, she was using food as an excuse to see him again.

The sun shone bright, and the temperature climbed near eighty. A city park employee watered a flowerpot. Sunlight hit the arching water creating a rainbow.

That morning Kelly had woken hearing the shower start. The warmth beside her had vanished. She had hurriedly thrown back the blankets to join Ben. She had moved the curtain, peeking at his gloriously naked body. With his eyes closed, he had rinsed his hair. Suds had snaked their way down, from his ripped biceps past his sculpted abs to his big feet. After he had noticed her watching, he had pulled her into his wet embrace under the spray of hot water. Caresses had soon become frenzied, and he had pressed her against the tile. They had made love until the warm water ran out.

During the encounter, she had made the flippant comment, "I wish your lips could be two places at once." Ben's face had contorted with extreme thought. His brow had furrowed, and he froze. She'd had to wiggle against him to get him going. Kelly chuckled at the memory of his face, as if he could somehow remedy it.

Kelly pulled open the police headquarters' door and saw Ivy typing at her desk. In a tan shirt, Ivy glanced up then down. She jerked up again as recognition dawned. She smiled in greeting and waved Kelly over.

"Hey girl, what are you doing here on a Saturday?" Ivy pointed to a vacant desk chair next to the desk.

Kelly sunk into the seat, balancing the foil-covered plate on her thighs. Her face heated, and she fiddled with a hangnail. "I'm here to visit Ben. Is he in his office?"

Kelly glanced at Ivy and saw she wasn't surprised. Triple crap! Kelly sighed, figuring the whole town knew about her and Ben's relationship.

It also meant her mother knew, and she'd been suspiciously quiet. Kelly straightened, chewing her lip.

"Ben's out on a call. Somewhere near the elementary school again. Indigo asked for backup."

Kelly jumped up, the plate landing upside down on the floor. Her heart hammered and she couldn't breathe.

"Calm down. It's just routine. We'll hear from them soon." Ivy motioned with both hands for Kelly to sit. She picked up the plate and set it right side up on the desktop. "Wow, you really like him."

Kelly covered her heart as if her hand would slow it. Would life with an officer always feel like this? She'd never thought about Ben in danger. This was Fortuna, a small town, not Houston or Dallas. But Fortuna had men like Ricardo.

"I brought him cookies." Kelly glanced around the narrow room that looked more like a hallway. She'd never had a reason to visit the police station before.

"Come on. We'll take them to his office." The chair scraped the vinyl-tiled floor as Ivy stood. Boots clacking, Kelly followed her to the small room about the size of her bedroom. Four desks were pushed together forming a center island.

"This is Ben's," Ivy said pointing to the only desk without family photos or even a plant. The tan walls and muted beige tiles were bland. Only the wood desks, a naked coat tree, and black chairs offered any color.

Kelly placed the plate on the center of his desk. "This is an ugly office."

"Isn't it, though?" Ivy giggled. Her light hair framed her heart-shaped face, softening her pointed features. Her cheeks seemed more ruddy than usual, a pleasant, healthy plumpness.

Kelly narrowed her gaze, inspecting her sister-in-law. "What's going on?"

"I'm happy for you. Ben's a good guy." Ivy put a hand on her stomach.

"Oh, my God! You're pregnant, aren't you?" Kelly stepped closer and Ivy's grin grew.

She nodded, and the women hugged. "You can't tell a soul," Ivy insisted. "We're waiting until we reach the second trimester."

"I won't tell, but you're glowing; people will figure it out. Especially Mom."

"I know." Ivy rolled her eyes. "Your mother has a nose for stuff like this or asking needling questions until something slips."

"Speaking of which…" Kelly glanced out the door, making sure they were alone. "Mom has said nothing about Ben. She's been unusually quiet. If you heard, then I know she must have found out from someone."

Ivy put her hand on Kelly's arm. "I don't know if she knows. Ben told me you guys started dating. I guess he wanted me to find out from the source so it wouldn't be weird." She shrugged. "He was shy about it, with him shuffling his feet and face red as a lobster. After he told me you've had several dates, I asked him if he thought it could get serious."

"What did he say?" asked Kelly, breathless. She tugged on her braid.

"He just grinned, stuck his hands in his pockets, and walked away." Ivy giggled and glanced at the door before leaning in slightly. "I think he really likes you. I know my opinion doesn't matter, but I think you two are a good fit."

It was Kelly's turn to giggle. "I like him too. We're friends, unlike some of my relationships in the past."

★ ★ ★

As Kelly left the station, a squad car whizzed past. Indigo drove, he spied her and gave a stoic salute. From the back window, Ricardo glared at her. Her mouth hung open long after the car rounded the building.

Horrified at the jubilation she felt at his arrest, she opened her car. Heat rolled out. Poor Mierda. Hopefully Ricardo wouldn't blame his problems on his wife.

Kelly took the long way to her apartment. The detour would pass the Dungogh house. She pulled into the quiet neighborhood and at once felt peaceful. Boys threw a ball in a yard. Several people worked outside. Children rode bikes.

Another turn and she was on Stagecoach Drive. If she and Ben could afford the Dungogh house, then they could be a part of the cozy community. Around a curve, the house came into view. Stopping at the front curb, Kelly tried to visualize a fresh coat of paint, new porch steps and flowers climbing the veranda. A couple rocking chairs on the porch would be a nice touch, too.

The house's door opened and a short thick woman emerged, heading for the for sale sign. Kelly's heart raced, and she fumbled with the car door handle. She pushed it open and stumbled out. "Excuse me," she called, waving her hands and smiling.

"Oh hello, Kelly," Sandy Beach, one of Fortuna's busiest realtors and her mother's classmate, said. She smiled and extended her hand.

"Sandy, you remember me?" Kelly's cheeks heated, and she glanced back at the street as a jogger passed.

"This house has fascinated you since your grandmother lived around the corner." Sandy's nose and eyes crinkled with a smile. "I loved Myrtle Greene. That woman could bake."

"Yes, ma'am. Everyone loved her cookies."

"Snicker doodles. Mmm." Sandy closed her eyes and lifted her nose as if smelling them. She held a metal price reduced sign.

Kelly's mind raced. She had a career now, maybe she could afford the payments. The price had dropped since the building needed repairs.

"Keep watching for the open house and please come," Sandy said her hands on her hips.

"I wouldn't miss it for anything in the world." Kelly helped Sandy push the sign's feet into the hard, dry ground. "Would you mind if I look in the front door?"

"No, honey, go right ahead." Sandy glanced at her watch then tapped it. "I have another showing or I'd take you through the house."

"It's okay, Sandy. I will see you on Sunday." Kelly hopped up the steps, joy creeping into her pores. Maybe she could do it. She waved as Sandy left. The drone of a lawn mower and effervescent laughter of children playing made her giddy. She hugged herself and her phone vibrated. Pulling it out added to her joy. Ben.

"Thanks for the cookies," he had texted.

"You're welcome. Are you okay?"

"Fine and dandy. Will I see you later?" he asked.

Her stomach flip-flopped. She might die of happiness. "Will you make dinner?"

"Only if you make dessert."

She giggled. "Deal."

Humming, she rubbed the hem of her blouse on the filthy glass. She cupped her hands to view the dingy foyer. The oak stairwell ascended and curved out of sight. The foyer floor needed stripped and polished, and the threadbare mauve carpet in the living room needed removed. How much damage had the underlying hardwood floors attained from the carpet?

Debris, papers and dust bunnies littered the ground. Cobwebs hung in every corner, ceiling and floor.

The ten-foot walls had yellowed over time but had once been cream-colored. The grimy hue she blamed on age and nicotine. Kelly backed away from the door and closed her eyes. This place needed someone to love it. She could be that someone.

She inhaled and blew out a long breath. Opening her eyes, she studied the large wooden entry door. It had beveled glass windows with beveled sidelights. Because of neglect the windows appeared to be stained glass in various shades of dirt.

Kelly circled the property, her heart sinking. The weeds had overgrown the roses. It would take years to restore the gardens. She could pull everything and start over, but the yellow roses might be as old as the house.

A poorly constructed deck had been installed over a crumbling concrete patio. Recalling a visit she and her mother had made, Mrs. Dungogh had a white cast iron table and chair set. Kelly's feet hadn't touched the ground when she sat.

"You look pretty, but there's no need to be so fancy," Mrs. Dungogh had said.

"Thanks," little Kelly had replied, jumping up. "Watch me twirl." She had spun in several circles.

"Gramma Myrtle bought it for me after I told her I was going to the princess house."

Mrs. Dungogh's stern face had remained smile-free, however her eyes had crinkled. "No, princess lives here."

Kelly remembered feeling sad.

"Only a queen lives here." Mrs. Dungogh had met Kelly's gaze then winked.

"Oh!" Kelly had stared up at the giant doll house. "Do you have a room full of treasure?"

"Yes, of course." The old woman had waved her hand. "One on each floor."

"How 'bout a secret passageway?" Kelly had taken a scone from the plate and nibbled. It hadn't been as sweet as a cookie.

"What kind of queen doesn't have one?" Mrs. Dungogh had leaned toward Kelly and asked, "Do you know what else we have?"

Kelly had shaken her head, her braids flying.

"A dungeon."

Little Kelly had sat wide-eyed and fearful to ask anything else.

Kelly rubbed her face. "Maybe Ben would be interested in installing a dungeon?" She chuckled and studied the remaining fruit trees.

The old detached garage might have been a carriage house. The peak's gingerbread trim matched the house's. Someone had painted it a nasty shade of green, probably a mistint in the bargain bin at Nailed.

The house whispered hints of its former glory. She could imagine it. Working full time, would she have the time to make all the necessary repairs? Could she afford the house on her salary alone? *If she and Ben together…*

She swallowed and closed her eyes. *Stop it, Kelly. You thought this way about Sawyer and look how that turned out.* She ached when she thought of that frustrating man. She'd given him her heart, and he hadn't treasured it. Oh, he never mistreated her, unless you could count flirting with every living thing that had a vagina. They hadn't jived the way she and Ben did.

Ben regarded her as a woman, his woman, not just a play toy. A toy, that was how Sawyer had treated her. Something he desired when he wanted it and nothing more. Their relationship had no depth.

Thank God she had found Ben. She giggled; she'd been planning their future today.

Kelly circumvented the rotting deck and came around to the side and tried to peer though the bow window, but heavy draperies covered the panes. It truly was a magnificent architectural detail that extended to the top floor; the master bedroom, if she remembered correctly.

She sighed and returned to her car. She didn't know how or when, but someday she'd own her fantasy house.

CHAPTER 17

Ben

"MMM." BEN POPPED ANOTHER CHOCOLATE chip cookie into his mouth. He could taste salt, butter, sugar, and chocolate. From behind him, Indigo moved like a snake to strike and pluck one off the plate before Ben could react.

"Oh, God," Indigo moaned as he chewed. He plopped down at his desk across from Ben and eyed the remaining cookies.

Ben recovered the cookies with foil and pulled the plate toward him with a growl.

"Are you sure this girl is into you?" Indigo asked then licked chocolate off his finger.

Ben leaned back in his chair, crossing his arms he waited for his friend to continue. Indigo had a somber expression. Hell, he usually looked serious.

"Maybe I should see if she likes me better. I could get fat eating these."

Ben chuckled and studied the other officer. "Sorry, Buddy, she's mine. Don't even try to take her."

Indigo's brow raised in a Spock-like manner, a hint of a grin on his thin lips. "No problem. Does she have a sister?"

"Actually, she does. She's in college and cute. Just as feisty as Kelly, from what I've heard." Ben shrugged and pointed out the door. "I'm sure Ivy can answer any questions you have about Olivia."

Indigo's gaze strayed to the plate once more. "Too young." He sighed, focused on his computer screen, and began typing a report.

Ben considered Indigo. With Kelly and Piper best friends and Cole and Indigo cousins, Kelly and Indigo had many opportunities to start a relationship. Ben rubbed his chin, grateful Piper's matchmaking juices hadn't kicked in earlier.

Kelly hadn't hooked up with Indigo and Ben smiled, feeling warmth in his chest. Ben sent her a text.

They planned to rendezvous later, but first he needed to visit Hammered and have a word with Sawyer Hickey. Having the discussion in public might be awkward, but the restaurant was neutral ground.

He messaged Sawyer and asked him to meet him for a beer.

The reply came almost instantly. It was a go. He swallowed and tugged on his collar.

★★★

Hunched over the bar, Hickey flipped the page of the book before him. He'd rolled the sleeves of his plaid shirt up, exposing his tanned forearms and calloused hands. Hickey had gone cowboy, taking a position at the Big Deal ranch. He took care of the property and a herd of longhorns. The man had even moved into the bunkhouse.

One booted heel hooked on the stool, Hickey turned to meet Ben. A half smirk tweaked Hickey's lips but purple bags hung under listless eyes. While Kelly's ex was a few years younger than Ben, tonight Hickey seemed old and worn.

Ben took the stool beside Hickey and signaled Holden. The rotund man waddled over, drying a glass with a white towel. "Ben, we haven't seen you around much lately." He wiggled his brows. "I heard you got a new filly."

So Holden Dix wasn't the most subtle man. Ben refrained from groaning and shot a look at Hickey.

Hickey frowned and closed his book. "Yeah, he's got my girl." He pushed the novel away and turned, watching Parker Ford study the spines of books on the bookcase.

Holden's round cheeks looked like shiny red apples. "Oh, I'm sorry. I didn't mean to bring up any bad blood," Holden sputtered.

"No worries, Holden," Hickey said. He stood and slapped Ben hard on the back. "Ben's a better man, and Kelly deserves someone who'll treat her right." He sat again and finished his beer. He tapped the side of the glass stein, signaling Holden for a fresh one.

Holden set two frosted glass mugs full of amber ale in front of the brooding men. He smiled. "On the house."

Ben ate a burger, and between bites, he asked Hickey about his life on the Big Deal ranch. The other man shrugged a shoulder while watching the flat screen. After a prolonged moment of silence, Ben continued to munch. His far-fetched idea of fulfilling one of Kelly's fantasies dimmed. *Might as well flush it down the toilet.*

"I like it," Hickey finally admitted. He pulled the novel close again and stared at the couple on the cover. He had picked a book with Kelly's likeness. Sadistic. A muscled cowboy in a black hat held a cute long-haired woman dressed in a frilly short skirt and boots.

Recognizing Hickey still cared for Kelly, Ben lost his appetite and pushed his plate back. He took a steading breath, realizing his plan could still come to fruition.

"It's hard work, but it's good. I sleep heavy at night. Even with Curly and Gimme snoring."

Hickey swiveled in this seat and faced Ben, gazing at him with sunken hazel eyes. "I had to try something different. When Kelly left me, I needed to get away from town. I wanted to work myself to oblivion. I knew when she said goodbye the last time there was no going back. And she was right. I'm no good for her. I'm not much into commitment, and that's what women want." He grabbed his beer and took a long pull, closed his eyes, and swallowed.

"You still care about her." Ben stated the fact quietly.

With a curt nod, Hickey jerked to face Ben again. "Yes, I do." Jabbing Ben's chest, he continued, "And if I find out you've hurt her…" The threat hung between them.

But Ben understood. He felt the same way. "What happened between you? How could you—"

"Let her go?" Hickey took another drink. "I kick my own ass everyday asking myself that question. I don't know. I fed it up."

The fact Hickey still cared for Kelly could work in Ben's favor but it could also backfire, especially if Kelly fell for Hickey again. Based on her continued reaction to Hickey's name in conversation, Ben had nothing to worry about but there was always a chance… He rubbed his gut. "Aren't you seeing Mona now?"

Hickey's brow rose. "You aren't still sweet on her?"

Ben snorted and then chuckled. He recalled his initial attraction to her fiery boldness. But now she appeared a floozy to him. "Nah. At one time I thought maybe, but once we went out… We didn't fit. She knew it, I knew it. We moved on."

"Mona's fun but too much like me. We aren't an item as much as you see us playing that way." He took another long pull, his brow heavy over his eyes. "I like her, don't get me wrong, but I'm not ready for a new girlfriend. I'm alone and, for now, I'm okay with that."

"I love Kelly," Ben breathed. The words escaped unfettered.

"Well, hell. Congratulations and all that shit."

Ben's mouth flopped open like a fish. He ran his fingers through his hair. "Thanks." He chuckled uneasily.

"Does she know?"

Ben shook his head, and both hands gripped the mug as if holding on would keep him rooted in real life. "No. I can't say anything yet." He closed his eyes and hoped he didn't look like a lovesick teenager, mooning over a crush.

"Why the hell not?"

"Supposedly we've only started dating. You don't do that right away, and I can't do anything to scare her off."

Hickey crinkled his nose and smirked. "Supposedly? So you've been seeing her on the sly." He glanced at Ben's knee bumping up and down. "Don't sweat it. Chicks love when you tell them that. She will too. Kelly likes commitment."

"I don't know." Ben didn't understand how confiding in Kelly's ex-boyfriend could help their relationship but he felt comfortable talking to Sawyer. "She's changed since she dated you. She hasn't wanted anyone to know we're together, especially her family."

"You mean her mom."

"Jessie and Piper, too."

"That's new." Hickey sighed, scrubbing his face. "I'm sorry, man, that's probably my fault."

"Yes, it is." Ben chuckled quietly when Sawyer growled.

Ben blew out a long breath and squared his shoulders. "I have a question for you. If you had one more chance to show Kelly how you feel about her, would you take it? Would you tell her with words or would you take her to bed?"

CHAPTER 18

Kelly

KELLY CLOSED HER LESSON PLAN, unable to focus. She rubbed her temples, her thoughts constantly shifting toward Ben. The last few times they had been together he'd been distracted.

The past week the police arrested two drag racers on Fortuna Elementary's street. They had crashed, nothing serious, but enough noise and damage to alert the neighbors to call emergency dispatch.

"No rest for the wicked," she had quipped, feeling the ache in her heart before he had even left.

"No rest for the weary," he had replied with a smirk before kissing her forehead and rushing out of her apartment.

Kelly rubbed her eyes and leaned back in her chair. Ben took the threat to the school seriously, but was his quiet demeanor something more? Something to do with them?

The school day had concluded and Kelly sanitized the room. The beginning of the school year brought cold and viruses out in full force. The kids not only shared them with each other but with the staff too. She pulled a tissue out and blew her nose.

She checked her email and replied to the parents then straightened the bookshelf.

A quiet knock sounded at the door. "Ms. Greene?" the soft voice of a child called.

"Yes?" Kelly stood, dusting her palms, meeting Howie at the doorway. "What are you still doing here?"

"I forgot my homework. Dad is talking to my teacher. He'll be here in a minute. I wanted to say hi."

"It's good to see you. How are you liking the third grade?" Kelly asked, noting how he'd grown.

"It's okay. I miss seeing you and all my friends." Howie looked around the room. "You changed seats."

"Remember, we did that last year too. After Christmas."

"Oh, yeah." He stepped deeper into her classroom, inspecting a new poster about cars. His head tilted to the side. "Ms. Greene. I like these cars. Which one is the fastest?"

"I'm not sure. This one is a sports car, it's made for racing." Her finger touched a red low profile car then moved to the opposite quadrant. "This one, with the bars, is called a Baja racer. The bars are part of a cage to protect the driver."

"How does it protect him? It doesn't have a roof." His bright blue eyes gazed at her. This was the part of teaching she loved. The kid longed for knowledge.

Kelly placed a hand on his shoulder and explained, "Sometimes during races cars can bump each other or break down. The cars could crash and if they turn over, then the thick bar protects the driver and keeps them from being crushed."

"Howie, are you bothering Ms. Greene?" Andy Felterbush stood in the doorway with his hands on his hips and a sly grin on his face. "I thought you needed your homework."

The boy looked around the floor like he had dropped something. "Uh oh." He ran to the door. "I left it on my desk again. I'll go get it, Daddy."

"Will do, kiddo. Hurry." His little legs worked overtime as he rounded the corner out of sight.

"He's probably enjoying running through the halls. Kids aren't supposed to run inside during the school day." Kelly chuckled.

"Thanks for talking with him." Andy advanced into the room and closer to her. He wore a turquoise polo shirt that brought out the color of his eyes. He had changed. Last year Andy had been disheveled, and now he appeared to model for GQ magazine.

Even Howie was better dressed. Andy must have noticed her inspecting him, because he approached with a confident smile.

She stepped behind a desk to keep space between them. "He's a great kid. He's changed and grown so much from last year."

"Thanks to your guidance." Andy reached his hand out to touch her face.

Kelly panicked and stepped backward, reaching in her pocket for lip balm. She didn't want to hurt his feelings, but if he encroached in her personal space again, she would give him a piece of her mind. She inhaled deeply. Picking up folders and her bag, Kelly walked to the door and waited for Andy to exit the room before she turned off the light.

"So," Andy started, his hands in his pockets, "would you like to get coffee sometime?" His cheeks flushed, and he smiled timidly.

"That's—"

"Kelly," an excited voice called from down the hall. Ben beamed as he hurried toward her.

She sighed happily, raising her hand. "Ben."

Ben took her into his arms, squishing the folders between them, and kissed her hard. She melted against him. "God, I've missed you," she mumbled against his chest after he'd released her.

"Oh, Ben, you remember Andy and his son, Howie." She felt hot all over and knew she was the color of a ripe tomato.

"Afternoon, gentlemen."

Howie's mouth hung open. He tugged on his dad's arm. "I thought Ms. Greene was going to be your date." Wide-eyed, Andy froze as color crept to his face.

"Sorry, sport," Ben said, kneeling to Howie's level but gazed up at Andy. "Ms. Greene is my girlfriend."

A thrill ran down Kelly's spine; she belonged to Ben, and he was claiming her. Her heart sped up, and she reached out and touched Ben's shoulder, squeezing it gently. His hand came up and their fingers laced. Hopefully Andy would get the message. Poor Howie.

A loud screech echoed through the hallway followed by a rumbling engine. Then the screaming started.

Ben ran toward the doors at the end of the hall. He shouldered the door open before the sunlight swallowed him. Kelly hurried after him. Andy, holding Howie's hand, cautiously followed her out.

A yellow sports car had stopped nose down in the drainage ditch in the schoolyard. Across the street, a young dark-haired man and Walter Mellan hurled insults.

"Learn to drive, you slimy little weasel!"

"What did you call me, numbnuts?"

"You've murdered Banjo!"

"Stupid dog shouldn't have been in the middle of the street!"

Two houses down a large dog lay on its side on the road.

Ben jogged up to the men, and the yelling subsided. Ben pointed to the car, and the kid nodded.

Kelly approached the car reading "beast" as the custom license plate. On the dented front bumper was black fur. The kid hit it so hard he swerved off the road.

"I'll go over with Ben," Andy said. "I can be a witness if he needs me. Stay with Ms. Greene," Andy said to his son then crossed the street and joined Ben.

Howie paced the sidewalk next to Kelly.

"I bet he doesn't have insurance," Walter yelled.

"Whatever, dickweed," the young man returned.

Ben took control of the conversation again and Walter walked a few feet away. Andy stayed at his side, lending an ear while the older man talked, waving his arms.

The young man and Ben spoke. The kid crossed his arms and stared at the ground while nodding.

"What's happening, Ms. Greene?" Howie's big blue eyes stared over at his father.

"Ben is talking to the men to find out what happened. That's just one job the police do."

"Will that guy go to jail?" he asked, pointing across the street.

"I don't know. Probably not. I bet he'll get a ticket, though."

The driver reached for his back pocket but shrugged then pointed toward the yellow car. Ben nodded, and the young man crossed the street toward his car. He sat in the driver's seat, leaned and bent down as if reaching into the glove-box.

Ben glanced over at Kelly. She waved, then his gaze snapped to young man.

The car engine revved then the driver threw it into reverse. The young man looked out the rear window.

Hands over his ears, Howie lurched forward toward his dad. Kelly gasped, failing to snag the boy. Ashen, Andy called out, but the roaring engine swallowed all sound.

The car jerked, flinging dirt clods into the air. On the pavement, he shifted gears. The throaty yellow beast shot forward.

Midway across the street, Howie fell to his knees. He glanced up, pouting.

Kelly's voice failed her. She froze, horrified. The driver did not slow.

Like a lightning strike, Ben scooped up Howie then rolled out of the way. Ben's lips pulled tight in a grim line and he shook. He glanced down at the little boy and loosened his grip. His eyes hardened as he watched the sport car speed away.

Kelly opened her arms and took Howie. "Go get that bastard, Ben."

Ben flashed a wicked smile then shot through the schoolyard, sliding over the hood of his squad car Dukes of Hazzard style. Lights on and sirens blaring, he sped out of the parking lot.

The sound faded. Kelly bit her lip, her heart still hammering in her ears.

"Is the little fellow all right?" Walter asked.

Kelly glanced at Howie. She set him down then kneeled next to him. His breath came in hiccuping sobs. He'd scraped both knees, but not too bad. Both his palms bled. He jerked away hissing when she touched his right hand. She wiped his face.

"Andy, he might need a trip to the urgent care. His wrist is sore." Kelly glanced at the father who ran fingers through his hair. When he looked at the bloodied knees, the tall man paled.

"Howie, I think you need to stop bleeding. Your dad's not looking so good."

The boy sniffed and wiped his nose on the back of his hand. "Daddy doesn't like blood. It makes him sick. He says it belongs on the inside and should stay there."

Kelly chuckled and winked at the boy. "He's right, usually it's on the inside but sometimes it has a special job to do." She stood him up and helped to dust the debris off his legs and hands. "When you get little holes in your skin the blood comes out, plugging the holes so the germs don't get in."

"That's cool." He examined his palm. "Do you think I can see my bone if I look good?"

"Kelly, could you come with us to the doctor? Just in case…"

She laughed and nodded. It wasn't exactly how she expected to spend her evening but Howie needed support and Andy might need smelling salts.

"I'll call the station and let Officer Moore know where you are," Walter said.

★ ★ ★

While the doctor assessed Howie's injuries, Kelly sat in the waiting room. She wrung her hands as she paced. When her phone rang, she fumbled with getting it out of her purse. Ben's face appeared on the screen.

"Hey Kelly, is the boy all right?"

"Oh Ben," she breathed, the sound of his voice bringing joy to the very essence of her soul. "I was so worried about you." Tears sprang to her eyes.

"I'm good. I'm more than good," he chuckled. "We caught that punk."

"Howie is being seen by the doctors. He has a few scrapes and bruises, but they're concerned about his arm."

"I'm glad he's not hurt to badly. Another few feet and—"

"The car would have killed you both," she finished.

"Colin is headed your way. He needs to get statements from you." Ben sighed. "I wish I could be there with you, but…"

"I know. You've got work to do. It's okay, Ben. Catching bad guys is an important job."

Andy leaned against the doorjamb with his arms crossed. He nodded when she caught his eye.

Kelly stowed her phone and explained about the chief coming to the urgent care.

"Kelly, would you mind coming back with me?" Andy glanced around

96

the room with a frown.

"Medical facilities unnerve me."

"Sure." Kelly followed him to a curtained room.

The bed seemed to swallow Howie's little body. The soft injuries had been cleaned and bandaged. They waited for the X-ray technician to come get Howie. Andy paced the place in a U shape, touching Howie's head in a caress with each pass.

"Andy," Kelly said in a soft voice. He faced her. "You're doing great. He's going to be fine, you know that, right?"

Andy shook his head as a wave of emotion scrolled over his face. He tried to blink back the tears. Kelly took his hands and pulled him away from the nurse and Howie talking about pets. She hugged him and he broke down.

"He could have died," Andy whispered, sounding in agony.

"But he didn't," Kelly soothed, rubbing circles on his back. "He'll be fine. Everything will heal and Howie will have a great story to tell when people ask him about his adventure."

Andy closed his eyes and sighed. "Your boyfriend saved my son." As if suddenly realizing he was too close, he backed away but kept his hands on her shoulders. "He's a hero."

"Yes," she agreed softly. If Ben hadn't intervened, Howie could have been crushed, if not killed.

The technician came for Howie and wheeled him to X-ray.

As Andy was paying his co-pay, Ben strolled through the door. Howie spied him first, dropped his dad's hand, and ran to Ben before Kelly could.

Ben swung the little boy up, mindful of his wounds, and then set him down. "Hey, sport, did they give you any robot parts?"

Howie giggled and shook his head. "They took me in this cool room and took a picture of my bones." He stuck the temporary sling out. "I got a broke wrist—that's my hand."

Andy extended a hand, "Thank you for saving my son." The emotion scratched the surface again and his voice sounded gravelly when he said, "Please let me buy you both dinner."

Kelly exchanged a glance with Ben.

"That'd be great, but I need to change first," he replied, taking Kelly's hand.

"Can we get a pizza, Daddy?" whined Howie.

Andy nodded. "That's a great idea, buddy. Why don't we meet you at Aim for 'Za Pie in forty-five minutes?"

Ben drove Kelly home in his Charger. She relaxed in the seat, closing her eyes. "Andy is emotional about having almost lost his son. I think Howie will get his way for a while."

Ben pulled into a spot. "Did you leave the living room light on?" he asked.

"Uh oh," she said softly, rubbing her arm. "Mierda."

"I'm going with you. I want to make sure you're safe." He led the way, using her key to open the door.

Mierda and Cali sat on the sofa, both asleep. Kelly blew out a breath she hadn't realized she'd been holding.

Ben kissed her on the cheek and whispered, "I'm going to take a quick shower and change my clothes." He tiptoed to the bedroom and closed the door. She went to the kitchen and opened a bottle of wine.

The clock read after nine. She sipped from a plastic cup, the epitome of class, but she didn't care a flying flip.

Ben emerged damp and smelling fresh. He wore navy basketball shorts and a T-shirt—a sexy man with a five o'clock shadow and short cropped hair she'd like to play with. But not tonight. She sighed and took another drink.

Ben smiled and took her hand, raising it to his lips. Only when he ran his tongue over her skin did she crack a smile. "Kiss me,' he whispered. As soon as he had her in his arms, he placed her hand over his rigid length and she melted against him.

In the other room, Cali coughed, reminding Kelly she had guests. Cali rubbed her eyes and yawned. She blinked and waved when she saw Kelly. She carefully slid off the sofa. Her dirty pink shirt, a size too small, showed her belly. She tugged at it as she shyly approached Kelly, eying Ben suspiciously.

"Hello, Cali, are you hungry?" Kelly asked. The little girl nodded. "We're going to get some pizza, would you and your mom like to come?"

Her eyes widened, and she ran to her mother. "Mommy, Mommy, wake up. Ms. Greene wants to go get some pizza. They want us to come. Pizza. At a store."

Ben placed his arm around Kelly's waist. "Get them to come. They need to get some decent food in them and get away from this place for a while."

Kelly's heart warmed as she glowed with fulfillment. She planted a kiss on his cheek.

That night Mierda and her daughter, Andy and his son, Kelly and Officer Moore all ate a late meal.

They laughed and heard Howie's version of the rescue story several times.

Ben sat back. "I was only doing my job."

"I want to be a policeman," Howie declared.

"Me too," Cali said, drawing on her paper placemat.

Ben rubbed his knuckles against his scruffy chin. "You know the funniest part? The kid crashed by the furniture store because he was reading one of the prankster's signs."

"Oh, no. Was anyone in town hurt?" Kelly bit her lip.

"No, the idiot saw the sign and not the curb. He hit it and over-corrected into a fire hydrant."

"What did the sign say?" Andy asked.

Ben chuckled. "Free handcuffs with every bed frame."

"Can we get some, Daddy?" Howie asked with big blue eyes.

"Um." Andy glanced at Ben.

Mierda's laughter rang like tinkling bells. Kelly joined her and soon the whole table had a case of the giggle fits.

CHAPTER 19

Ben

HALLOWEEN NIGHT, BEN SAT IN his squad car near an intersection by the school. Earlier both the police and fire departments had toured the subdivisions, handing out candy.

A little red car pulled up behind him. Kelly approached his car and tapped on the glass. The crisp evening air blew in as he lowered the window.

"I know you said I shouldn't come by but..." Kelly thrust A Hole In One bag toward him. "Here you go. I thought you could use a treat. They're fresh."

"Thank you. But you know I'm off in less than an hour," he chuckled.

Kelly shrugged, blushing. "I got you something to wash it down with, too." She held a large soda.

Ben exited his car, setting the donut bag on the roof. He pulled Kelly into his arms and she sighed against him.

"Did you have a lot of trick-or-treaters?" Ben asked before taking a bite of his favorite glazed donut.

"Not a ton. Cali came by. She was a unicorn. They rolled up paper and colored it for the horn." Kelly smiled but it fell off when another squad car pulled parallel to Ben's. "Oh. Will I get you in trouble?"

Indigo leaned over the roof of Ben's car. "Kelly, Ben's been in trouble since day one with you."

Ben laughed.

She tilted her head, her gaze volleying between the men. "There's another donut in the bag, Indigo."

Indigo rubbed his chin. "Now I'm in trouble."

Ben took her elbow and tugged her into his arms. "Kelly's my kind of trouble. Get your own."

Kelly giggled, wrapping her arms around his back.

Indigo glanced at the time. "Shouldn't you be off duty? If you'd like to work my shift, you can."

"He can't," Kelly blurted and returned to her car.

"See you in a few," Ben called. She waved as she passed.

"Quiet night?" Indigo asked. He took the donut bag and peered inside.

"Yes. No racing or vandalism. Hardly any cars, actually," Ben said, scratching his head.

"Get out of here. Don't keep the lady waiting."

Ben saluted his friend then drove to the station to get his car. He had invited Kelly to stay the night at his place. She had been over for dinner or to hang out, but had never stayed over. Ben had scrubbed the house spotless in anticipation of his guest. He hoped Indigo picked up his dirty workout clothes that afternoon.

Kelly waited in his driveway. "What took you so long?" She hugged him and they practically fell into the house.

He turned on music and cuddled with her on the couch. Slow lingering kisses transformed into hard passion. Kelly couldn't keep her hands to herself and he indulged. She nibbled his neck and earlobe while unzipping his pants. Ben hummed. His hands worked on her clothes.

Suddenly his phone rang, vibrating the table. Indigo. He wouldn't interrupt unless it was important.

"Yeah," Ben said.

"You better get to Kelly's place."

"What's going on?" Ben sat up.

"Trouble. There's been a break in."

"Oh, shit." Ben leaned forward and rubbed his face. "Thanks, man. We'll be there soon." Ben ended the call and stood. He found and handed Kelly her shirt. "We need to go back to your place. Seems there's a problem."

Kelly nodded and pulled her shirt overhead, covering an exquisite bra holding the most perfect set of breasts he'd ever seen.

He sighed, hoping he and Kelly wouldn't be awake all night.

Kelly was unusually quiet on the drive. She didn't ask questions. He wouldn't have had the answers anyway. He took her hand, and she held on with a death grip.

The apartment door stood wide open with every light on. Colin and Rick O'Shea stood talking. Indigo took notes from one of Kelly's neighbors. The plump woman wore fuzzy Grinch pajama pants and an oversized T-shirt. She shook her head and pointed somewhere.

Ben pushed past the onlookers and entered the living area with Kelly on his tail. It appeared as if a bomb had gone off. Everything was askew. Tables overturned, the sofa cushions tossed across the room, all the potted plants knocked to the ground and dirt everywhere. She stepped past him and into the hall. She covered her mouth with a hand and a tear escaped.

They had yanked the kitchen drawers out and scattered the contents; the glass top dining table had been shattered and the microwave smashed. Plates didn't survive the fall.

Ben put an arm around Kelly's shoulder as she stared into the bedroom. They had ransacked all her drawers, including the toy drawer. The mattress was cut, and the bed pulled apart. It appeared someone punched the dresser mirror.

"What were they looking for?" she whispered. Ben's arms reached around her and held her. The tears came, and she burrowed into his chest.

"I don't know." Ben drew her tighter against him. His emotions warred. He shook with pent up anger, yet Kelly needed him to comfort her, and thoughts of gratitude had him rejoicing she was safe. "I'm glad you were with me tonight."

"Excuse me, Ms. Greene, can I have a word?" Colin asked in a quiet tone. She glanced through red-rimmed eyes and nodded. "Do you notice anything missing? Any valuables?"

Kelly blinked the tears back and pushed away from Ben. Her lips pressed in a firm line, she entered the chaos of debris, wading through the mess.

"Laptop?" Ben asked.

"My trunk," Kelly replied, lifting a shredded towel.

"I have a few pieces of jewelry from my grandmother, but I kept it with the costume jewelry." She kneeled on the bedroom carpet, searching. "I found the necklace."

Ben pulled Colin into the other room away from Kelly's ears. "Did anyone hear anything? These thugs had to have made a lot of noise."

Colin rubbed his head. "The one lady did, but everyone else didn't think twice about a little racket."

"I haven't found anything missing." Kelly said, coming into the living room. She sat on the one undamaged dining chair and wilted.

"Did you have any enemies?" Colin's mustache twitched.

She shook her head.

"How about someone who'd like to scare you?"

Kelly squeezed her lips shut then pressed her hands to her face. Ben pulled her into his arms and kissed her cheek. "Breathe, Kelly-bean. We'll figure this out." She nodded, clutching his shirt.

"Ben, have you noticed anything or anyone out of place?"

Ben's thoughts raced backwards; the only other people he'd seen at her apartment had been Mierda and her daughter. An angry, abusive husband could lash out at Mierda's only friend.

"Colin, check under the front mat for a key."

Kelly gasped, and they followed the officer to the door. He picked up the mat but didn't know the secret pocket. Ben searched and came up empty. "It's gone."

They searched the apartment for the key but could not find it. And there was no sign of forced entry.

"Who knows about the key?" Colin asked.

Kelly swallowed. "Ben, my parents, brother and sister-in-law, my sister Olivia. Jessie and Piper." She glanced at Ben. "Mierda," Kelly whispered.

"Who's that?" Colin asked Ben.

"A neighbor who has an abusive husband. Kelly's been nice enough to hire the woman to clean her apartment so she can have money to buy food for the little girl to eat."

"Could she have done it?"

Ben rubbed his chin. "I don't think Mierda would violate Kelly's trust. But she would have taken things to sell." He glanced at Kelly, her nose red and face blotchy. What would have happened if she would have been home? He shivered, anger rolling over him anew. "No. I don't think Mierda is capable, but her husband and his cronies are. He was brought down to the station a few weeks ago. Ricardo Vaso."

Colin nodded, "That punk? Yeah, I can see it."

After the police left, Ben helped put the furniture right. Kelly turned off the lights. She sat in the dark staring at the door, the deadbolt and regular locks engaged. She leaned against Ben, her head on his shoulder. Reba laid by her side, loaded. She yawned, and he squeezed her hand.

"It's okay, Kelly. Get some sleep, I'll protect you." Ben kissed her forehead, and she nodded.

Kelly's breathing deepened. Ben held her petite body against him. His mind whirled, straining to remember the times he had visited the apartment, searching for anything amiss. Frustrated, he blew out a long breath. Nothing extraordinary stuck out.

He contemplated his choices, but if Kelly wouldn't leave that meant Ben was staying.

CHAPTER 20

Kelly

"I MISSED THE OPEN HOUSE!" Kelly hiccuped, tears streaking her face. She covered her mouth, squeezing her eyes shut.

"It will be fine, Kelly," Ben said, holding her while she sobbed.

"No, it won't." She felt foolish whining to the point of crying.

"It's not your fault someone broke into your apartment," Ben soothed.

Kelly sniffed and wiped her eyes. After the tumult of the break-in, the event had slipped her mind. That weekend with the help of Jessie, Piper, and their husbands, she and Ben had cleaned up her home then transported a new table and mattress to her apartment.

"I know. Still." She wiped her eyes again. "Sandy said someone made an offer. I'm too late. It should have been me," she huffed, crossing her arms like a little girl. "I went to the bank to talk with the loan officer. Two incomes would've been better, but now we'll never know." Kelly paced the living room, volleying between cursing her bad luck and the buyer.

"It will be fine, Kelly-bean. I promise. Did you finish filling out the incident report?"

"Yes, and I signed all those papers too. The report won't be any different from yours since we arrived at the same time." She crossed her arms.

"I know. It's routine." Ben hugged her then gathered the paperwork and left.

Kelly blinked at the closed door. *Why did I have to go off on a tangent?* She groaned, her head in her hands.

She had even hinted a combined income could have doubled her chance at affording it. Geez, was she trying to scare Ben away for life?

Sawyer would have laughed about the pipe dream then ignored her for days just to drive home the point. Ben wasn't Sawyer, though.

Kelly's heart ached. Her childhood dream had evaporated in the span of a phone call.

Sandy must have suspected Kelly's despair because she said, "It isn't a done deal. I'll let you know if it falls through."

That whisper of hope kept her from a total breakdown. She sighed, chewing on a nail.

Kelly glanced in the corner at a bag of hand-me-downs, but she hadn't seen Mierda since the break in. Cali had been absent from school, too. While Kelly hoped that Mierda left Ricardo, she couldn't help but think the worse.

★★★

Kelly couldn't believe her life. Between having a boyfriend focused on fulfilling her wildest fantasies, her apartment ransacked, elementary school kids believing Ben was a superhero, and her mother not dragging her to get fitted for a wedding dress, Kelly would pick her mother as the most astonishing. Her mother hadn't asked about Ben. Not a single question. Kelly likened it to a Christmas miracle.

Like her mother, the drag racers had stayed quiet, but since Howie's narrow escape Principal Utzmeld had his hands full. Despite the emergency protocols, parents concerned about their children's safety called at all hours. The number of drop-offs and pickups dramatically increased, creating long lines. The parent lines overflowed onto the street, slowing traffic and potentially keeping the racers away from school during peak times.

Kelly entered her apartment and put her purse down to lock the door. She fished inside her purse for the book she picked up on her way home from work. The busty woman on the cover wore a police hat while twirling handcuffs. *Under Covers* looked fun and something she and Ben could read together. The Gift Spot had sexy cop costumes. Maybe she'd get to use the fuzzy cuffs she had bought for cosplay.

She snapped a picture of the novel and sent it.

"Are you thinking of joining the academy?" Her mother responded in a text.

"Oh, God," Kelly uttered, realizing her mistake.

Before she could respond, her mother replied, "Call me."

Kelly groaned and dialed. "Hi, Mom. What's up?"

"I wanted to talk about Thanksgiving."

Flooded with relief, Kelly dropped onto the sofa. "Okay. I'm off the whole weekend, remember?" She glanced at her horse calendar, noting the date of the holiday. Her mother would reveal the dish she needed to bring

105

any moment.

"That's lovely dear, but your father and I are going to Austin. Your Aunt Barb invited us down. Uncle Frank isn't well. This will be his last holiday season. I hope you don't mind, but you and your brother and sister are on your own."

Holy flying turdballs! "No, no, it's fine." The words stammered out. What the hell would she do now? "Give Aunt Barb and Uncle Frank a hug from me."

"Yes, dear."

Kelly sat in the dark for a few minutes. Her mother had never given someone else possession of her turkey dinner. Fridays after were open to anyone but not Thursday. Odd. She shrugged and sent a text to Forrest.

"Sorry, Kel," Forrest replied, "Ivy and I are going to Ivy's parents. And Olivia is going to her roommate's parents' place."

Kelly was truly on her own. She sent Ben a text, but he worked and wouldn't immediately respond. Glancing at the dusty end table, she stood. Kelly turned up her music while she dusted, then vacuumed. Cleaning was therapeutic, but it reminded her of her missing friend.

She mopped the kitchen floor then moved into the bathroom. Wiping down the mirror and counters, she remembered Ben's last stay. They'd showered together, having a little fun before the necessity of cleaning. Just thinking about that man's body made her hot for him. After scrubbing the shower and toilet she felt exhausted. She sat at her small kitchenette and sipped a glass of wine. Checking her phone, she smiled. Ben had texted more than once. The first one was casual but by the third he sounded alarmed.

First text: I get off late. Is it okay if I come over and stay the night? I have a surprise I want to try on you.

Second: You can go to bed and I'll wake you for the surprise. Let me know.

Third: Kelly, are you all right?

She warmed, pleased that he cared. She responded, "Sorry. Was cleaning and had the music up. I'll be home. I love surprises. Will you be wearing clothes?"

Ben had a key to both new locks and was welcome in her home and bed.

As hard as she tried, he wouldn't spill the details other than he'd be late, as in two am or later. She ate something then took a bath. She shaved all pertinent areas.

Kelly lit a vanilla jar candle and slathered lotion on her legs. Opening her lingerie drawer, she stared at the options. White, red, and black lace, Ben loved all equally. But a garter belt and stockings weren't the most comfortable to sleep in; neither was the teddy, although she'd love to give

Ben a surprise of her own. The more practical options were gowns. She had clingy, lacy, sleek, sheer, prints, and solids and a variety of combinations. She picked out a racer back strap pale periwinkle gown. The front dipped low in an empire waist with a tiny bow. Edged with lace, the bodice was soft. She had matching thongs, again not the most comfortable to sleep in but she'd make the sacrifice.

She lay down, turned out the light and watched the candle flicker. Her lids grew heavy, and she dreamed.

A weight shifted on her bed and Kelly raised to a sitting position, her thoughts a jumbled up ball of tangled yarn. If she could find an end, she could start to unravel the mess but it was illusive.

A man, edged by golden candlelight, kneeled beside her. The bathroom light bathed the man in light. His hair was sexy messy, like men could get away with, and his muscled abs she could play like a xylophone and his erection waved hello. Christ, he was hot and in her bed.

There was one problem: it was Sawyer Hickey. Her ex-boyfriend shouldn't invade her dreams, her thoughts, or her bedroom.

She frowned, but, like her brain, her mouth wasn't working. She couldn't question the grinning man who touched himself. *What the hell?*

A click. Kelly turned to the bathroom. Maybe her college sweetheart would jump out with his junk swinging free.

A masculine silhouette crowded the doorway, the backlight creating a Heiligenschein "Hello, Kelly," Ben said. She swallowed and rubbed her eyes. He leaned against the doorjamb, arms folded against his chest, also naked.

"Mmm," she hummed. What a sexy beast. Her brain rationalized him.

Sawyer hadn't disappeared, though. The past and present collided in her bedroom; no wonder her brain felt like exploding, this situation created a time paradox.

Kelly shook her head and rubbed her eyes. Her mouth loosened, "This is a crazy dream."

"This isn't a dream, Kelly-bean." Ben turned off the light, pushed off the door frame, and stepped toward the bed. The warm glow of the candle caressed his body and illuminated the unmistakable hunger in his eyes. Her gaze dropped to his crotch, and she swallowed. He walked slowly, stalking her as if afraid she would bolt.

Kelly glanced at the candle, now liquid wax. She gulped.

Wide-eyed, she examined Sawyer again, then poked him, finding him to be flesh. Kelly scrambled out of the bed and rushed to Ben. Her voice failed her, and she had a hard time forming words. Ben rubbed up and down her arms. Finally, her jaw loosened. "What's going on?"

"Don't worry."

"He's here." She thumbed over her shoulder but jumped, finding

Sawyer standing behind her. "What's he doing here?" she squeaked.

"Surprise."

"I don't...why? It's not." She beat her head against Ben's chest and her hands slid around to his back and linked. "I want you. I only need you."

"I know but let me do this for you. I want to fulfill your fantasy."

She'd never said she desired Sawyer in any way, shape or form. Just Ben. "When did I ask for this?" Nothing had come to mind.

Having two naked hotter-than-sin men want her turned her on. Her panties needed changed from her being in the middle of a penis sandwich.

"In the shower the other day. You wanted me in two places and I couldn't give that to you." His voice lowered, as if ashamed.

Kelly took his face in her hands. "Benjamin Thomas Moore, it's you I love."

His sultry brown eyes filled, and he sucked in his lip, biting it. What anguish had Ben gone through to get Sawyer here?

"I appreciate your eagerness to grant my fantasies," she admitted. "But he's my past you're my future." She took a deep breath and released it.

Ben tipped his head pressing his lips to hers. His hands slid to her hips. He kissed his way to her ear.

Kelly rested a hand on Ben's chest. She nuzzled him, smelling his spicy masculinity. "Are you always going to try to grant my fantasies?"

"If you'll let me," he whispered in her ear. He pulled her tight against him and sighed.

Sawyer touched her shoulder and Kelly twisted in Ben's arms.

"What did Ben say to get you to agree to this?" she asked.

"Ben offered me one more chance to show you how I feel, darlin'."

Kelly squeezed her eyes shut. How much pride had Ben swallowed in order to convince Sawyer to join them for a night of fun? A night with two sexy men sent her imagination into overdrive. Fantasizing was one thing but reality was another. Her future held Ben—not Sawyer.

Kelly shook her head, having an epiphany. "Ben made you promise to stay until morning, didn't he? It was part of your deal."

Sawyer blinked, then his grin turned cocky. "You're pretty damn smart."

Ben knew Sawyer had vanished into the darkness without a trace. It had always left her feeling alone, used, and empty.

Ben was the opposite; he valued her and made her feel loved. She wanted to see him first thing every morning. She turned into Ben's arms. Snuggling into his firm chest, a faint hint of his cologne lingered on his warm smooth skin. She sighed and wrapped her arms around him.

She heard Sawyer walking around, then the bedroom door shut. After a moment, the front door closed, loudly signaling his departure. Ben wormed out of her embrace and left to lock the deadbolt again.

Kelly turned on the shower. The hot water bounced off her hand as she tested the temperature. Ben found her there, watching the water swirl around the drain.

"Kelly." He touched her arm. "Are you okay?"

Her eyes glistened with tears, making his worried face blurry but she smiled at him. "You are an amazing man. I'm glad you're mine." She kissed his chin and hugged him tight.

"I love you."

"I know."

He chuckled.

She grabbed his face, pulling him close. "Don't do that again, Ben. Don't you bring another person into our love. I don't want to share you with anyone. Got it?"

He saluted. "Yes, ma'am."

CHAPTER 21

Ben

HAND POISED ON HIS GLOCK, Ben walked to the driver's door of a gold 1970 Cadillac DeVille. The window slowly lowered. Inside, the wrinkled doe-eyed face of Desire Hardmann gazed at him with feigned innocence.

"Afternoon, Ms. Hardmann." He grinned at the ornery old woman. "Do you know why I pulled you over today?"

Her eyes darted to the side then back with a wicked smile spread over her bright pink lips. "You're in need of sexual favors?"

He coughed to cover his laughter. "No, ma'am. Not today."

"That's a shame," she pouted. "Perhaps another time."

Ben watched a car slow. The driver stared as she drove past. One of the stylists from Tease Me Salon and More. Joy Ryder or Derry Yare; he couldn't remember her name but her scandalized expression made him chuckle.

The elderly woman rested her hand on the door edge and Ben stepped back, keeping his crotch out of her reach.

"You look mighty-fine in a uniform, Officer Moore." She wiggled her penciled brows then mumbled, "Would probably look better out of it, though."

He cleared his throat. "Ma'am, as to why I pulled you over...you were speeding."

"Oh well. I'm sorry, I have a lot on my mind." Desire shook her head, and not a hair on her black-dyed Vulcan-do stirred. She gripped her primary yellow handbag with both hands. "Oh, my, my, my. I don't know how I became so distracted." Reaching in the bag, she plucked out a paper and fanned herself.

"Are you all right?"

All he needed was the woman to have a heart attack because he stopped her. She closed her eyes and continued to fan herself. "Oh, my, my, my," she repeated. She opened one eye and peeked at him. "Aren't you curious what distracted me?"

Ben smirked and shifted his pad. The old coot had been playing him. "Yes, ma'am. What, in all of Texas, has distracted you on this fine day?"

"Sex."

Shit. He turned around and laughed. He took deep breaths and stared toward the heavens to keep from losing it. Finally, he faced Ms. Hardmann again.

She didn't appear happy; in fact, those penciled brows now formed a V and seemed to sharpen each other. "Son, it's not a laughing matter," she harrumphed. "Sex is a serious thing, a state of mind, a place of being."

She sounded like a sexual yogi. He found it hard to keep a straight face. "Ma'am, it's not safe to be distracted by anything."

"Not even safe sex?"

"Nope."

She put the paper away and sat her purse back on the seat. "Are you going to arrest me?"

Why would she think that? Ah ha. Handcuffs. He bit his tongue and inspected the lines on his pad. "I'm going to give you a warning today. Keep your thoughts on the road."

Her hands gripped the wheel. "Oh, all right, but it's hard when you're listening to naughty books on tape. The car becomes a steamy place."

"Have a good day, Ms. Hardmann."

Before he registered what he had seen on her back seat, Desire had driven away. Several cans of spray paint and a few black letters from street signs. He rubbed his chin and returned to his squad car.

Ben's phone vibrated in his pocket. He glanced at the screen. Les. He debated not answering, but his brother never called him. He sighed and pushed the button, hoping his impatience wouldn't be evident.

"Hey, Ben, you'll never believe who visited me yesterday." Les paused a micro-second to suck in a refueling breath before he continued, "Mom. Can you believe it? I can't. I'm still trying to wrap my head around it."

"Did she want money?" Ben scratched his head. Usually their mother came to him, the son with the regular paycheck.

Les chuckled. "That'd be a switch, huh? No, she didn't."

"Wow." Ben had been more of a parent to Les than his mother. His brother had always resented his parental influence. His mother lived paycheck to paycheck, when she even had a job, and usually lived with the boyfriend of the week. Honestly, Ben found it hard to believe that he and

Les had the same father.

"I know, right? She looked good." Les sighed and his voice softened. "Sober and clean. She smiled and hugged me."

Ben's mother always liked Les the best, especially when she was sober. Their free spirits related to one another, but also cramped each other's style.

"Wow," Ben repeated. Attention without wanting something in return was contrary to his mother's behavior. "Anything come up missing?"

"No, man. I was working. She snuck into the back kitchen to talk." Les chuckled. "Luckily, it's my kitchen. I put Vince in charge for five then went on a much-needed break."

"How's work?"

"I've got a good team. It makes working easier when you can count on people to do their jobs. And the owners are cool. They give me free rein. We've been working on creating a rotating weekend special. So far the gorgonzola steak has been the best seller." Les's pride manifested in his tone.

"Sounds good." Ben's stomach rumbled.

"You'd like it. It comes with a side of steamed asparagus or smashed potatoes and rice. The restaurant has been getting great online reviews. I want to create a barbecue item for one weekend, but I haven't got it sorted yet."

"It feels good to like what you do, doesn't it?" Ben relaxed back in the seat.

"Yes, sir. I can understand why you enjoy your job if it gives you this much gratification. I had a couple celebrating their fiftieth call me out to tell me they'd just ate the best steak they've ever had, and it made their anniversary."

"That's awesome. You're earning loyal customers."

"Yeah, Mary and John have returned once a week since." After an awkward pause, Les asked, "So how's Kelly doing? Did you catch the thief?"

"She's still rattled." Ben's jaw clenched, then he sighed. "No, luck on the perp yet."

"You'll get him."

Ben appreciated his brother's confidence.

"Are you going to a big family shindig with Kelly?" Les asked, a hint of tease in his voice.

"No. Her parents are going out of town and leaving the kids to fend for themselves. Kelly's siblings have other plans."

"At least, you won't get interviewed. This time," Les chuckled.

"Yeah. We don't have plans. I think Kelly feels lost. Her sister-in-law works in the office and she told me the Greenes' trip is out of the ordinary." A woman pushing a stroller walked past and Ben waved. "I don't know what we're going to do."

"Ben, this is a no brainer." Les made a strange clucking noise. "Make dinner for her."

"I don't think that's—" A roast was one thing, but a turkey dinner… Ben coughed.

"She's a teacher and has the weekend off, right? Stay at a hotel somewhere for a few nights or take her camping and pack turkey sandwiches."

"Camping on Thanksgiving?" Ben drummed his fingers on the steering wheel.

"You and your woman under the stars." Les sighed then spoke louder in response to background noise. "Sounds relaxing."

Who would have thought his little brother was a romantic? Ben chuckled and shook his head. "Yeah, it does. I'll see what I can do. Maybe you should start a dating service."

"Maybe. Let's get you happily hitched first," Les laughed.

Tires screeched. Ben straightened and glanced in the side mirror. Two cars raced toward him.

"Shit. Got to go." Ben ended the call then radioed the race into the station. Only a few streets away, Indigo and Rick joined the hunt, planning to head the racers off.

The throaty engines vibrated the windows, begging for spectators. The black and white cars grew larger in the mirror as they barreled toward him.

Ben spotted a woman in high heels, short shorts, and a low-cut belly shirt wave as the men passed. Her long, honey-colored hair ruffled in the wake and she clasped her hands while jumping up and down excitedly.

A black Toyota with a rusted out quarter panel zoomed past ahead of a white Honda with a wide purple stripe. Ben hit the lights and sirens and pulled onto the street. The racers kept their pace until Indigo blocked the road. The black car swerved, missing Indigo's car by inches.

Sweat beaded on Ben's forehead. The high-speed pursuit raced into the country, on a state route headed toward the neighboring town of Nockerville. The white Honda took the lead.

A state trooper and Colin joined the hunt. Nockerville officers blocked roads, corralling the speeding vehicles, driving them to less populated areas.

The Toyota bumped the Honda and blew a tire. It tried to recover but shot off-road into a ditch, smoke rising from the hood.

The Honda charged forward, taking a curve too fast. It spun out, hitting a mailbox. Like vultures and carrion, the lawmen surrounded the car, guns trained on the driver.

Smirking, Ricardo Vaso finally stepped out of his car, hands raised.

"On the ground," Colin ordered. He handcuffed Vaso then pulled him to his feet. Ben lowered his weapon. Indigo walked him toward a cruiser's rear door.

Vaso stopped and jerked his elbow out of Indigo's hand. With a sneer, he yelled at Ben, "Where's your girlfriend?"

Bile rushed into his mouth as Ben stepped forward. His jaw tightened but Indigo pressed Ricardo's head down stuffing the man in to the back of the squad car.

"Where's your wife?" Ben countered fighting the urge to go call Kelly.

Vaso smiled with dead eyes. "She left me."

"Smart woman," Ben said.

Vaso snarled and jumped at Ben, but Indigo closed the door.

CHAPTER 22

Ben

"HELLO, COLE. I HAVE A question for you." Ben swallowed and steeled himself for a strange conversation.

"Shoot."

"What are you doing this year for Thanksgiving?" Ben asked.

"Pipes and I are going to Chicago to visit her mom and step-dad, her brother, Fletcher, and his family. I've never been to the Windy City. I expect we'll do some touristy things. She has places she wants to visit that she misses. Some pizza place in particular. Man, she raves about it." Cole chuckled then quieted. "I've never been on a plane before. I'm kind of nervous. Have you flown?"

"Sure have. The most exciting part is also the most frightening. It's takeoff and landing. Here's a tip. The pressure changes so before takeoff, chew gum. It helps your ears pop and to alleviate the uncomfortable feeling."

"Thanks. Now that you know my itinerary, is there something I can do for you? What are you doing?" Cole asked.

"Nothing really," Ben said, "that's why I called."

"I'm sorry, Ben, if we were staying home you'd be invited over."

"Thank you, but that's not the reason I called." Ben cleared his throat. "I think I'd like to do a little fishing and camping Thanksgiving weekend."

"Camping?" Cole seemed to snort. "What about Kelly's family? Ah, too soon, huh?"

"They have plans." It wasn't a lie. "I might take her with me for a night. She's gone fishing before. I just want some time away from work and the norm. Is there somewhere, a back roads kind of place, you know of? I'd

115

love to go off the beaten track."

"I've got a spot on my property. There's a small field surrounded by trees, near a spring-fed creek. The water's like ice but there's some good fishin'." Cole paused and Ben heard some shuffling. "If you can meet me this evening, I'll show it to you."

"That sounds great." Ben made arrangements. When he ended the call, he smiled. Step one complete.

Step two. "Hey, Kelly-bean. Don't make any plans Thanksgiving weekend. You're mine."

"Another fantasy?" she asked in a breathy voice.

"Mmhmm."

"Yours or mine?" Her tone had lowered and his heart sped up.

He chuckled and pulled into the driveway of the Dungogh house. "It's a surprise. Got to run." He'd wet her whistle. Perhaps more, he grinned.

Looking at the dilapidated old building, he inwardly cringed. Band-Aids wouldn't do; the old thing needed cosmetic surgery. The superficial stuff wouldn't be cheap, but it'd probably be cheaper compared to the bones of the house, if they needed repaired. He swallowed, climbed the stairs onto the porch, and glanced in the dusty windows.

"Hello, Ben," Sandy Beach greeted from a wicker rocker.

"Thanks for meeting me on short notice." Ben offered his hand.

She nodded and pulled out a large wad of keys. They clanked as she ticked them off, finally settling on a dull brassy one. She jabbed it into the hole, twisting her wrist. Turning the knob, she pushed the wide wooden door. The hinges creaked, starting deep and ending high, as the door yawned open.

Someone had painted the walls a flat off-white, but the coat wasn't even and had burnished in a few places. The fresh paint probably helped mask the decrepit odor of age.

"The stairwell is a cool architectural element," Ben said, visually following it upwards.

Sandy walked under a door frame and pointed to the corner. "All the wood trim has bullseye accents."

She moved into a room. "This is the sitting room. There are oak floors under this...worn carpet and Rookwood tiles around the firebox. Very stylish for the time. Most of the glass in the windows is original." Sandy put her hands on her hips. "I won't lie to you, Ben. This place needs a lot of work. It's going to take elbow grease to bring it back to its glory."

Ben examined the walls, electrical outlets and the ceiling. The dining room connected to the living area and wrapped around to the kitchen. Sliding glass doors opened off the dining room onto a death trap deck.

The kitchen looked like pictures he had seen of his grandparent's home from the seventies. Christ, harvest gold refrigerator, an avocado green stove, and a brown dishwasher. The cherry red microwave oven stuck out like a sore thumb.

"Was the previous owner color blind?" Ben asked.

Sandy laughed and opened the folder. "Maybe. The owner is the grandchild of Ms. Dungogh. He rented it for a while but now he wants to move and doesn't want to be an out-of-state landlord."

"I can understand that." Ben opened cabinets and inspected their underside. The musty scent of age bombarded his sinuses. "Does this place have a basement?" he asked, wiping his hand on his pants.

"It's a cellar."

"Let's go."

Sandy frowned and rummaged through the keys again. They stepped a few steps into the garage. She unlocked an unusually small wooden door. He would have walked past it.

He took hold of the spaghetti-like railing and stepped onto the narrow gray-painted stairs. At the bottom he tugged on the string attached to the bulb on the ceiling. Against the back wall, covered in dust and grime were rows of wine racks. "Wine?"

"Oh, this place had a vineyard at one point. There are still a few surviving vines out near the fence line."

Did Kelly mention the vines? Ben had a vague recollection but couldn't remember exactly.

He would love to restore the house and live there with her. A grin formed as he imagined handing her the big ball of keys.

"I don't see any cracks," Sandy said, pulling Ben out of his daydream. They glanced around the foundation then returned upstairs.

Ben made a mental checklist of things and took pictures. He had already visited the bank just to see if they'd laugh him out the door. He ran his fingers through his hair.

Restoring the old house would create memories, oodles of them. The house was perfect for raising a family. He could see a swing set and trampoline in the yard. Either a new paver patio with a grill, or a stone patio with a barbecue pit. He smiled; the house was growing on him.

He followed Sandy up the curving staircase. The open balcony overlooked the long entry hall. Kelly could deck the halls, winding pine garland around the banister.

The master suite was above the living room and shared the bay window. Beams of south-western light gave the room a warm, homey glow. Ben could picture a king four-poster bed fitting in the space. He pushed open a door and found a large mostly remodeled bathroom: beige marble tiles in a state-of-the-art shower. The sink and basin looked like a chest of drawers. A small door opened into a long narrow closet.

Two large bedrooms shared a bathroom. The dated wallpaper had to go.

He grimaced at the shade of Pepto-Bismol pink on the walls.

Continuing down the hallway led to two smaller bedrooms. The fourth bedroom had a pull down ladder.

"There's the attic," she pointed.

"Have you been up there?" Ben asked, tugging the cord. It stubbornly remained closed.

"Heavens no. I'm afraid there are dead bodies up there." She chuckled nervously.

Ben yanked harder. The hatch gave, raining mummified carcasses of dead bugs. "Nasty."

Sandy attempted to brush him off without touching him. After the dust settled, he glanced into the gaping black hole and swallowed. "I don't have a flashlight and my phone's battery is low."

"Here, use this." Sandy had clicked on a small pen flashlight.

Ben took it and frowned, his only excuse extinguished by the light. He sighed and tested his weight on the ladder step by step. Ignoring the things that crunched under his fingers, he rose into the super-heated, cramped space. Sweat trickled down his back as he peered inside. Old gray insulation yawned between the wood beams. Plywood sheets paved a path along the floor. The ceiling jutted in odd angles because of the strange pitched roof. He narrowed his gaze and spotted a few trunks toward the back, where a hacked up body could fit. He shined the light on something hanging in the corner and gasped.

"Dear God, what is it?" she said from under him.

"My imagination." Ben studied the shape and relief washed over him. "It's a dress bag. It's dark; it looked human shaped."

"Do you see any evidence of water damage or rodents?"

"Not offhand." He wanted to exit the oven before he had heatstroke. Climbing down the ladder lowered the temperature by twenty degrees. "That's better."

At the end of the hallway was another full bath. Stepping into the bathroom was like leaping back in time. The floor had white oval octagon tiles with black squares and a claw-foot bathtub. It needed a deep clean and a new shower curtain. Ben prayed the plumbing worked.

"So what do you think?" Sandy asked as they returned downstairs.

"It has potential." Ben shook his head. "Honestly, I don't know if I could afford both the house and all the work it needs. I'll have to do some math." He grinned and together they exited the house. He shook her hand and turned toward the house once more.

Kelly loved the place. Potential, he'd said. And Kelly had recognized it even as a kid. If Ben had the power to make it happen, he would.

CHAPTER 23

Kelly

KELLY'S PHONE RANG, STARTLING HER. Jessie. She sighed and hit the button. "Hey, girl. What's going on?"

"How are you doing?" Jessie asked.

"I'm good. And no, Ben hasn't caught the dickwad who broke in." Kelly rubbed her arm.

"Bummer. I know you'd call and tell me if that bastard had been caught."

Ben had cautioned Kelly to have her gun close by her side at the apartment. The small metal object sat on the cushion, a comfort, yet causing anxiety because it was needed.

Kelly switched the subject. "Are you hosting the holiday this year?"

"God no, we're supposed to be going to Dallas to one of Josiah's uncles. They rotate hosting every year. I can't remember who's having it, the dentist or the doctor. He has such a huge family. It's weird being with a group that large after it being just Dad and I."

"You'll have fun. They'll love you like Josiah does."

"Yeah," Jessie paused and took a deep breath. "What do you think about the long gown? You've had it a while now."

Kelly's brain stalled. Maybe this was the real reason for the call. She glanced at the clock on the wall, wondering if Ben would show up and save her from this topic. She didn't want to hurt Jessie's feelings. Her voice tentative, "It's a beautiful gown, Jess."

Jessie sighed. "Just give it to me straight, Kel. Tell me what you liked and what you hated. It won't hurt my feelings. It's why I gave it to you to test."

119

"Okay, sorry." Kelly shifted the phone to her other ear. "Truly, it is breath-taking material and looks stunning on while you're standing there, but when you lay down, it doesn't move with you. My girls fell out every night. I'd suggest adjustable straps for women who aren't so endowed as you. The fabric is prone to static electricity, and it made my hair crazy. I had to sleep with it in a ponytail. Maybe you could find a similar material that isn't so clingy."

"How did it launder?" Jessie asked.

"I put it in with my other delicates and washed it on cold. It's a solidly made garment. It even got dried in the dryer once and there's nothing wrong. It'd be perfect for a wedding night or some other special occasion. You know, one where it's on the ground before you hit the bed."

Jessie laughed. "That's an idea, but if I add the adjustable straps, I'd be able to use it as a selling point," she squeaked happily. Her words rushed together with excitement, "This is awesome, Kel. Great idea."

Kelly rolled her eyes. Jessie always thought her complaints were great ideas. She chuckled. "Happy to help. You know what's also awesome—that condom pocket."

"Oh!" Jessie drew out the word like a song. "Did Ben find it convenient?" she teased.

Ignoring the comment about Ben, Kelly said, "I think it's brilliant to not have to get up or stop just to retrieve one from the dresser, nightstand, wallet or whatever. It's a great feature. Hidden on the seam. I didn't feel it at all."

"Yeah, I like it too." Jessie giggled.

They talked more about Jessie's business and the new building. She had acquired the permits, and the remodeling was nearly complete. Jessie was working on creating stock for a grand opening.

"It's almost ready," Jessie said, joy radiating through the phone. "Piper suggested a fitting room. Why didn't I think of that?"

"Are you going to get a sidewalk sign?" Kelly asked.

"I hadn't thought about it." Jessie giggled. "Imagine if the prankster punked me."

"Get intimate with your Double Ds," Kelly said in an announcer voice. "It would be hilarious."

"I'm waiting on an order of sewing busts to arrive, and I've interviewed a lady to help me." Jessie said.

"How did you find her?" Kelly asked.

"Desire called me and recommended her. She's a single mom, trying to make it on her own. You know how Desire is about helping women better themselves."

Desire took Gloria Sass on as a receptionist even though she hadn't graduated high school and had no work experience. "I hope she's not grouchy like Gloria," Kelly said.

"No, not at all," Jessie said, then giggled. "She's shy and soft-spoken. I gave her a few patterns to try with the new material and when she returned the next day, she'd assembled them perfectly. She even showed me a few timesaving tips. She'll be an asset. The only drawback is she can't work a full day because of her daughter's schooling."

"How old is the girl?"

"I believe the child is little but I'm not sure. Anyway, I want someone full time so Piper isn't there alone."

Kelly sat up and stretched. "Where will you be?"

"Most of the time there, but sometimes Desire and I will go to Austin. While I'm in Dallas, I'm going to check out a few boutiques on Black Friday."

"I'm sure Josiah won't mind if you return with a few skimpy souvenirs." Kelly giggled. She could picture Jessie's face bright red.

"No, he won't. I'll return with some ideas for new sexy stuff."

"Good. I need some new stuff to try."

"Going to try it out on Ben?" Jessie asked.

"We'll see. We have to get the opportunity to, uh—"

"Have sex?" Jessie laughed. "Have you had a visitation yet?"

Kelly had a visitation all right, with two men, but that wasn't what Jessie had referred to. In the town's favorite novel *The Visitation*, the hero wore angel wings and visited his love interest while she slept. He whispered into her ears for months. She finally fell for him.

Fortuna men took to sneaking into their sweetheart's bedroom at night in nothing but angel wings. A few had even got caught in their birthday suit and wings at the park, trying to please their ladies. The women of those men were the envy of others in town.

"No feathers, not yet."

"Your turn is coming." Jessie encouraged. "Why don't you come to the store for a visit?"

"That sounds great." Kelly picked up Reba. "I'll see you in a bit."

★★★

Kelly couldn't resist the temptation to drive past the Dungogh house on the way to Jessie's. The uneventful drive gave her time to flip on her favorite station and sing a few songs while trying not to cry. It felt as if she lost a lifelong friend and was attending the funeral.

Recognizing Sandy's car, Kelly pulled into the driveway. There were two parked cars, Sandy's and a blue Charger similar to Ben's.

"Hey, Kelly," Sandy said from the porch. "Come on in."

Befuddled, she followed the path to the door. Sandy held a long metal sign with the word "sold" on it. Kelly's heart sank. She sucked in her bottom lip so it wouldn't quiver. Her eyes filled as Sandy sashayed out to the yard sign and slid it into place. Grinning, the woman nearly skipped back to Kelly. "Come on in," she said again.

"I guess I can say goodbye," Kelly mumbled.

Sandy turned, putting a hand on Kelly's shoulder. "Oh honey, don't you know who bought it?"

"Nope. I don't want to know." She shook her head and tried to blink the tears away.

Through the blur of tears, Kelly noticed a blue ladder. The electrician capped wires near the ceiling.

"Oh!" she gasped. The clean gleaming crystals of the newly polished chandelier caught her focus. A throwback to the glory days, the opulent fixture once more found purpose. It gave the house a new look, as if it had taken a large breath and wanted to keep living. And the light wasn't on yet.

Kelly glanced at the man and found Ben staring down. His eyebrows lifted and jaw dropped.

"What are you doing here? Did the new owner ask you to do handyman jobs?" Kelly asked, unable to think of other reasons.

"Uh, yeah, I'm trying to earn a little extra money so I can take my girlfriend out to the movies." He grinned then returned to work.

"So you know the owner?" she asked, staring into the living room looking for other updates.

"Yep," Ben said with a grunt and snapped the cover back into place. "Known him for a long time. I can do small things like this, but when it comes to the big stuff, like the kitchen or the deck, I'm no good." He climbed down the ladder. He tugged her into his arms and kissed her. "Hey Kel, I need to flip the breaker back on. Stand by this switch and turn it on when I tell you."

She took her position next to the wall switch and waited.

"Okay. Try it," he yelled from somewhere.

Kelly toggled the switch, and the chandelier flicked to life. "Yes! It's beautiful." When entering the house, instead of the dingy walls everyone would stare at the majestic light fixture.

Sandy smiled and clapped her hands. "This is wonderful. This house needed the right buyer and I'm quite confident I've found him." She picked up her large purse and fished around until she pulled out a ball of keys.

"Are all those to this place?" Kelly asked, trying to count them.

"Yes, but I've only used five to get into the house and outbuildings."

"Maybe there's a secret room?" Kelly couldn't help her imagination. She had been inventing stories about the home since her childhood.

"There'll have to be at least a dozen to match all these keys," Sandy laughed, jangling the keyring. "Tell Ben I'll be in the kitchen if he needs me."

Kelly nodded. She stepped under the chandelier and twirled as she stared up at the dazzling crystals.

From around the corner, Ben appeared with a grin and dust streaked across his face.

"Sandy's in the kitchen if you need the keys to lock up," Kelly said.

"I don't need anyone but you," Ben said, pulling her close.

Kelly breathed in his spicy scent and snuggled against his chest. The moment was perfect. She pushed the negative thoughts to the furthest recesses of her mind and savored Ben's touch. Her man in her house.

CHAPTER 24

Ben

CONCLUDING HIS VISIT WITH SANDY, Ben headed to Cole and Piper's small cabin they rented from the owner of the Big Deal ranch. On the porch, Piper sat in a rocking chair with her feet curled under her, reading a novel. She glanced up and waved when he parked.

Ben had to drive cautiously on the primitive road getting to the cabin. Dust coated his low profile car.

"Cole, your date is here," Piper called over her shoulder.

"Pipes, I'd never cheat on you, even with a good-looking guy like Ben." He bent and kissed his wife.

"I don't know," she laughed. "I've seen the way you stare at his gun."

Both Cole and Ben chuckled. "Men are always jealous of my piece and women swoon when they see it," Ben shrugged.

"That I don't doubt." Piper put her feet on the floor and stood. She set the book down and disappeared into the cabin. She returned with a bottle of water for each man and a large bag of chips.

"Thanks, Pipes." Cole started his truck and set the refreshments inside.

Ben climbed in the passenger seat and studied the dash. "I like your new truck. It beats the old one."

"You mean, big and shiny versus small, rusty and beat to hell?" Cole asked. Acquiring the truck had come with a price. The truck had to remind Cole of what he'd lost: his vehicle, house, and his uncle.

The day of the storm, Ben arrived on the scene where they'd found the bodies, a couple from Nockerville and Arlon Topp. He glanced out the side window, hoping Cole wouldn't sense his melancholy.

After twenty minutes of back roads, they pulled off into a gravel drive.

About thirty feet in they encountered a chain crossing the road. A no hunting/trespassing sign hung in the center and swayed with the wind. Cole exited and unlocked a padlock letting the chain drop. He picked up the lock and climbed back in then drove over the chain.

"This is all your land?" Ben asked.

"Yes," Cole said. He gripped the wheel tightly for a second then relaxed.

"Arlon was a generous man."

"Yes, he was." Cole sighed and stared to the right. He slowed and pointed to a knoll in the distance. "See that ridge? That's where Arlon used to live. He had a trailer, but the storm that killed him shredded the thing. We don't really want to build there. Piper wants the house closer to the woods." He picked up speed and turned off into a field. They bumped and hollered until Cole stopped near a row of trees.

He grinned and blew out a long breath. "Don't tell my wife."

Ben laughed. "Why, because she will be mad you went four-wheeling without her?"

"You know her well." Cole started forward again. "This is where we are thinking about building. We'd have to install a septic tank, because we're too far out for sewer. We can put a drive through those trees over there and it'd come out near my mom and dad's place."

"No shit." Ben looked over at the thick wooded area. "Is it a narrow strip of land?"

"Yes, my property is shaped like Oklahoma."

Cole slowed the truck and turned onto a narrow tree-lined lane. The light waned as the trees grew in density and size. The woods opened to a grassy meadow, and Cole turned the truck off. They sat there enclosed by evergreen sentinels. Ben opened his door first. Birdsong along with the symphony of wind swirled through the boughs overhead. The green of the trees created a ring around the flawless blue sky. He breathed in the fresh pine scent. The plush grass grew to his ankles.

"This is a perfect place to pitch a tent." Cole spoke in a hushed tone. "Follow me." He walked with sure steps and a clipped pace, entering the woods on a faded trail. Ben tripped over roots a few times because he kept looking up. The trail turned left then descended. The babbling of water tickled Ben's hearing.

"We're not far now. There's a great spot to fish down here."

"How in the world did you find this place?" Ben asked.

"Arlon brought me here to fish a few times. He'd drive that ol' jalopy of a Jeep of his, and we'd park in the field then haul our fishing gear and beer down here." Cole slowed, and the path widened so Ben could walk beside him. The brook grew louder, and they broke out from the woods. The small creek meandered between medium-sized boulders and the trees.

"This way." Cole motioned up past a two-foot waterfall and around the bend.

Past a car-sized boulder, a deep pool sparkled the reflected sunlight. Fish swam in the clear water. "You can cast from up there or from here." Cole rounded the large rock. On the other side, a nature-made sandstone dock edged into the water.

In the total privacy of the secluded wood, Ben could attempt skinny dipping with Kelly. They could make love on the warm stone after swimming. He rubbed his hands together.

"How deep is it?" Ben couldn't judge the depth.

Cole stroked his chin. "Maybe three feet here, so don't dive in. Out in the center it might be over your head. It depends on the rains."

"We aren't supposed to get rain until Saturday." Ben shrugged his shoulder. "I might not stay that long."

"You can bathe in the stream." Cole spun around excited. "Oh. Piper bought a new shampoo and soap. It's green and safe for the environment. You can try it."

"Green? Not the color," Ben teased.

"Piper's on a kick. She's being all earthy and whatnot. I don't care as long as it works and smells like the old one."

On the way back to Cole's cabin, his phone chimed. At a stop sign, he glanced at the screen and chuckled. He rubbed his face; his cheeks looked sun-kissed.

"Does Piper want to slurp your love-noodle?" Ben teased. The ruddiness of Cole's cheeks deepened and his lips twisted into a wide grin.

"Pretty much."

Ben fantasized about the camping trip, the supplies he needed and how he could pleasure Kelly under the stars. He couldn't stop smiling when he walked in the front door of his home. Indigo reclined, watching TV. He glanced up long enough to catch Ben's goofy grin.

"What's up with you?" Indigo asked.

"I have a date. I need to get my car washed first." Ben glanced at the wall clock.

"Man, why do you go to those cheap car wash places?"

"Maybe I shouldn't get it washed. I'm going fishing on Cole's property out in the woods." Ben frowned and scratched his head.

"Paved roads?" Indigo sat up.

"No roads."

"What?" Indigo stood and faced Ben. "You can't take your car out there; you'll tear it up. You'll ruin your sweet ride."

Ben inwardly chuckled and put his hands on his hips. "I'm going for the weekend, remember? And I have to drive something. Who's going to let me switch vehicles with them for a few days? I guess I could rent an SUV."

"Save your money for that dilapidated shack." Indigo shook his head.

"You can take my truck."

"Wow. Thanks." Ben smiled. "You'll be okay driving my car for a few days?"

"Hell, yeah." Indigo chuckled and dropped to the sofa. A slight grin lounged on his lips.

★★★

Wednesday after his shift, Ben went home and showered. He let the hot water wash away his anxiety about Vaso taking revenge out on Kelly.

Vaso had been released on bail that afternoon. Ben wanted Kelly away from the apartment for a while. Luckily, he'd talked her into meeting him at his place. From there they'd take Indigo's truck to the Dart property.

Ben checked things off a mental list. He had aired out the tent, packed his fishing supplies, sunscreen, bedding and food. Planning this fantasy of hers quickly became something he longed for.

He wanted casual, sensual, and memory making fun. The weekend included a game he had read about in a romance novel. Early that week Ben checked on Kelly at her apartment. He chuckled, remembering her priceless expression when he asked to, "dump all your toys from the magic drawer into this bag."

"Will I see them again?" she had said with a smirk.

"Yes ma'am," he'd assured, then wiggled his brows, "and maybe a few more." She had grinned and grabbed the brown paper bag, returning almost as fast as she'd left.

Ben packed the sack full of toys first thing after he and Indigo traded vehicles. The tent, cooler and fishing pole were in the back of the truck as were the food, firewood and cooking supplies.

He tugged on a T-shirt and basketball shorts. The doorbell rang. He hurried to the door and pulled it open. Kelly stood there, holding a small backpack. She swayed side to side, a shy grin spread across her lips. She wore a cute red bandanna patterned skirt and a plain white tank top, a matching red bandanna holding her hair back. The tank top showed her red bra through the thin material and he swallowed.

Her gaze traveled his body, stopping at his bare feet. "I was just finishing getting ready. Come on in." He held the door, taking her backpack as she passed.

"Do we need this bug spray?" Kelly pointed to the kitchen counter where a small pile of stuff sat in plain sight. The box of bandages might come in handy; hopefully not.

"Thanks," he said, hugging her. "We're going to have fun."

"I can't believe you have the entire weekend off. That was cool of your boss." Her arms snaked around his back and he nuzzled her hair.

"Indigo took a shift for me on his day off. It's nice to have a workaholic friend who likes my car." He slid the supplies on the counter into a bag and picked up her backpack. Indigo's truck had a dual cab. It was perfect for the small bags of stuff they'd need. He double checked he had Cole's key, then locked the front door. They climbed into the cab and the diesel rumbled to life.

"This is weird, being up so high." She stared out the side window.

He drove to Chatwell field, a remote locale but not out of the way. Unfortunately, it was the wrong time of the year to see the butterflies.

"Okay. Time for surprise number one." He cut the engine, exited, and then opened the door for her. She stood next to the vehicle, corralled between the door and Ben. She put her hands on her hips.

"Ben, I can see you're dying to say something. Wipe that grin off your face and tell me." If she would have stomped her foot for effect, he would have laughed.

He felt his lips; yep, that smile was causing his face to hurt. "It's time to strip."

"Strip what?"

"All your clothes."

"My what? Are you crazy? Right here in broad daylight? Anyone could drive by and see us."

"Look around. The road is vacant. There aren't any houses within sight and we're elevated, so if there were deer in the fields we'd see them first. You're sheltered between the door and truck. I'm guarding the opening."

"If we get naked then what? We aren't camping here, are we?" She glanced through the window into the field of milkweed plants.

"I can think of a few things we can do naked." He chuckled when she stepped closer to him and touched his chest. "We'll get back in the car and drive."

"Drive naked?" she asked skeptically. "Isn't it illegal? What if someone sees in?"

"Technically, it's not illegal. Indigo's truck is higher than the average vehicle. They won't be able to see in, plus we're not going very far."

To convince her of his seriousness, he tugged off his shirt and threw it into the cab. Then he stepped out of his gym shoes and then pushed down his shorts. He sprang free. She leaned to touch him but he stopped her. With a wicked grin he said, "Your turn."

CHAPTER 25

Kelly

FINE. IF BEN WANTS TO *play hard to get, game on.*

Kelly unzipped the side zipper, and as it fell the skirt ballooned around her boots. Her tank top hid the little red G-string. She toyed with the hem, pulling it up to show the lace and string side, her belly button, and part of her hip as she twisted sideways. He gasped, and she tossed a coy glance then shook her bottom, tempting him.

Ben's mouth hung open and his hand gripped the door with white knuckles.

Kelly faced him again. Slowly, she shimmied the tank upward, revealing the red bra. The demi cups were half sheer and edged with lace, a Double D Intimates' work of art. She opened the front clasp bit by bit, exposing her breasts. Kelly swung the bra like a lasso and released in into the truck.

To see if he'd lose his cool, Kelly sucked on her index fingers then swirled them around her areolas. He stared bug-eyed but didn't move.

"Impressive control," she said with a wink, then climbed up into the seat and lifted a booted foot to Ben. He removed both boots in haste as if he feared fire. She lifted her hips, and he glided the thong down her legs but once he slid it off one foot, she kicked her leg into the air. The thong hung on her toes. She shifted, offering him the full view of her sweet spot.

"Holy hell, Kelly. I want you something bad," Ben hissed through clenched teeth.

"Are you making me wait until we get there or are you taking me right here?"

"Not yet." His lips pressed into a line as he yanked the thong, balling it in his fist. He slammed the door and hurried to the driver's side.

They drove slowly at first then picked up speed. Approaching a four-way stop, she pointed to a small car opposite them. Ben motioned for the Chevy to proceed. Kelly crossed her arms. Ben waved as the car passed and Kelly giggled. The people couldn't see they were sans clothes.

As they turned, the seatbelt bit into her skin. She never thought she would miss her bra. The lap belt didn't cover her view of Ben's one-eyed wonder worm. It dipped and swayed to the rhythm of the road, hypnotizing her. She reached out to stroke it but only made it mid-thigh.

"I can't touch you," Kelly pouted. "This truck is too big."

"It's probably a good thing," Ben said. His gaze raked her body then snapped back to the road. "I'd hate to crash Indigo's truck."

"Or explain how?" Kelly giggled again.

"We're here." Ben turned the truck onto a dirt road.

"Where's here?" The lane narrowed to tire tracks.

A chain blocked the way and Ben stopped. "This is Cole's property. I'll show you where they want to build." He plucked a key from the cup holder with a grin. Walking gingerly to the chain, he fiddled with the lock.

Settled in the truck once more, his gaze dropped to her breasts, and he swallowed. Unbelted, Kelly leaned toward him and caught his kiss. He pinched her nipple, and she squeaked, not breaking their connection. She reached between his legs, tugging his shaft.

"That feels good, but I don't think Indigo would appreciate the stain." Ben pushed her hand away then drove slowly along the primitive road.

Refastening the seatbelt, she gazed out the windows at the field. Ben followed a set of tracks disappearing into the weeds, veering off. Kelly bounced up and down in the seat. Grabbing the handle above her head, she held on tight. Ben called "yahoo" and did a donut.

It felt weird not having a bra on. The poor girls were getting jiggled all over the place. Kelly had to admit it felt freeing to be without clothes. She shouted along with Ben, loving the adventure. She felt free to be herself with him, and she grabbed his hand.

After he hit the same dip three times, she glanced over and caught him watching her breasts bounce. "Seriously?"

Red-faced, he smiled like a little boy. With a shrug, he slowed. "I like your boobs."

Her core heated, enjoying the power to turn him on. "Again?"

He nodded and stomped on the gas, jerking the wheel. "Yeehaw!"

Ben's gaze mirrored the sway of the twins. After a few donuts with his gaze hardly leaving her body, he stopped the truck, closing his eyes, drawing a ragged breath.

She righted herself. "Are we camping in the field?"

Ben's eyes popped open. "No, why?"

"Why don't we get to the camp and make it?" Kelly glanced toward the west.

"Make it?" One brow raised, he stomped on the gas pedal. They both yelled as they bounded across the field, heading for a line of trees. He slowed again and turned into a narrow, barely a road, trail. She clutched his arm, leaning closer to him. He chuckled again. "Claustrophobic much?"

"It's really tight. This is a big monster truck. How are you doing?" Kelly chewed her lip.

"So far so good, mom," he said concentrating.

Kelly smacked his arm. "I don't think Indigo would like scratches either."

The path opened to a grassy glen; she sucked in a surprised breath. The sunlight shimmered off the fluttering leaves, giving the area a greenish cast. The space was roughly the size of a soccer field but oval.

Ben stopped the truck, this time turning off the engine. She left the cab, stepping on a carpet of cool springy grass. She pranced around to his side then pressed him against the truck, rubbing their bodies together. His lips consumed hers in a needy soul-sucking kiss.

Kelly pulled away breathless. "We're going to sleep here?" she asked, pointing to the trees behind him.

"Under the stars, tangled together, no clothes, all weekend."

"No clothes all weekend?" She chuckled and walked into the field. "Like Adam and Eve."

Ben shook his head and lowered the tailgate. He jumped up and pulled things to the edge. First the cooler and then the tent. He carried the tent to a flat place and unfolded the material. Kelly helped when he asked and together they pitched the tent. As they unloaded the truck, she enjoyed the teasing and flirting.

Nude and free, she rubbed her arm as her gaze explored the dips and contours of Ben's lean body. She should feel weird without her clothes, but instead she felt comfortable and at ease. Ben accepted her, flaws and all.

Ben set up the fire pit. He used an air compressor powered by the truck to blow up an air mattress. Kelly covered the full size mattress with a sheet then added pillows and a quilt while he brought other supplies over. A folded brown paper bag sat on a red cooler.

"S'mores?" Kelly asked, pointing to the bag.

"Better."

Kelly gasped. What was better at a campfire than s'mores? Wanting to find out, she stepped toward the bag.

"Later." Ben held his fishing pole and tackle box. "Come on, you've got to see this."

She followed him to the tree line where a trail disappeared into the shadows. The forest floor was covered with dirt, pine needles, sticks, and probably deer poop. *And he wants me to walk in there?*

Kelly glanced back at the bright orange tent with its bed waiting. She sighed and stepped into the coolness of the shade.

"Don't worry. At the end of the trail there's a surprise."

"Sex on a stick?"

Ben laughed then tripped. "Shit. Watch for the roots."

"I'll watch them." But she stared at his perfect butt cheeks. The path widened, allowing them to walk side by side.

A pristine creek shimmered in the sunlight. Large boulders dotted the water's edge, making sitting places for fishermen and their girlfriends. Upstream a waterfall cascaded down several levels.

"I love the sound of waterfalls," she hummed. "I can sleep here."

Ben continued toward the waterfall and she followed, trying to walk on sand and pebbles, not mud. Ben rounded a large man-high rock and on the other side a pond appeared.

"That's weird."

"Yeah, I'm glad Cole showed me this place, or I never would have found it." Ben set the olive green tackle box on the bank and opened it. "Hope you like fish. That's what I plan on fixing for dinner."

"You need to catch them first." She teased and sat down on the flat sun-warmed rock. She tested the water then stuck both feet in. Ben cast his line and perched next to her. She put her head on his shoulder and sighed. He got a nibble, but the hook didn't set. So they waited.

She watched the water, his crotch, his face, his crotch, and the sky. Finally she offered, "Let me hold your pole." She grabbed his manhood, and he nearly dropped his rod. The fiery way his eyes consumed her, like his insides were burning, and the way he took his pole and jammed in into the mud made her think he had something other than fishing on his mind. He stuck his hand into the tackle box and pulled out a condom, then wiggled his brows. As his palm slid between her legs, his kiss held a promise of more. Whatever he had in store for her she wanted.

★ ★ ★

The firelight played with the shadows flickering over their naked bodies. Reclining on a blanket, her arms behind her head, she stared up at the star-spangled sky. They'd made love only once by the water, but all the flirting and teasing was fun. She reached for him, where he sat on another blanket, with his back against the cooler, and touched his leg.

The fire shifted, sending amber embers heavenward. Ben straightened and faced her. "I have a surprise."

"Another one?" Kelly sat up, a smirk on her lips. "Really?"

Ben retrieved the paper bag. Her gaze caressed his backside. As he turned toward her once more she licked her lips and his manhood twitched.

He sat the paper bag between them. She reached for it.

"Wait." Ben's dark eyes sparkled with mischief.

Kelly paused with her head tilted.

"This is a game. There are objects in here for us to use. When it's your turn you reach in, pick the first one you touch. Don't search around or that'll ruin the surprise. Also, you can use the item up to three times before it's the next person's turn."

Kelly sat up on her knees, trying not to let her gaze stray into the bag. Her heart rate jumped. Rubbing her hands, she asked, "Who goes first?"

"Rock, paper, scissors?" They slapped their fists on their palms three times. Ben kept his fist intact, forming a rock, while she flattened her hand, making paper.

"Yes!" Kelly said, clapping. "I'm going to win."

Chuckling, Ben held the bag high and shook it. She wiggled, rubbing her hands together. Then her hand slithered into the bag and she gasped. "Oh my God." She pulled out the glittering lavender toy. Her brow furrowed, and she held it up with her fingers.

In an announcer's voice Ben said, "Congratulations, Kelly! You picked the magical unicorn dong. What are you going to do with it?" He set the bag aside.

"Am I supposed to use this on you or me?" Kelly cocked her brows upward.

"Either," he said, but handed her a pillow. "Lay back on that."

She swallowed and rested her head on the pillow. Ben leaned forward, a grin tweaking his lips. Butterflies flitted in her stomach. He had watched her before, but she'd been in charge then.

Kelly sucked in a deep breath. Bending her knees, she spread her legs, offering Ben a front row view. She pressed the button, and it vibrated in her hand. She eased it in then slipped it out. His gaze scorched. Twice more she inserted and pulled it out.

Kelly sat up, cross-legged.

"Here, I'll take the toy." Kelly handed the toy to Ben, and he took a wipe and cleaned it.

"Your turn," she said.

Ben reached into the bag and removed a baggie of three grapes. He met her gaze. Heat crept to her face.

"Open your mouth and hold this in your teeth." Ben passed a grape, and she obeyed.

Ben leaned in, covering her mouth with his. He used his tongue to pry the fruit free, then chewed it. A hand flew to her chest as if to keep her heart there.

"Lay back." Kelly rested back on the pillow, her hands behind her head and ankles crossed. Like a golf ball on a tee, Ben placed the next grape on her belly button. His warm breath fanned her abdomen as he licked and nibbled the area before consuming the juicy orb.

Ben rolled the last grape between his fingers, scanning her body. Wiggling his brows, his gaze froze at her legs' pinnacle. She shivered even though her blood felt like lava. He dropped the grape at her apex and without warning dove at it.

Kelly gasped as his tongue lapped at her crevasse. He pushed her thigh, granting him more room.

"Ben," she moaned, thrusting her fingers into his short hair.

"I never knew you were grape flavored," he stated, his whiskers tickling her as he chuckled.

"I love this game," Kelly rasped.

He withdrew. "Your turn," he said, wiping his chin.

Kelly popped upright and stole a kiss. Her hand rummaged in the bag, pulling out a red cone shaped lid. Ben grinned and opened the cooler and handed her the whipped cream.

"It's a good thing we're not lactose intolerant." She giggled, shaking the can.

Her gaze narrowed on his groin. Then she met his gaze, aiming the tip of the can at her nipple. She sprayed, covering the tip. He lunged, smearing the whipped cream and latched on. Kelly arched her back and his hand slid between her legs, probing. One final lick and he pulled away. She whimpered at his withdraw.

"Two more shots."

With another shake, she aimed the nozzle. He licked his lips as she sprayed her crease. He went in a little rough but, damn, he could play her body like an instrument. Her eyes rolled back, and she groaned and writhed under his administrations. The whipped cream long gone, her body shuddered as she climaxed into his mouth.

Winded, she glanced at him and breathed, "Best game ever."

"One more."

She sat up and claimed his mouth again. His kiss made her insides melt into goo. While she kissed him she squirted the can.

"Woody has a hat," Ben said and Woody nodded.

"I think he looks hot," Kelly said, critically inspecting his crotch.

"Literally or figuratively?" Ben asked.

She tilted her head. "Both."

Kelly bent over him, licking the edge, getting every molecule of dairy. She slurped him in like a large hard noodle. He fisted her hair and moaned.

"You better stop. I—wait."

Kelly examined him; she couldn't help swirling around his head one last time.

"Your turn." She shook the bag.

Glancing at the sky, he reached inside and pulled out a small clear cap. "It's the chocolate sauce. I think I'll redeem this tomorrow down by the water. We'll probably need to bathe after we use it."

Kelly's eyes narrowed, and she stabbed him in the chest with a finger. "You just want more time to figure out how to use it."

He licked his lips then leaned and breathed next to her ear, "Don't you know it. You will think about my tongue all night. And what chocolaty goodness awaits."

She giggled. "Promises, promises."

Ben's arms encircled her, pulling her against him. His palms dipped lower, massaging her buttocks the way she liked. She melted against him.

"I love you," he murmured, ruffling her hair.

Kelly sighed, caressing his face. "Thank you for planning the camping trip."

After a while she rolled away from him. "It's my turn."

Kelly reached for the bag, but Ben set it on the other side of him. He edged toward her and she grinned and skittered back. He crawled, and she stood. Then he was chasing her around the campfire. She ran behind the tent and into the darkness of the glen.

"You can't run away, Kelly-bean. I've got a built-in divining rod." Her laughter rang out, but she kept out of his arms reach, dodging two grabs. The third time he caught her wrist and spun her. He pulled her to him. She tried to shoot past, but he wouldn't let go. Giggling, he scooped her into his arms and hoisted her toward the campsite.

She licked his earlobe, and he hissed. "Kelly, you have two options. Make love by the fire or in the tent."

"You choose."

"Fire. It's closer." He sat her down on the blanket and fished in the paper bag. He acquired a condom. With languid eyes she watched him sheath himself. Chest heaving, she crooked her finger. She wrapped her legs around him and he drove hard with pent-up passion. He nosed the crook of her neck; together they worked to reach the crescendo. Heat pooled then erupted, her muscles clenched, and she climaxed. Riding her euphoria, Ben joined her.

After disposing of the used condom, he lay with his head on the pillow, Kelly cuddled up against his chest. He pulled a light blanket over them and they watched the fire slowly die and more stars wink into existence.

They talked about the kids in her class, the people they worked with, the spinster church ladies, Jessie's talented eye for the skimpy, and the speed demons.

Eventually, she found the courage to ask Ben about the Dungogh house. "How do you know who bought the house?"

He hesitated, then kissed her forehead. "I was in the neighborhood, for work, and saw Sandy Beach standing in the driveway waving to a car as it drove away. I knew you liked the house, so I stopped and talked to her." He shrugged and touched her hair, running his fingers through it.

She sighed, playing with the hair around his belly button. She worked her way downward. "Ben?"

"Hmm?"

"I could see us living there," Kelly admitted, closing her eyes.

"Together with a family?"

"Yes. Does that scare you?" Her heart raced, and she wondered if he could feel it.

"Which part? Rehabbing that old house or making babies with you?"

Kelly giggled and turned, placing her chin on his chest. "The together part."

"Hell, no." Ben held her face tenderly. "I can see it too. Us, together for the long haul. Making babies and filling an old house like that relic you love. But honestly, as long as I'm with you, I'd be happy."

Tears welled, and she kissed him. A sweet chaste kiss. "I love you."

He rolled on top of her. "I love you too. Let's practice making babies. You know, for when we try for real so we get it right."

"Oh." Kelly stared at the sky. "I saw a shooting star."

Ben sat up and tugged her into a sitting position. "Make a wish." He opened the cooler and fished out a bottle of chilled wine with a screw off cap. He poured them each a glass. "Let's toast. To your wish. May it come true."

"Cheers." They bumped glasses and sipped.

Kelly gulped down another drink, realizing Ben had already professed her hopes and dreams.

CHAPTER 26

Ben

BEN SAT ON THE EDGE of the stream as tickling rivulets of water ran down his chest and back. The faint smell of chocolate lingered, and he hoped Kelly had washed it all out of his hair. He rubbed his chin with the towel, watching her wash. She dunked under the water then popped above and squeezed her hair. He leaned back on his palms and soaked up the afternoon sun.

It was the last day of their trip, and he wanted to air dry before dressing.

Squawking birds shot out from the trees. The crunching of ground debris made him sit up and turn downstream. He waved his arm, motioning for Kelly to move toward a trio of medium-sized boulders. Wide-eyed, she hesitated, then voices floated over the babbling rapids. The pool was deep enough for her to kneel with her head above the water.

Men laughed. Ben frowned as he grabbed his tackle box and pulled it close. Slowly, he opened the lid and moved the recognizable condom box to the bottom.

Ben slipped his Glock under the towel on his lap.

Downstream, the men stepped into view. Ben's gaze zeroed in on their faces, namely the short lanky man in camouflage. His profile, with a long hooked nose, seemed familiar. When he turned to the larger man, Ben recognized him. He talked in a high pitched voice but turned away, and most of the words became lost in the torrent of the brook.

Ben shifted his gaze to Kelly. She stared at him expectantly and was smart enough to wait for him to signal. His face must have worn a grave expression, since she sucked in her bottom lip and pressed further into the shadow.

"I should have brought more money," the short man whined, kicking the loose gravel along the creek bed.

Ben strained to remember the squeaky man's name. He was an acquaintance of Ricardo Vaso's, and he had a record of minor incidents with the law. Roberto something-or-other.

"You should have seen their faces," Roberto said, reaching his arms up, stretching. His bushy hair stuck out from a John Deere ball cap.

"I would never bet on Ricardo." The second man was beefy with wide shoulders, a double chin, and a deep rumbling voice.

Ben swallowed. He glanced at Kelly, who kept hidden.

The big guy handed Roberto a shotgun then unzipped his pants. He stepped up to the water and pissed into the stream. "Do you think we'll find the wild boar soon?"

Roberto glanced at his phone, frowned, then slipped it into a pocket. When he turned, his profile reminded Ben of a vulture.

It was a miracle they hadn't spotted him yet. It was only a matter of time until his presence became known. He glanced at Kelly once more then pressed his lips together. His priority was to get the men to move along without noticing Kelly. He intended to be quick.

The spring water felt refreshing at first but could turn chilly. Kelly's lips would turn blue. He didn't want her to freeze.

Ben cleared his throat.

Both men turned in his direction. Roberto's jaw dropped open.

"Howdy, boys," Ben drawled. "It's a mighty fine day for fishing, don't you think?"

"Hey," the larger man greeted, stepping closer. His gaze held an amused twinkle. Ben had to look ridiculous with only a towel covering his nether regions.

Roberto scrabbled after his friend. "This here's Ben Moore. He's a Fortuna policeman."

The men's gazes raked his torso and took in his gear.

"Did you come to fish?" Ben asked.

"No, we're hunting." The large man shifted the shotgun.

Ben needed to be diplomatic. He could easily become a victim, and he didn't want to leave Kelly alone with these goons, especially not knowing their intent. The men stopped directly across from him on the edge of the pool. Roberto stared into the water and pointed. "Look at that big ass fish."

"Did Cole Dart give you permission to hunt here?" Ben asked.

Roberto and his friend glanced at each other. "Of course he did," Roberto said, nodding and smiling.

Ben rubbed his face. "I didn't know Cole had others planning to use the property. I'll have to call him to see if any more will be venturing onto his land." Ben opened his tackle box and found his phone.

"You can't get a signal in these woods," Roberto said with a sneer.

Ben held up the phone. "It's a special satellite phone. I have great coverage."

The men glanced at each other again. "Well, you don't have to bother the Darts while they are celebrating the holiday."

Ben lowered the phone, hoping his guests had decided to leave. The big man took a step closer to Kelly's hiding space.

Refusing to look at Kelly, Ben asked, "Who's your friend, Robbie?"

"This is Nick, my ah, my cousin." Roberto tugged on his shirt. "He's in town from California. Too many leftovers. We got stuffed like the turkey then got bored. Too many aunts and cousins pinching my cheeks and wanting to marry me off." He rolled his eyes.

"Why aren't you with family?" Nick asked in a suspicious tone.

Roberto blew out a laugh. "Everyone in Fortuna knows Ben don't have a family."

Ben's eyes narrowed.

"That doesn't explain why he's in the middle of this godforsaken forest."

"Yeah, why are you here? You aren't fishing, you're naked." Roberto's eyes squinted once more, inspecting him.

Ben smiled and rolled his shoulders. "You're right. I don't have family obligations, so I decided to go camping." He stretched. "You just missed the show. I was taking a bath."

"Camping?"

"For days." Ben smelled his underarm. "I was starting to smell ripe."

"Nice towel. Are you alone?" Nick glanced up and down the stream.

Ben straightened the towel covering his groin.

"Pretty pink," Roberto teased and Nick laughed.

"I didn't want to use my good towels, so I took this old one. It used to be red a long time ago. You're right. I can't believe how it's faded." Ben hoped they bought the lie. He prayed the men would get bored and leave.

Without taking his gaze off them, Ben reached for his fishing pole. Neither man reached for a gun, and an awkward silence stretched. He checked the line then cast it. The lure caught the sunlight, and it cut through the water as he reeled it in.

Roberto put his hands on his hips and shook his head. "There are some big 'uns in there. If they get hungry, you'll be set."

Nick nodded then nudged Roberto. "We should get going. Nice meeting you." He held a hand up and waved.

"Same. Enjoy your family time." Ben gave a wave and recast the line as the two disappeared into the woods where they appeared. He glanced at Kelly and met her eyes. She blew out a long breath and moved away from the rock alcove but not into the open. He smiled at her common sense.

After another ten minutes of fishing, he stood up, dropping the towel. He slipped his shirt, boxers, and shorts on then sat back down and fished once more. Something tugged on the line. He yanked it and reeled it in. A wriggling bass tried to escape. After putting the fish in a bucket for later, he motioned for Kelly to come and put on her clothes.

As she swam over, Ben ventured downstream to cross at a shallow part. Hopping across rocks, he examined the woods where Roberto had emerged. He glanced over his shoulder and found Kelly already dressed. She'd cast the line again. She gave him a thumbs up, and he replied with a nod.

I should have put on my shoes. Ben moved through the trees, searching the ground for footprints. He listened and watched for movement. The men had vanished. He paused near the gnarled trunk of a live oak tree. The birds had resumed twittering, and he breathed a sigh of relief and started back to the stream.

When he pushed through the tree line he witnessed Kelly, her feet in the water, sitting holding his rod. A sweet smile rested on her lips. Her cheeks tinged pink from the sun, and her hair was drying with a few wisps floating on the breeze.

The rod dipped, and she grabbed it with both hands. "Holy smoke," she muttered with a yank. A fish came flying out of the water, and she screeched when it landed on her lap.

Ben laughed and jumped on the stones back to her side.

"Nice catch," he teased.

"I know," she said glancing up at him with hooded eyes. "I don't aim to let you off the hook."

He rolled back with a simpleton grin. "I'm not looking to get let go."

"Good."

"Thanks for holding my pole," Ben said, blushing.

Kelly winked. "Anytime. I mean it."

★★★

Ben pulled the door open at the Tease Me Salon and More. Desire Hardmann had called the station and requested he stopped by to talk. He'd put the visit off until after lunch and made sure to leave his cuffs in the car.

The receptionist Gloria Sass glanced up at him with wide eyes. A handset was pinched between her head and shoulder, and she jotted something down on the schedule.

"Thank you, Molly. Yes, you have a nice day too." She hung up and closed the book before glancing at Ben once more.

He didn't understand Gloria; she always looked constipated, but the tone she'd taken with the client had been polite.

She opened her mouth, "What—?" The phone rang, and she gave him an apologetic shrug. "Hello, Tease Me Salon. This is Gloria, how can I help you?"

Again, her tone surprised him. Gloria must not be as crotchety as she let on, or maybe she had a chronic case of resting bitch face. He crossed his arms and watched her print neatly within the small square.

"Officer Moore," Desire called from the hallway. Her penciled brows rose as she scanned his body from scalp to boots. A toothy grin lit her face. "Thank you for coming. Follow me."

The petite woman sashayed down the hallway toward her office. She put an extra wiggle in her sway just for him. Once they turned the corner, she pushed open the office door, exposing a dark-haired woman sitting in a chair. Her hair cascaded over her face, covering it from view. Her shoulders were moving as if she laughed, but from all the wadded tissues on the desk Ben suspected she was upset. Sitting across from the crying woman was Morgan Topp, Fortuna's social worker.

He tipped his hat. "Ladies."

Ben waited as Desire tapped the crying woman's shoulder. She glanced up and sniffed. Her red eyes seemed to see past him. She swallowed and straightened, then her eyes widened. The skin of her face was blotchy and her nose red.

"Hello, Mierda," Ben said.

"Ben, do you know Mierda's situation?" Morgan asked.

"I'm familiar with her relationship with Kelly." He didn't want Mierda to feel betrayed by Kelly. "How can I help you today? I know Rick O'Shea spoke with her husband." He glanced around the small office, noticing that Mierda's daughter wasn't present. His heart sank.

"We wanted to include you." Desire put a hand on his arm. "Her man is no good."

Mierda glanced down at her lap again. "He hit Cali," she whispered.

Morgan reached across the table and squeezed Mierda's hand. "Mierda wants out, and Ricardo threatened her and Cali. She doesn't feel safe."

"She's staying with me upstairs in my apartment," Desire said. "They are welcome as long as she needs a place."

"Thank you, Miss Desire," Mierda whispered.

"Don't you never mind," Desire patted her arm. "I love having y'all."

Ben looked the three women over, honored they included him in their discussion. Vaso could easily find them, and even though Desire's mouth was strong, the rest of her wouldn't be much protection from a jilted lover.

"She's moved out and is homeschooling Cali until the divorce is final. He's fighting it." Morgan said.

"It's dangerous," Ben said, rubbing his face.

"I don't have any money," Mierda croaked.

"Do you have family or friends out of town somewhere?" Ben asked.

Mierda's dark hair swished as she shook her head. "No one. I wasn't allowed to have friends, and he kept me from my family."

Ben grit his teeth and balled his fists. He inhaled deeply, then released it.

"I got a job," Mierda said. Her face lit up. "Jessie Barnes hired me."

Ben's heart warmed. "That was kind of her. I hear her business is booming." He nodded. Then an idea hit him. The Dungogh house had a large yard and plenty of rooms. Ben pivoted and pushed the door closed. He turned to face the women.

"Can I tell you a secret?" he asked in a serious tone. When they all agreed, he took a large breath and blew it out. "You can't tell a soul. Especially Kelly Jo Greene."

CHAPTER 27

Kelly

SINCE THEIR CAMPING TRIP, BEN had been acting different. Not rude or upset, but introspective and tired. She made dinner, and they'd turned on a movie. Ten minutes into the movie Ben had fallen asleep.

Worry gnawed at her. *Is he bored with our relationship?*

Saturday after Ben left for work, Kelly visited Jessie and Piper at the Double D Intimates store. The small stairway opened into the remodeled showroom. The large front windows and overhead lighting made the displays pop. Exposed brick and the painted tin ceiling added to the nostalgic yet modern vibe. A few four-way racks held gowns available for purchase.

Kelly stalked up to a teal spaghetti-strap gown. It was short with side slits. She touched the satiny material and envisioned Ben's reaction to her wearing it. His eyes would light up and a sappy grin would form. He'd point to his tight pants.

"Kelly?"

She jumped, and the hanger dropped to the floor. Kelly covered her heart with her palm. "Piper, you scared me to death." Kelly bent to retrieve the gown.

Piper smirked with her arms crossed. "So that goofy grin you've been wearing came from Ben all along?"

Kelly felt her face. Her cheeks ached from the smile residing there. It only grew bigger when she gave a noncommittal shrug. "Maybe."

Piper's eyes narrowed then she laughed. "Come on into the back. We're getting organized."

Piper's shoes clacked as she walked. Her floral sundress bellowed around her legs with each step.

As Kelly rounded the corner from the sales floor to the work zone, she was stunned. A large metal rack lined one wall. It held several bolts of fabric like a gift wrap dispenser. There were work stations with sewing and serging machines. Jessie sorted a tub with different U-shaped wires. Kelly recognized the under wires from bras.

"Hey girl," Jessie said, glancing up. "Help me find a C cup. It's this color." She held up a wire sheathed in clear plastic with a tiny green sticker on it. They sorted the box, finding three others. "Oh snap, I need to order more."

"I can do that, Mrs. Barnes," a voice said from behind Kelly.

Kelly swiveled around and gasped. "Mierda!" She jumped toward her friend and hugged her neck. "Oh my God. You're alive! How are you? Where's Cali? Are you okay? What happened? Where've you been? I've been so worried."

Mierda blushed at the attention but smiled shyly. "Kelly, it's good to see you." She hugged Kelly again, this time holding on until the tears came.

"I'm sorry. I didn't mean to make you cry," Kelly said, biting her bottom lip.

"I hired Mierda," Jessie said. "She's been working here a few weeks."

Mierda nodded and sniffed. "Mrs. Barnes has been kind to me."

Jessie waved her hand and clucked her tongue. "I'm lucky to have you. You've got some mad sewing skills. You are a blessing, Mierda."

Mierda teared up again, but a smile broke out. "Thank you."

"Mad sewing skills, huh?" Kelly asked.

Mierda stepped back with a shrug. She tucked a strand of her long brown hair behind an ear. "I'll order those wires for you."

"No, that's my job," Piper teased from the doorway. "Why don't you count the others and see if we need any more sizes."

Mierda continued to sort the wire packages while Jessie pulled Kelly over to the fabrics. She reached and touched the shimmery material. There were several solid colors but the contemporary pattern with red, white, and black caught her eye. "I love this, Jess."

"I'm glad," Jessie pointed to another work table. "Look at this lace. Which one do you think would work best?"

Kelly touched the intricate black lace. It was beautiful but stiff. The white was sheer but almost as itchy. Her fingers skimmed the scarlet red lace. It was bolder, almost as if it had been embroidered. It didn't stretch, but it was pliable. "This one." She brought the lace to her face and closed her eyes. "I wouldn't mind this touching my intimate places."

Jessie snorted. "Intimate places? So your hoo-hoo would like it?"

Kelly's lids popped open, and she grinned. "No, I said my coochie *wouldn't mind it*. Not like the other material." She shuddered, imagining the stiff itchy lace next to her skin. "I was thinking along the lines of butt-floss."

Mierda tried to hide her giggles by turning away.

"We can still hear you, you know," Kelly said, putting her hands on her hips.

"Bet you didn't know about Kelly's sensitive booty did you, Mierda?" Jessie asked.

Kelly smacked Jessie's arm and Mierda bent over laughing. Seeing Mierda's face crinkled in mirth cheered Kelly. She hoped Mierda could continue her life filled with laughter and not pain.

"How much butt-floss have you threaded down there to make your cheeks insensitive?" Kelly asked as she nudged Jessie.

Jessie blinked owl eyes before blushing and bursting into another giggle-fit. Tears streamed down her face.

"What're y'all doing to my wife?" Josiah asked from the entry.

Mierda and Kelly glanced at each other. Mierda hid her mouth with her hands and ran to the storefront. Once out of sight, a loud guffaw echoed off the ceiling.

"I'll let Jessie explain," Kelly said, following Mierda. She left Josiah quizzically staring at the tear-stained face of his chuckling wife.

Piper stood next to a table that served as a checkout counter. One of Bunny Hopkin's daughters glanced over Piper's shoulder as she learned the tablet's functions. Mierda had plucked up the feather duster and cleaned off the bottoms of the four-ways. Jessie's business had grown from a small one-woman home-based show to a full-blown store with employees.

Kelly wandered over to the large windows and leaned against the wall, staring out at the street. The small green space in the middle of town had a fountain. A few people crossed through, heading to their destinations. Kids pulled their parents toward The Tin Soldier toy store. A squad car passed and Kelly sighed.

Mierda touched her arm. "How are you and Ben doing?"

Kelly bit her lip. For the first time since she had committed to Ben doubt bubbled up. "I don't know." Hugging herself, she forced her gaze to the street below. "He's been distant lately."

Mierda shook her head. "Don't you doubt his love, Kelly." Her vehement tone made Kelly turn and stand straight. "He is head over heels in love with you."

Mierda glanced away and in a wistful voice said, "He's a good man. He won't let you down." She wiped a tear from the corner of her eye then folded her arms over her chest.

Kelly nodded. She decided she needed to talk with him and be open about her concerns. "Thank you, Mierda. I needed to hear that."

★ ★ ★

Kelly found a space at the end of the full lot and parked. She headed toward the large white building. It had been a while since she'd visited Twin Peaks, the Nockerville country club. Her father had summoned her to lunch. Near the front, she spotted a sporty sedan looking a lot like Ben's. Her heart skipped a beat then went into overdrive. What would her father want with Ben other than to read him the riot act?

She hurried up the steps and through the large wooden doors. The foyer opened into a wide hallway with a tall ceiling outlined with crown molding. The walls were adorned with gilded framed portraits of important people and the fairways. She passed the entries to banquet rooms and turned down the narrower hallway toward the pro shop.

A man held open a door, and she thanked him as she slipped out onto the patio. Scanning the tables, she found her family. Under a red umbrella, her father, Forrest, and Ivy sat with Ben. She sighed and inspected them. Ivy had a hand on Forrest's leg and a serene smile graced her lips. Forrest sipped a drink and leaned forward as if listening to a joke or an antidote. Her father tipped his head in laughter then slapped Ben on the back. Ben stood and her father and brother offered him their hands.

Next thing Kelly knew, she was beside Ben. "What's going on?" she asked.

"Hi, Kelly-bean," Ben took her into his arms in a tight hug. He nuzzled her hair with his nose, breathing in deeply. "You smell good."

She closed her eyes and relaxed against him. Her stomach fluttered, and she longed to sing. "That didn't answer my question."

"I played golf with Colin and your father today," he smirked.

She pushed back to inspect his face. Her eyes narrowed. "Work, huh?"

He shrugged then kissed her nose.

Forrest cleared his throat. Kelly blushed and turned. "What are you doing here?"

Forrest pointed to himself. "Me? Dad's buying. I'm here for the free food."

"I'm here so I don't have to cook," Ivy chimed in.

"I need to head out for real work." Ben squeezed her gently, capturing her attention once more.

Kelly tried not to, but she knew her lip stuck out in a pout. "Don't go yet," she whispered.

"Not yet. I need to do this first." Ben tipped her head and his lips claimed hers. Her arms circled his waist, and she pulled him tightly against her. He teased her lips, and she opened for him. His fingers entangled with her hair, holding her in place. She forgot they stood in the middle of the country club's outside dining area with a front row view for her family.

Everything fell away. Only Ben existed, his body claiming hers. She heated, wanting time to stop.

He ended the kiss and stepped back, but she kept her head tilted toward him. Tempting him, yes but needy and craving more.

"Bravo!" Forrest started clapping and soon others joined in.

Kelly squeaked and covered her face. Ben pulled out a chair for her and she sat. He leaned and kissed her on the cheek. "I'll see you tonight."

She nodded. "Promise?"

"You have my word." He winked and was gone.

Kelly relaxed back into her chair. She examined each member of her family. Her father had pink cheeks and smirked, while her brother tried to hide a cheesy grin. "What?" she asked him.

"Nothing." But his smile only grew.

Her family remained silent, and she drummed her fingers on the table. Something was amiss. Her father's hasty lunch summons, so out of character for him, and brother and Ivy being present. "Where's Mom?" she asked.

Her dad glanced down at the wrapped flatware while Forrest stared at Ivy. Kelly sat up. "What's wrong?" Her stomach flip-flopped as dire thoughts scrolled through her brain.

"Nothing." Her father echoed Forrest. "Your mother is fine."

"Okay. What's going on?" She crossed her arms.

Her dad sputtered over his words, a sure sign of being caught.

"Don't worry about Kelly," Ivy said. All heads glanced at her. She rubbed Forrest's leg again. "She already knows."

Forrest swallowed. "She does?"

Ivy placed her hand on her tummy and patted.

"Congratulations," Kelly said. She relaxed back now, understanding why her mother wasn't present. She would flutter over Ivy and want to plan showers and visit the doctor with her. "So when's your due date?"

Her father had a fish-like expression, and his voice gurgled. Forrest's brow dipped as he continued to stare at Ivy. "The first week of July."

"Oh, wow," Kelly said, raising her iced tea. "To a safe and healthy pregnancy and baby."

CHAPTER 28

Ben

BEN REACHED IN, TRYING TO get the wrench into the tight spot between the wall and the pipe. His back ached from the awkward position under the sink.

"You should have hired a plumber," Indigo said. He stood near Ben's feet.

"I should have, but I didn't," Ben said, his words sounding muffled in the tight space.

Indigo snorted. "I finished spackling the holes in the parlor. Who the hell has a parlor anymore?"

"Thanks, man." The wrench slipped and his knuckles slammed into the pipe. Ben cursed and crawled out. His scraped knuckles throbbed.

"This place is shaping up." Indigo said, sitting next to Ben on the floor. "You shouldn't decorate too much, should you? Leave the fun stuff for Kelly."

His dry tone made Ben question Indigo's idea of fun. "Don't worry, I wasn't going to ask you to help me pick out sheets," Ben smirked.

Indigo blinked. "Anything but flannel."

Ben laughed and stood, wiping dust off his jeans.

The doorbell rang. Indigo followed Ben to the door. He pulled it open. Mierda glanced at him with wide brown eyes as she held Cali's hand.

"Hiya, Ben," the little girl said.

"Cali, what did I say?" Mierda scolded with a frown.

The little girl glanced at her shoes. "I'm sorry, Mommy. I'm sorry, po-leez man Moore." Mierda nodded, and a faint smile fluttered over her lips.

"Mierda, Cali, welcome to your new home," Ben threw his arm out and

148

moved back, offering them a view of the sweeping stairwell. "Come on in."

Cali pulled a wheeled monkey backpack behind her as she stepped over the threshold. Mierda followed, glancing up at the sparkling chandelier. "Wow, this is beautiful."

"You haven't seen the rest of the place," Indigo mumbled.

Mierda jumped, having not noticed him before. "Oh."

"This is Indigo Black. He works with me at the station." Ben thumbed over his shoulder to his friend.

"I also help him fulfill his delusional fantasies. Like bringing this dump back from the dead."

Mierda rubbed her hand on the banister. "This old lady was once belle of the ball. I can see why Kelly loves it so." She turned in a circle, her eyes taking in the architectural details.

"Feel free to explore." Ben led them toward the kitchen. "I haven't moved in yet, but my room will be on the right at the top of the stairs."

"Where's my room?" Cali asked, shuffling her worn gym shoes.

"Cali," Mierda sternly corrected.

"It's fine. That's a good question. Would you like to see your rooms?"

"Rooms?" She covered her mouth and turned toward her mother. She hopped up and down then took a big breath. She stepped close to Ben and took his hand. "Okay. I'm ready."

The small hand clasped his in utter trust. He stared into Cali's innocent big brown eyes, trying to forget what an asshat her father had been. He smiled and led the parade down the hall to the kitchen. "Over there is the breakfast nook. I have to get a table. Out the sliding doors is a patio. It's uneven, so be careful if you walk outside. This is the pantry," Ben said, pulling open a door. The shelves were stocked with dry goods. "Help yourself."

"That won't be necessary. We can get our own food," Mierda said. Her eyes took inventory.

"I'm not much of a chef. You are welcome to use whatever I have or it might go bad. I'd hate to waste it." Ben pulled the door closed. "Also, if you ever need me to pick something up at the grocery, an ingredient or whatever, I don't mind stopping if I'm near the store. Plus, we don't want you potentially running into you-know-who."

At the end of a short hall past the door to the garage and a half bath was Mierda and Cali's room. The L shaped room, while large, was cozy too. Ben had intended it to be an office but for now it would be a safe house. He'd found a bunk bed with a full for the lower bed. He'd emptied his own night table and dresser and used Indigo's truck to move them. Desire had donated a small loveseat and a coffee table. Somehow he'd fit a kid's desk into the corner near the sofa.

Mierda put a fist to her lips and squeezed her eyes shut. A tear escaped.

She shook her head. "This is—," she croaked. She cleared her throat and tried again. "Thank you for what you've done for me. For us." She walked to the window and glanced out at the yard.

"Mommy, look at me." Cali had climbed to the top bunk. "Can I sleep here?"

"There is the full bathroom," Ben pointed to a door then twisted the knob of another, "and the closet is here. Cali, I think I saw something for you inside."

"Me? Oh!" She scrambled down and flew to Ben's side. "What is it?"

Ben chuckled and reached for the door handle. "Let's find out." He yanked open the door. From the side of a yellow gift bag a unicorn, sporting a rainbow mane, flashed a toothy grin.

"Ah," Cali tiptoed to the gift and tugged on the tag. "It says 'for Cali'." She glanced up with a gummy smile. "That's me!" She clasped her hands together and spun around.

"Open it," Indigo said. He peeked over Mierda and Ben's shoulders.

Cali kneeled and pulled out the tissue paper one at a time, as if savoring the experience. Finally she glanced into the depths and squealed. "Oh my gosh!" She reached in. Her tiny hand retrieved a giant puff of white fur. "Ah, it's a kitty." She hugged it against her and rocked side to side. "I love it."

"There's more," Ben said, then held his breath.

Cali extricated a thick animal coloring book and a box of crayons. "Wow! That's the biggest box of crayons I ever seen." Without dropping the stuffed cat, she ran to Ben and hugged his leg. "Thank you, Ben."

"Cali."

"Ben is fine," Ben said.

Cali lumbered to her new desk and set the coloring book, crayons, and kitty in front of her, then sat in the little chair. She began flipping the pages.

While she colored Mierda paced around the room. "This is very generous of you, Ben."

"What's wrong?" Ben glanced at Indigo, who lingered by the door.

"You've been so good to us. I don't know how to repay you." Mierda sat on the edge of the bed.

"Mierda, you're doing me a favor. I want it to look like someone lives here." He blew out a breath. He needed to keep the rouse from Kelly just a little while longer. "The phone is in the kitchen. My number and others are listed there."

Mierda nodded. "The desk…"

"You said you were homeschooling Cali now." He cocked his head and studied the young mother. The bags under her eyes and her drooping shoulders reminded him he should probably leave them to settle in. He stepped toward the door.

150

"Thank you. We've been going to the library before or after my work. We can walk there."

The Double D Intimates' building was close to the library, but the sidewalk was open in the main part of town. Anyone could see them and it could get back to Ricardo. "Be careful."

Mierda's head tipped up. "We wear hats and different jackets."

The doorbell rang again. Mierda cringed.

"Who can that be?" Ben mumbled.

"That's the plumber," Indigo said. "Come on. I called Rick to fix your sink. He'll do a much better job. It will be fast and won't flood Mierda and Cali out of their new home."

★★★

Ben parked next to the courthouse. He carried a handful of books back to the bookshelf. He placed the pile on top while he searched for new titles. He picked one up. The woman held a riding crop. His heart kicked into gear when he envisioned Kelly posing like that. He pocketed the book and returned to his car.

Driving toward the station, he waved as he passed Mierda holding a skipping Cali's hand.

At the station, tension hung in the air. Indigo ran toward his car. "Ivy just received a call from Walter Mellan. There is a race happening now!"

Ben trailed Indigo. He flipped his lights and sped toward the neighborhood. Indigo, Rick, and Colin all approached the street from different entry points.

Unfortunately, the racers had vanished. Dueling ruts across several yards and through the corner lot of the school had Ben's temper rising. He balled his fists and slammed the steering wheel.

With three of the four squad cars parked in front of the school, kids pressed their faces to the windows. He waved at Kelly's window, thinking he saw her with her arms crossed.

Glancing down the street Ben saw curtains move. Colin spoke with Principal Utzmeld on the school lawn while Indigo took a statement from Walter Mellan. Ben made eye contact with Indigo and pointed down the street.

Ben surveyed the single-story stucco home. As he approached the curtain swayed again. He knocked and no one came. "I know you're in there. I'd like to ask you some questions."

The lock disengaged, and the door opened a crack. A young woman with long bleached hair and a smarmy smile leaned against the jamb in a tank crop top and jean shorts. She lazily rubbed her exposed stomach. "Would you like my number?" she asked seductively.

"Actually, miss, let's start with your name." Ben clicked his pen. After getting her basic information, she begged off knowing about the disturbance. "You didn't hear or see the cars?"

"I like to listen to music loud."

"A beautiful woman like you must have many admirers." He watched as she blushed and looked away, fluttering her lashes. "I'm sure many men try to impress you. Racing could be one way."

"Race? You mean people have been racing here?"

Ben tried to keep his tone neutral. "A little boy was almost run over because of these racers."

The girl threw her hands up and covered her cheeks. "That's horrible."

Ben returned to his car to find Indigo parked beside him. "What do you think about her?" he asked, thumbing toward the house.

"Nothing new." Ben shook his head then rubbed his face.

Indigo pointed at the house, starting at one window then the garage door. "What's your gut say?"

"She's involved somehow."

Indigo now pointed at the front window with the rustling curtains.

"What are you doing?" Ben asked.

"Trying to intimidate her." Indigo flashed a wicked smile. "I spy with my little eye something green."

"The front door?" Ben laughed.

"No, and you have to point."

Ben inspected the home for green items. He raised his hand and pointed to the corner. "The hose?"

"Yes. Your turn."

After a rousing game of I Spy they returned to the station to complete their reports. He looked forward to dinner with Kelly, then he would visit his Victorian house and the hidden family within.

★ ★ ★

Getting into a routine of balancing his work, girlfriend, and house repairs, things progressed with the house in small conquering bits. Cosmetic things he could afford, but big remodels he couldn't do and wouldn't start until Kelly had a say.

Christmas fast approached, and he wanted to help Cali and Mierda have a happy holiday. More importantly, he wanted them to remain safely hidden from Vaso.

There hadn't been a drag race in days, and Fortuna was almost boring.

Ben pushed a file aside and rubbed his temples. His office phone rang.

"Ben, she's gone! I can't find her," Mierda's hysterical voice cried.

"Take a deep breath and slow down. Tell me what happened." Ben stood, waved and signaled to Ivy to listen in.

"Cali's gone. We were sitting at the study tables and I sent her to put a book in the return slot at the library. It's by the main desk and the front door. She never came back, and she's not in the bathroom. He has her." Mierda mumbled other words he couldn't understand.

"I'm coming to the library. Hold tight." Ben grabbed his hat and ran out the door.

He jerked the car to a stop in the parking lot. He hurried toward the library entrance, but on the sidewalk he spotted Kelly. He waved, and she hustled over. It was nearly five o'clock, and she'd been out of class for a few hours and, from the look of the pile in her hands, collecting romance books.

"Where's the fire?" she said with a laugh.

"Cali's gone missing from the library. I'm on my way to talk to Mierda." He glanced at the building, then around the perimeter. "I have an idea—can you go to the Double D Intimates store? That's somewhere Cali and Mierda have been today and it's familiar."

"I don't know why Cali would leave her mother, but I'll check. I'll call you if—when—I find anything." Shifting the books, she placed her small hand on his arm. Her brow dipped. "Tell Mierda we'll find her."

"I love you, Kelly." Ben stooped and pecked her lips. She rewarded him with a smile. "I've got to run, but I need to talk with you tonight." She nodded, and he hurried toward the library. As he pulled open the double doors, Kelly shut her car door. He scanned the area, watching Kelly cross the street. He turned away before the sway of her skirt mesmerized him. He worried Vaso might see Kelly as a target, too.

The door shut, and he lost view of Kelly.

CHAPTER 29

Kelly

KELLY TOOK THE STAIRS TWO at a time. Her chest heaved when she reached the top. Beads of sweat had broken out on her forehead. She glanced around frantically while gulping large breaths.

"Are you okay?" Piper asked, hurrying over.

"I'm looking—" Kelly shook her head, sticking a finger in the air. She sucked in a few more deep breaths. "Have you seen Cali Vaso?"

"Yes."

"Thank God." Kelly sighed and drooped against the sales counter. "Where is she?"

"You just missed Cali and Mierda. They left for the library." Piper glanced at the wall clock, tapping her chin. "You could probably catch them. It's only been a few minutes."

Kelly groaned, doubling over. "Oh, no." She ran to the window and scanned the street.

"What's wrong?" Piper asked, wringing her hands.

"A minute ago, I ran into Ben and he said Cali's gone missing from the library. He asked me to come see if she was here." Kelly sent a quick text to Ben. She bit her lip and studied the parked cars.

"Poor Mierda. It's probably that piece-of-crap Ricardo," Piper muttered, crossing her arms.

"You're right," Kelly mumbled. She narrowed her eyes, spotting a vehicle way down the street outside of Hammered. Abruptly, she swiveled and faced Piper. "Call Desire and get her first pew ladies calling everyone to look for Cali."

"Okay," Piper scurried toward the counter phone.

Kelly ran down the steps and out the door. She hastily crossed the road, looking around her, then toward the car. She slowed and pretended to window shop while inspecting the white Honda. As she closed in on it, movement in the backseat caught her attention. Her heart sank.

The driver had left the windows rolled up most of the way. One more glance down the street. She stilled her heart; there was no one around. She shifted diagonally between the parked Honda and a tall pickup. Cupping her hands, she glanced through the tinted glass.

"Ms. Greene," Cali called, waving.

Kelly gasped. Unusually hot for December, Cali could easily dehydrate and succumb to the heat.

Cali wiggled trying to move the car seat straps off her shoulders but the straps appeared to be wrapped with some kind of tape. The two-door car's backseat was tiny but large enough to accommodate the base of a car seat.

Hold the phone. Jade's car seat is just like that and she's a toddler. Poor Cali is so much bigger.

Kelly shook with anger. She tried the driver's door, but it was locked. "Hold on, Cali."

"Ms. Greene, I'm hot," Cali said, pulling at the strap again.

Kelly dashed to the passenger side. Locked. The window was open a crack. Holding her breath, she squeezed her arm through the tight space. She angled her hand, fingertips touching the lock button. "Come on," she hissed as the glass bit into her bicep. It popped. Grateful for her skinny arms, she opened the door.

A wave of heat rolled over her. Poor Cali.

"Your mommy is sad she can't find you," Kelly said, trying to wedge behind the lowered seat back. The wind blew the door shut.

Cali's face was dewy. "Poppy said she didn't want me anymore." Cali started crying.

"Hey," Kelly touched her little knee. *Unbelievable.* Ricardo, the lying jerk-face. "Your mommy is worried about you. She wants you back and called Ben to find you. Let's get you out of here and go find your mom, okay?"

Cali rubbed her eyes. "'Kay."

Familiar with her niece's harness, she went to push the release button. "Oh, no."

"What's wrong?"

Kelly pasted a smile on her lips. "It's stuck."

Ricardo had wrapped the strap and locking mechanism together with thick blue tape so it would close. He'd made sure Cali was safe but now she couldn't get out without meticulously cutting the tape so it wouldn't ruin the belt or cutting the strap and scrapping the child seat altogether.

Kelly tugged, loosening it.

"Here comes Poppy. He will hurt you if he sees you." Cali whimpered, trying to remove the shoulder straps again.

Kelly sucked in a breath and glanced out the window. Some distance away yet, Ricardo and another man sauntered toward the car. However, Kelly couldn't exit without being seen. She swallowed, noticing a bulge under Ricardo's jacket, a jacket he shouldn't be wearing in the heatwave.

Unfortunately, there was no one else near for Kelly to call and get help.

The glowering men had words, then shook hands. Kelly tried again to pull Cali free but no good. She couldn't let the deadbeat dad kidnap Cali. Mierda would never see her again.

"Cali, you can't talk to me. Can you keep quiet?" Kelly asked as Ricardo pulled open the door. Kelly squatted in the tiny space behind the passenger's seat, praying the men would leave again. Her knees squashed fast food trash as she tried to disappear under the reclined passenger seat's back. She leaned away from his view as he entered.

"Hey Cali," Ricardo said in a sticky-sweet voice. "How's my princess?"

Cali pouted and crossed her arms. "I am not your princess." She kicked her feet. "I'm hot and I've got to tinkle."

Kelly had to shift toward the center when Ricardo's friend knocked on the passenger window then pulled open the door. He sat with a huff and Kelly held her breath.

"I'm going to ride with you to the rendezvous," he said.

"What? Don't trust me, Nick?" Ricardo asked.

"You bet your sweet ass I don't."

Ricardo laughed and started the car. "Have it your way."

The engine rumbled and Cali covered her ears. Kelly raised herself enough to see out of the side window. They passed the Double D store front, and she waved hoping to catch someone's eye. She wanted to shout, then they turned away from the library.

Her heart sank when they left downtown Fortuna. She shifted with every curve. Her legs ached and feet tingled. She bit her tongue when the passenger shoved the seat back.

"You are going down, Ricardo. You better have your money ready," Nick said.

"In your dreams. I won't owe you squat. You and your goons will owe me and I'll laugh all the way to Mexico."

Ricardo stopped, and both men exited. Kelly took a moment to stretch. "Where are they now?" she asked Cali.

"Over by a blue car." She wiggled in her seat. "I really need to tinkle."

"Oh my God," Kelly said, remembering her phone. She sent her location to Ben then snapped a picture of Cali. She angled her phone and took a picture of the people by the other car.

She shifted the trash to the other side and found a plastic knife. She held it up and grinned. "Let's get you out of there."

"Kay." Cali smiled back.

Kelly began sawing on the tape. She worked fast but couldn't apply much pressure to the flimsy plastic. "Come on." One strap came loose. "Yes."

"Here comes Poppy!"

Kelly shrunk into her hole.

Ricardo opened the door and pulled the hood latch. "Arrogant rich Californian, your stock car is no match for me."

With the men gathered around the opened engine, Kelly thought she could finish working on Cali's restraint and hopefully flee the area, but several people grouped around the engine. Men and a few women had flocked to the car.

Kelly froze, else the movement would catch someone's attention. Frustrated, she sighed and hung her head.

"The fat man is getting in the blue car," Cali said, straining her neck. "The peoples got dollars."

The door opened and Ricardo turned the engine over. He mumbled words Kelly hoped Cali wouldn't understand.

"Poppy, I need to tinkle," Cali said, wiggling.

"Not now. First, we need to win this race then we can leave Fortuna for good."

"I don't wanna leave Mommy." Cali kicked her feet and started crying. Kelly recognized the full-blown tantrum.

"Shut up." Ricardo maneuvered the car. It idled a minute. A gun shot startled Kelly. Ricardo floored it, and Kelly flopped on the backseat. She bobbed as he shifted gears,

"No, Poppy!" Cali screamed wide-eyed.

"I told you to shut up." Ricardo growled. Suddenly thumping bass drowned out the little girl's screams.

The car jerked left and Kelly squeaked as her head hit the passenger door. The music covered her noise. A car honk sounded and bounced as if it ran something over. Something hit the side of the Honda. Metal crunched.

Kelly's heart lurched every time something hit the car. She closed her eyes and took a deep breath.

"You aren't going to win, cheater!" Ricardo shouted.

Sirens echoed in the distance. At least, Kelly thought it was a siren.

The car jerked right and bumped off the other car. "Take that, asshole."

Ricardo yelled obscenities and downshifted as he rounded a property, hugging the corner. The tops of trees whizzed by. Kelly closed her eyes and prayed.

Kelly chanced a glance at Ricardo. He gripped the steering wheel with a sneer. His wild gaze flicked from the rearview mirror to the road.

"Son of a bitch, how the hell did the cops find us?" He didn't slow.

With one hand pressing the bench seat and the other against the side, she wedged against the passenger seat back.

"No. No. No. You will not pass me," Ricardo growled. He cursed and once more sped up, ignoring the police. They rounded another corner. "There's the finish. Oh shit. Cops."

The sirens became louder. Ricardo let off the gas. Kelly's head jerked when he slammed on the brake then turned the wheel. Her shoulder smashed into the door. Then he punched it again.

"Po-leez cars!" Cali yelled, pointing to the side.

Kelly chanced a glance out the window. The blue car careened parallel to them.

She reached to pat Cali's leg. The little girl cried. Tears and snot streaked her face. The front of her shirt and pants were wet.

Kelly's thoughts raced. The noise. All the jarring.

Car chases ended with one of those tire flattening strips. The police were the sheep dogs and the racers where the lambs being herded.

Ricardo yanked the wheel again, and Kelly fell over the transmission hump between the seats.

"What the hell?" surprised, he jerked again. "You bitch." The blue car rammed them again. A tire exploded.

The car flew off the pavement into the berm. Cali gripped the straps, her teeth bared. As if in slow motion, the vehicle rolled onto its side, groaning as it bumped down a slope.

Kelly bounced around like a pinball in a pinball machine. Glass shattered. Metal ripped.

The car lurched to a stop, throwing Kelly into the front.

The engine hissed. An acrid scent of burning oil hung in the air. The music continued to thump bass, but it sounded sickly. She lay on her back, her one leg twisted under her, wet warmth trickling through her hair. She rubbed her forehead and winced. Taking a big breath, she groaned. Everything hurt.

"Ms. Greene," Cali whimpered.

Kelly's lids popped open. Cali hung above her. Her tears dripped and hit Kelly's arm. She raised bloody fingers, and Cali touched her fingertips. She tried to move but white stars blinded her. Her foot throbbed.

Ricardo groaned. She couldn't see him. He must have been ejected from the vehicle. Outside she saw shadows and heard voices.

"Kelly!"

Ben? His frantic voice floated over the noise of pain. She swallowed and tried to speak. "Here."

A tingling sensation along her neck. She frowned and tried to shoo it away. "It's the EMTs. Let them assess you." They lifted her shoulders and slid the backboard under her.

"Ow!" Kelly gasped, tears welling. "Get Cali first."

"We can't get Cali until we move you." The EMT Canon Berns said. "Can you tell me what hurts?"

She laughed then groaned. "Everything," she hissed. "My head and shoulder. My foot."

Once out of the Honda, Ben leaned over her with a frown. He picked glass fragments and other debris from her hair and clothes. Kelly took a deep breath of fresh air and winced. A rescuer cut Cali's car seat free and then sawed the straps holding her in. Another EMT took the little girl to the waiting ambulance.

Canon felt the sides of Kelly's neck; she fought the blackness trying to close in.

"Her shoulder is dislocated," Canon said. A slight probing pressure and white stars exploded.

Ben's warm hand held her arm, and he leaned over her. "Stay with me, Kelly."

"I—" then all became silent as a blanket of darkness covered her.

CHAPTER 30

Ben

BEN PACED IN THE HOSPITAL waiting room. The tapping of his shoes on the tile rang in his ears like the ticking of a clock. Every time a door opened he spun, expecting a doctor.

They had rushed Kelly to get X-rays or a CT scan. He wasn't sure which, but her head injury was the primary concern. As he waited, her mother and father hurried up the hall toward him.

"Any word?" Mr. Greene asked, sticking his hands in his khaki pockets.

Mrs. Greene sucked in her bottom lip. She clutched the red strap to her purse.

Ben shook his head and glanced at the tan speckled floor. He found it hard to breathe. Suddenly, arms surrounded him. Mrs. Greene clung to him and she began to cry. When she could muster words she said, "Thank you for helping our girl."

"I wish I could have gotten there sooner," he mumbled, patting her back.

Together they walked toward the seating area at the end of the waiting room. Kelly's father sat and patted the teal vinyl sofa. Mrs. Greene lowered herself next to him.

"Kelly is always trying to help people," Mr. Greene said, rubbing his jaw. "I always said someday someone wouldn't appreciate her help, and she'd get hurt."

Mrs. Greene crinkled her brow and sighed. She turned to Ben. "Kelly has a sensitive heart. When she was young, if another child was alone Kelly would approach them and ask, 'do you want to be my friend?' or 'would you like to play?'"

"Yes, that's our Kelly. She always puts others first," said Mr. Greene, his voice tinged with pride.

"Kelly's the hero," Ben agreed. "She's the one who alerted me to her location. Kelly tried to get Cali out but Ricardo returned. Rather than leave the little girl with that bastard, she opted to stay by Cali's side." Ben rubbed his chin and sunk into a chair across from the Greenes.

Time passed. Turning pages of magazines filled the silence. Mrs. Greene stared at the clock and crossed her arms.

Ben stood, wiping his palms on his thighs. The door across the room burst open. Frantic footsteps made Ben turn as Mierda threw herself at him.

"Thank you for saving Cali!" She shook in his arms.

Toward the door, Ben noticed Andy Felterbush waiting. He dipped his head, acknowledging Ben.

"How is Cali?" Ben asked as Mierda straightened and wiped her eyes.

"She has a few cuts from the glass but they are minor. The nurses say there will be bruising from the seatbelt straps." Mierda waved her arms as she turned red. "What was Ricardo thinking? That seat was Cali's baby seat."

Ben had wondered the same thing. At least her husband had the foresight to use the duct tape, even if the original purpose was to restrain her. It had saved Cali's life.

Mierda quieted and stood still. "Ricardo has internal injuries. They don't know if he'll live." Her red-rimmed brown eyes met Ben's. "I should get back to Cali," she whispered.

"They're keeping Cali overnight for observation," Andy offered.

"That's good. Keep us informed if anything changes," Ben said, holding up his phone.

"Where's Kelly?" Andy asked, his brow pinched.

Ben opened his mouth, but the words clogged his throat refusing to come out.

"She's getting her head scanned," Mrs. Greene replied. "She probably has a concussion."

A woman in royal blue scrubs cleared her throat. "Are you with Kelly Greene?"

Ben's heart hammered, and he sauntered close. Her parents stood and nodded. Mr. Greene took his wife's hand.

"She's awake and if you'd like to see her, you can. Follow me." She motioned for them and turned. Ben waved at Andy and Mierda then fell into line behind Kelly's folks.

In Kelly's room her mother fussed over her, shifting her hair out of her face and handing her water. Her dad held her hand.

Ben caught Kelly's gaze and held it. His chest tightened. Her usually bright eyes appeared dulled by pain. Small cuts peppered the right side of her face. A large gash had butterfly bandages on her forehead. Under the florescent lighting, her skin seemed washed out.

The doctor reported her injuries. Concussion and contusion. Sprained ankle. Stress fractured bones in her foot. Dislocated shoulder. Cuts and bruises.

Ben's stomach churned. If only he could have solved the racing case sooner.

Kelly lifted her hand, summoning him. He took it then bent and kissed the back. Then careful of her wounds, he hugged her, placing his ear over her heart. The steady rhythm thrilled him.

What if I had lost her? He pushed the devastating thought away.

"I'll call Jessie and Piper." Mrs. Greene exited the room as she pulled out her phone.

"And I'll get us some coffee," Mr. Greene slapped Ben on the shoulder.

"How are you feeling?" Ben asked.

"I've been better." She grinned then winced. "Every muscle is sore."

"I'll bet. You tumbled around like clothes in a dryer." Ben held her face in his hands, longing to count every freckle on her nose. "Don't you do anything so foolhardy ever again." He sucked in a ragged breath. "I don't know what I would do if I lost you."

Kelly blinked. "I had to, Ben. I couldn't leave Cali alone." A sly grin appeared, and she asked, "What would you have done?"

He frowned and tweaked her nose.

★★★

Three days later they released Kelly. Out patrolling, Ben stopped by to check on her, his favorite Fortuna citizen. He knocked on her apartment door.

"Ben," Kelly said through the crack. She closed the door to unlock it then pulled it open again.

"Hello, gimpy," Ben teased.

"Hello, handsome," a voice said from behind Kelly.

Ben glanced around to find Desire Hardmann sitting on the sofa with her ankles crossed. "Howdy, Ms. Hardmann."

"Did you stop in to demonstrate the use of handcuffs?" Desire wiggled her brows and grinned like a hungry wolf.

"If you'd like," Ben said, reaching behind and unsnapping the container. He took the cuffs and swirled them on a finger.

"Oh, my." Desire fanned herself and Kelly giggled.

"How are you feeling?" Ben inspected Kelly.

"My foot aches a little." She glanced down to the air cast.

"You should probably sit down," he said, leading her to a chair.

"I was until somebody knocked on my door," Kelly replied with hands on her hips and a wry grin.

Ben blushed and swirled the cuffs again.

"It was worth it. I love a man in uniform," she said. Her gaze scanned him from hat to boots.

"Me too." Desire smiled as she picked up her glass of iced tea.

"I know you talked with Herb about your schedule, but I wanted you to know I spoke with him and our safety team. With the culprits caught and the racing ring busted, the danger for the school has lowered." Ben studied Kelly.

Her nose crinkled, and she frowned. "How was Mia?"

"Who? Oh." Ben recognized the green monster. "Pretty."

Kelly looked at her hands in her lap. Her lip trembled.

Ben continued, "Pretty dull. Pretty annoying. Pretty shallow. You know." He waved his hand. "She's nothing like you, Kelly-bean." He leaned and kissed her nose.

"I like you, Benjamin Moore." Desire wiggled a finger in his direction. "If Kelly didn't have her talons in you deep, I'd eat you up and then swallow."

Ben's jaw dropped and his gaze slid to Kelly, who hid a smile with her fist.

"Uh, thanks. I like her talons."

Kelly tapped her chin. "I might have to eat you up and swallow." Kelly lifted a delicate eyebrow.

Desire's witch-like cackle filled the room. "That's my girl!"

CHAPTER 31

Kelly

BEN OPENED THE PASSENGER DOOR and offered Kelly a hand. She remained seated, staring at the Dungogh house.

"Like it?" he asked.

She sputtered then gave up trying to form words. A large smile broke out on her lips. She took his extended hand, and he pulled her to her feet. One foot still encased in an air cast, she took his elbow and they strolled toward the door.

"I hope you don't mind stopping here," Ben said, glancing up at the decorations. White lights outlined each window, the bow window, the porch, and the strange pointed roof.

"It's nice that the owner is letting you have dinner here, but I guess since you've been helping them fix up the place they owed you," Kelly said. She held the rail and hopped gingerly up the steps. "It looks so festive. I can't wait to see inside."

"Kelly, there's something I need to tell you." Ben stopped her in front of the door. "It's about the house."

Her smile drooped, and she glanced into his eyes. "What is it?"

Ben hesitated then sighed. "Look up." A sprig of mistletoe hung above them.

"Oh, remind me to thank the new owner." She smiled then fisted his shirt, pulling him down to her level and claiming his lips.

Her greediness surprised him and all rational thought melted away. Someone cleared their throat. Breaking contact, he mumbled, "We have an audience."

"Kinky," she whispered against his mouth.

"I think you're turning into Desire Hardmann." Ben stepped back.

"Goals," Kelly grinned.

Mierda opened the door and swept out her arm. "Welcome to the Dungogh Inn, Fortuna's premiere bed-and-breakfast. If you would please step inside, your table awaits." She bowed and closed the door after Ben and Kelly walked into the room.

"So formal," Kelly said then hugged Mierda. "You look pretty tonight. That black dress is sexy."

"Thank you," she said and tucked a strand of hair behind an ear. "You look beautiful tonight. You're glowing. Although it might be all these lights." She giggled and glanced around at all the decorations.

"Oh, my!" Kelly gasped, staring at the banister. "The garland is lit and wrapped like I would have done."

"Really?" Ben grinned, rolling back on his booted heels.

"Check out the tree in there," Mierda said, pointing into the parlor. "Come and see me in the kitchen when you're hungry." She walked away from the couple.

Ben took Kelly's elbow and led her into the room. In the corner, a tall evergreen twinkled with lights. An angel christened the apex. Red bead garland, bows, ribbons, and ornaments decorated it. A scarlet embroidered tree skirt encircled the base. The beading detailed snowflakes.

"It's beautiful." She stepped closer, inspecting the ornaments. Ben held her hand, lacing their fingers. She closed her eyes and leaned against him.

"What are you thinking?" he asked.

Kelly sighed and a sweet smile appeared. "I'm envisioning children opening presents on Christmas day."

"Really?" he breathed.

Suddenly, she twisted in his arms and she asked, "Why is Mierda here?"

Ben tapped her nose. "Good question. The owner gave her a place to stay."

"Oh." Kelly stepped back, her gaze darting around. "That's nice."

"Are you hungry? Would you like to sit down?" Ben asked.

"Sure. Lead the way." She giggled when he bowed and swept his arm ostentatiously.

He pushed open the galley door, and she gasped again. Garland with red berries and lights edged the backsplash. The small kitchenette table had a round burgundy cloth, plates, flatware, and lit white candles. Tiny snowman salt and pepper shakers grinned up at them, even though Fortuna had never seen snow. Hunter green curtains covered the sliding glass window, blocking the view of the back yard.

"This is cozy," Kelly said taking a seat in the chair Ben had pulled out for her.

"I think so too," Ben said, sitting beside her.

Mierda came and filled their water glasses and then set a salad before them. They dined and talked. "What do you want for Christmas?" Ben asked Kelly.

She stared at her plate; her chest tightened. After a moment, she answered, "Nothing." She met his gaze. "I have everything I need."

Ben's expression softened, and he grinned.

"What do you want, Ben?"

His eyes misted, and he blinked back moisture. "You."

Kelly giggled and blushed. "You can have me anytime. You just have to act."

Ben patted his suit jacket pocket. He stood and his cloth napkin fell to the floor. His brow crinkled, he checked his back pockets, turning around.

"What is it? Do you have to go to the bathroom? It's down that hallway," Kelly said, pointing.

Tapping the left breast pocket, Ben smiled. "For Christmas, I want you." He dropped to one knee beside Kelly and presented a small, blue velvet box.

She blinked. Her hands flew to her face, and she gasped. "Oh, Ben." Overwhelmed, she found it hard to breathe.

"Kelly Jo Greene, will you marry me?" Ben opened the box, and a solitaire shimmered. "I never want to lose you. I want to honor and protect you. Kelly, I love you."

She leaned forward and touched his face. Tears streamed down her cheeks, and she nodded. "I love you too. I'd be honored to be your wife."

He closed his eyes and sighed, a goofy grin spreading over his face. He took the ring and slipped it on her finger, then pulled her into an embrace. They stood holding each other until the noise of clapping and catcalls overrode their heartbeats.

Kelly peered through the opened sliding glass door. Mierda had pulled back the curtain, and a crowd filled the back yard. She recognized her parents and siblings, Jessie and Piper and their husbands, Desire, school staff, Pastor Peacock, Indigo, and the police force. With two fingers in his mouth, Leslie Moore whistled. Her niece Jade held Cali's hand.

Kelly and Ben stepped down the stairs into the back yard under a party tent. All the happy faces congratulated the couple as they moved between them. Ben thanked everyone for coming and for sneaking around back.

Strings of lights lined the inside of a large white tent. Toward the rear, appetizers, desserts, and a punch bowl had been set out on tables. Round paper lanterns hung from the ceiling. All the twinkling lights reminded Kelly of a fairyland.

Ben took her hand and squeezed. Kelly turned to face him again. "You got me."

"That was my plan the whole time," he replied.

"You will never lose her if you use handcuffs!" Desire said, wiggling her brows.

Piper elbowed Jessie. "That big goofy grin is back."

Jessie put her hands on her hips. "Oh, my God. It was Ben the whole time, wasn't it?"

Kelly shrugged, her confident smile never faltering. She couldn't agree more. "We were destined to be together. We just had to find each other first."

Piper and Jessie shared a glance and grinned. They converged on Kelly with a group hug, collective "ahs" and then giggled.

"I can take partial credit for helping Ben impress Kelly. At least with food," Les said, slapping his brother on the back.

"Thank you," Kelly said. She tiptoed and kissed Les's cheek.

The large man blushed, rubbing the spot. He swallowed then grinned. "I get a sister out of this deal." He reached his tattooed arms around Kelly and pulled her into a breath-expelling bear hug. She giggled, holding her new brother. Although younger, he was anything but little.

Kelly's state of joy elevated her, and she floated from one person to another. Her cheeks ached from smiling but she couldn't turn it off if she tried.

Ben took her elbow and whispered into her ear. "There's something else for you inside."

"What is it?" Kelly asked as she stared into his twinkling dark eyes.

He chuckled. "You'll have to see."

"Okay." She turned to follow him.

"Not now," he said then he kissed her cheek. "After our guests leave."

"Ben," she said, her curiosity peaked. "Not fair." She stuck out her lip, hoping he would give in to her pout.

He closed in and his lips brushed against her skin as he spoke softly, "It will be worth the wait. I promise."

"Your word is gold," she acknowledged, and begrudgingly turned back to her mother. "Well, Mom, are you happy I landed the hottest man in Fortuna?"

Her mother took her hands. "I'm happy if you are happy. That's all your father and I ever wanted. We are so proud of you." She leaned in and hugged Kelly. Warmth spread as joy filled her soul. Laying her head on her mother's shoulder, she closed her eyes and fought tears.

After most of their guests left, Mierda, Les, Ivy, and Forrest helped clean up the yard. Ben led Kelly inside, back to the parlor. He closed the door behind them. They sat on a tan sofa and he took both her hands in his.

The diamond sparkled and her breath caught as the enormity of her engagement hit her. Tears welled.

Ben tipped her head up. "What's wrong?"

She smiled and wiped her eyes. "Nothing. I'm happy. You chose me."

Ben's chocolate brown eyes misted, and he touched his forehead to hers. "Forever."

"I love you."

Her lips met his, and she opened for him. He swept in and the room's temperature rose. Her hand slid up his thigh, and he moaned. When he broke the kiss, they were breathless.

Ben smirked and stood. She leaned back against the sofa and inspected the fit of his pants. He walked to the elaborately carved mantel. On top sat a wrapped present the size of a shoe box. He picked it up. The silver bow glittered in the light. He handed it to her then sat beside her once more.

"Open it," he said. He leaned forward with his hands on his knees.

"Yes, sir," she replied, tearing at the red gift wrap. She lifted the lid and pulled out a folded paper. Kelly glanced up into his eager eyes then unfolded it. She scanned the document.

"What the—?" she gasped. Forgetting her hurt foot, Kelly jumped to her feet, and the box tumbled to the floor. "This isn't possible." Her hand shook, making the paper rustle.

Ben sat on the edge of the sofa, his hands folded on his lap, chewing his lip.

Kelly spun, her heart hammered and words failed her. From the freshly painted plaster ceiling medallion and walls, to the sanded and refinished hardwood floors, the house was slowly returning to life.

"What do you think?" Ben asked, scooting to the edge of the sofa.

Kelly thrust the paper at him. "How is this possible? I never signed anything."

Ben glanced at his hands while he picked a nail. His face turned red as he said, "Yes, you did. It was in the paperwork after the break in."

"Ben." Kelly placed her empty hand on a cocked hip. "You tricked me."

Ben splayed his hands in surrender. "I didn't want to commit forgery." He swallowed and frowned. "So you don't like it?"

"It's not that. I'm overwhelmed. I can't believe my name is on the deed and we own the Dungogh house." She sunk on the sofa next to him.

Elbows on knees, he rubbed his hands together. "I only wanted to fulfill your biggest fantasy."

She jumped at him, pinning him against the sofa. Laying over him, she said, "It's a dream come true but—" She pecked his lips. "My biggest fantasy has changed."

Ben frowned, and she kissed him again. "It changed to our happily ever after—marrying you and living life together forever."

Ben's smile grew, and he ran his hands up her back and under her shirt. "Let's see if I can make you happy right now." His fingers fiddled with the bra back. "I can't find the hooks."

Kelly smiled. "Jessie gave me something new yesterday. It's a front hook."

Ben moved, careful of her bruises and foot, until Kelly lay under him. He lifted her shirt then hummed.

"I thought of a new fantasy," Kelly said. She placed her palms on his cheeks.

Ben's hooded eyes met hers. "What's that?"

"Making love to my fiancé in our house."

A slaphappy grin appeared. "I'll see what I can do." He took off his suit jacket and started unbuttoning his dress shirt.

"Ben," Kelly said, making him pause. "Do it faster."

He saluted. "Yes, ma'am."

EPILOGUE

Ben stood beside the window and gazed out onto the starlit nightscape. He rolled his shoulders, the harness biting his skin. Yanking the bedroom curtain closed, he turned away and stared at the petite woman swallowed by the king-sized bed. One hand lay flopped above her head on her pillow, making it perfect for him to reach. The gash on her forehead had faded to a barely visible scar.

He fumbled on the dresser for the lighter. Finding it, he lit the jar candle. The soft golden light caressed everything in the room.

Ben climbed onto the bed and kneeled next to Kelly. Her sleepy expression hinted of good dreams with a relaxed smile on her plump lips.

"Your visitation begins now," Ben breathed, reaching and stroking her cheek. Her satiny smooth skin, warm to the touch, called to be kissed. He leaned to her ear. "I love you, Kelly-bean." He placed a chaste kiss next to her ear, then trailed down her cheek to her lips.

Kelly sighed and stretched her arms above her head. "That hum...my turn," she mumbled, not waking completely.

She shifted and rolled to the side, trying to bring her arm under her head but it wouldn't move.

Ben pressed his lips together, stymieing a laugh as her brow crinkled and she pulled her arm.

Kelly's lids fluttered open and she glanced around, tugging her arm again. She stared at the wall and blinked. Slowly, she turned her head and gasped, noticing him for the first time. She shot upright, jerking her wrist again. The sheet dropped, exposing the most exquisite set of breasts.

"Ow! What the hell, Ben?"

She leaned over her wrist and stared. "Handcuffs? You want to use the fuzzy handcuffs now? What time is it, anyway?" She swiveled her head, searching for the time, but her gaze narrowed on the candle then swung toward him. "Oh!" she gasped again, honing in on the wings and his naked torso.

"Are you ready for a visitation?" Ben asked, tilting his head. "If you want to go back to sleep, you can."

"Oh hell no. You are not going to get out of it that easy. I'm ready." Her gaze dipped to his erection. "What do you want me to do?"

"Lay back down, hands above your head." Ben stood and rounded the bed to her side. She complied and watched as he removed the coverings from the bed.

"You've hinted that you wanted a visitation. I haven't ignored you; I was waiting for the right moment to act." Ben climbed onto the bed again.

Kelly's eyes trained onto the long white feather in his hand. "What are you—?"

He fanned her stomach with the feather and she giggled. "To celebrate the city's zoning of our house, I bought the wings."

"Because the bed-and-breakfast has been approved, you're going to tickle me to death?' she asked. The feather whispered over her breasts and she sucked in a deep breath. Her eyes narrowed. "You're no angel."

"You're right. I don't have any angelic plans for you. Muhahah." He rubbed his hands together.

Kelly rolled to the side and opened the side table drawer. She retrieved a balsa wood ruler then faced him, wielding it. "Two can play this game." She struck first slapping his thigh. The light wood didn't sting, but the noise and her assertiveness went straight to his groin.

"You're getting me excited," Ben said, waving the feather. Heat pooled between his legs.

Giggling, she tapped his thigh again.

Ben dropped the feather and fell on top of her. She squeaked and squirmed. He consumed her neck, starting near her ear and heading toward her breast.

Smack!

Ben lifted his head and stared wide-eyed into Kelly's mischievous emerald eyes. His buttocks stung.

"Did you like that?" Kelly smiled alluringly. "I'll do it again, but only when you're in me."

He caught her arm with a devilish glint and held it away while he devoured her breast. She writhed under him, mewling. "Ben, please," she begged.

Ben pushed up then leaned in, sucking her bottom lip. Her tongue darted out, inviting. He pulled back to gaze into her languid eyes, and angled his body. Her lips parted, and he plunged into her. She gasped and moaned, "Ben."

Arching her back, she synchronized with his movement. Ben sought her lips, and their tempo became frenzied. She tightened around him and climaxed. Then crack! She hit his rear again, and he exploded with a groan.

Ben retreated to the bathroom then returned and released Kelly's wrist. He used a wash cloth to clean her then retrieved the crumpled sheet, pulling it over them.

"When we open the bed-and-breakfast we won't be able to make as much noise as we just did," Kelly said, staring at the ceiling.

"This is our house—we can make noise if we want," Ben said, propping himself up on his elbow.

"What if we get honeymooners?" Kelly asked, turning to him.

Ben chuckled. "We are honeymooners."

"Not yet." She reached and touched the harness. "Is that itchy?"

"It is," Ben said, rubbing under the harness.

"Here, let me unhook it." Her fingers grazed his chest, unfastening the hooks.

The wings fell to the bed, and he pushed them to the floor. "Did you like your visitation?" Ben held his breath, hoping he'd exceeded her expectations.

"Yes." She snuggled against him. "I can't wait to tell Jessie and Piper. Wings and handcuffs in the same night."

Ben tried to hide his gasp and stared at the ceiling. The women compared visits? Of course they did or Parker Ford wouldn't be a Fortuna celebrity and his arrest unknown. "Not too much detail, I hope."

Kelly lifted her head, grinning. "No. Just wings and handcuffs. They'll be so jealous."

Ben smiled and put a hand behind his head. His chest swelled, full of love. He'd done good.

The End.

Love a book?

Please leave a review.

Reviews are like virtual hugs for authors

SNEAK PEEK

Municipal Liaisons

Book Clubs, Bureaucracy, and a Ghost.

Who'd have thought Michaela Arschfick would like Texas? Particularly some Podunk town with the mighty Fire Ant as its mascot. But from first glance, Fortuna captivates Michaela. With most of the residents, primarily men, keeping their noses glued to the pages of romance novels, they don't notice it needs a makeover. Michaela takes on the challenge of opening the eyes of City Hall to Fortuna's potential. The longer she stays in the cozy town the more it feels like home, especially with the sexy, young mayor giving her VIP treatment.

After his wife died in a flash flood, the mayor of Fortuna, Texas, Jasen Delay, delved into work. Two years later, he's still wearing the placating smile. In front of the courthouse, he spies an out-of-town entourage. The spring temperature rises like his curiosity. But nothing warms his soul like the beauty who steps out of the van and into the morning sunshine.

Determined to keep their relationship professional, Jasen and Michaela must stymie their blossoming feelings and focus on revitalizing Fortuna's downtown. A nosy newspaper reporter, a perverted prankster, and sightings of Jasen's wife's ghost have Michaela second guessing her choice to stay. Jasen will do anything to keep Michaela in town. Fortuna needs her but, more importantly, Jasen needs her.

With Jasen's help, can Michaela wade through small town bureaucracy, solve the mystery of the canyon ghost, and learn to trust to her heart?

Michaela

The restaurant's door opened and Darren strode in, followed by Rodney. Michaela shrunk into the booth, holding her breath. The men spotted their group and started toward the table, but when Darren saw her sitting with another man he changed direction.

His brow rose and his patented deal-closing smile appeared. Darren attempted to slide in next to her but Michaela wouldn't budge. He balanced precariously on the edge of the seat.

Across the room, Michaela caught Kim's attention. Kim rolled her eyes then pretended to yawn as Rodney and Chase carried on a lively discussion next to her.

"I'm Darren Arschfick, Mick's husband," he said, holding his hand out to shake Jasen's.

"Ex-husband." Michaela frowned and crossed her arms. She hated it when Darren claimed her, especially after he had neglected her during their marriage.

Jasen's gaze jumped from Darren to Michaela.

"So what's good to eat here?" Darren asked, glancing toward the bar.

"Nothing," Michaela said, giving Darren's shoulder a shove. "Jasen and I are going somewhere else."

She shoved again and, frowning, Darren stood. Michaela scooted out of the booth and pushed past Darren with her nose in the air. She hadn't intended to abandon Kim and threw her friend an apologetic smile.

Jasen stood and opened his wallet. He threw a five on the table and followed Michaela out of Hammered. In the sunlight and fresh air, she inhaled deeply.

"I'm sorry. I hope you don't mind?" she asked.

"It's okay." Jasen glanced up the street and pointed. "I know a place with great food. It's a food truck of sorts."

"Of sorts, huh?" She fell in step with his long strides as they headed away from Fortuna's central square.

"It's more of a wagon." He glanced at her. "You'll see."

They walked in companionable silence as she inspected the different Main Street buildings. They passed the steps leading up to the town hall. "Darren wanted to meet with the mayor today. A woman told us he isn't in this afternoon. I thought I might talk to him before Darren. Do you know him?"

Jasen caught his toe on the sidewalk and stumbled a few steps. "Me? Yeah sure, I know him."

"Do you think he would be open to an outside consulting firm cold-calling on him?"

"I suppose," Jasen said, rubbing his chin.

If she could get inside information before her ex, she'd really make him irate. Michaela smirked. "What's the mayor like?"

"He's a hot young thing."

Michaela turned toward a skinny, old woman with a cap of dark hair and an ornery grin. Jasen covered his face with his palm.

"He's young?" Michaela asked. Her father could be considered young compared to the woman.

"And hot," the lady reiterated, while wiggling her eyebrows.

"What's he like?" asked Michaela, trying to stymie a giggle.

"He's single." The woman fanned herself.

"Desire Hardmann, let me introduce you to Michaela Arschfick," Jasen said.

"Nice to meet you, Michaela. So why are you interested in the mayor?"

Michaela sighed, glancing behind Desire to where Darren poked his head out of the restaurant. Thank God, they were far enough away that he wouldn't hear the conversation.

Jasen and Mick shared a look before she answered, "I'd like to meet him."

Desire's gaze jumped to Jasen's, then back. "Okay." The old woman shook her head. "Haven't you met him?"

"No, she hasn't," Jasen said, then hastily continued, "We're walking down to Hamish's wagon for lunch. Would you like to join us?"

"Oh, that sounds heavenly. I haven't had Hamish's wiener schnitzel in a long time."

They continued down the street, passing an old fire station that looked abandoned. Weeds grew out of the foundation and window panes were cracked. "Is that building for sale?" Mick asked.

"The building is owned by the city and hasn't been used for anything other than storage since the eighties," Desire said.

Jasen nodded. "Christmas lights. Props for the high school play. Those types of things are stored there."

"That's a shame it's not utilized. It's a neat building." Sadness panged Michaela's heart.

Kim had been on the lookout for a building where she could start a coffee shop. The old firehouse would be perfect.

"It is." Jasen agreed. He led her across the street and a delectable scent had her stomach rumbling.

"Mm. That smells awesome," Michaela smiled at Jasen.

Turning a corner, she spotted a line wrapped around a chuck wagon shaped contraption enclosed in glass. Bags of chips hung on a line like laundry. "Burger's Kraut Wagon" was hand painted in an olde English font on a sign over the window.

Jasen introduced Michaela to an older man, Brad Davidson, and his daughter, Jessie, who stood in front of them in line.

"Brad's in my book club," Jasen said.

"Wait. The book club again," Michaela giggled.

"The men of this town are obsessed with my grandma's books," Jessie said.

"I'm waiting for someone to act out a hero for me," Desire said, staring at Brad. His gray mustache twitched.

Michaela spotted a man in camouflage pants sitting on a bench some distance from the wagon. He stared away from the people. Something about him made her suspect he was homeless. Before she knew what she was doing, she stood in front of him. He wore an old tattered T-shirt and a grimy backpack sat between his worn boots. His sunken eyes glanced up when she stopped and stuck out her hand.

"Hi, I'm Michaela," she smiled.

He hesitated, and then took her hand. A thin grin lifted his lips.

"Thank you for your service," she said.

He responded with a stiff nod and pulled back.

"Can I buy you lunch?" she asked.

His features hardened, and he shook his head. "No, thank you."

Michaela didn't want to push her luck or insult his pride so she nodded then returned to Jasen's side.

Desire smiled at the man taking orders. "I'll take the Fortuna fire dog," she said. "Hamish, have you seen the mayor lately? This young lady wants to meet him." She pointed to Michaela, but the man stared open-mouthed at Jasen.

"He's always around, Miss. I'm sure you'll talk with him soon," Hamish said.

Mick nodded, reading the menu. "What do you recommend for a newbie?"

Hamish grinned. "I've got you covered. Just tell me the size."

"As big as I can get," Michaela said, standing on her tiptoes trying to see into the wagon.

"Wow, and I thought I had an appetite for wieners," Desire said, taking the wrapped dog.

Jasen insisted on paying for Michaela's food. She placed a hand on his arm. "Thank you. Let's go sit by that man." She pointed to the homeless veteran.

Jasen carried the food while Michaela held the bottles of water. He sat on one side of the bench opposite the man. She sat between them.

"I hope you don't mind if we join you, Tom," Jasen said.

"No, not at all." Tom glanced away as they unwrapped the sandwiches.

Michaela bit into the sausage style meat with sauerkraut and other toppings. Flavors exploded in her mouth. She hummed as she chewed, making both men chuckle.

The conversation touched on Tom's service stint and then turned to Michaela's family.

"My grandpa was in the army. My dad too. He's a long-distance trucker now. I don't see him much because he travels across the country all the time. He loves the west."

Jasen's thigh rested against hers and as he moved to ball the sandwich wrapper, his arm brushed hers, sending tingles up it. She wished she didn't have to return to traveling companions.

"Thanks for being willing to leave the restaurant. I'm sorry I acted the way I did." Michaela glanced down at the sandwich, embarrassed she'd let Darren bring out the worst in her. She had eaten a quarter of it, but her appetite had fled.

"It's not a problem. I was craving the Kraut Wagon anyway."

She glanced hopefully toward Jasen. "Really?

"Actually, yes, but Darren acted like a conceited jerk. I don't blame you for wanting out of his space."

She nodded and glanced down again. Tears pricked her eyes. "He has a way of sucking all the oxygen from the room."

Jasen's arm fell along her shoulder and he squeezed her against him. Her wounded heart beat faster at his tender touch. She brushed a tear away. "You must think I'm crazy for working with him."

"You must love the work."

Michaela nodded again. "I do." She sucked in a deep breath and raised her head, focusing on the building across the narrow street. "We put plans together to revitalize small towns. We breathe life into them."

"You think Fortuna is dying?" Tom asked.

"No. But there are signs of decay." She twisted to face Tom. "This town has a steady heartbeat. It's crazy, but I feel it. I've never felt something in my gut like this. It's weird and scary."

Tom grinned and glanced over her head at Jasen. "It's home."

"Would either of you like the rest of this? I can't eat any more." She lifted it toward Jasen first.

"Sorry, I'm stuffed," he said, shaking his head.

Michaela lifted it to Tom. He smirked but took it. He made a similar humming sound while he chewed.

Jasen winked at Michaela; she felt her face heat. She wanted to speak with the mayor, but she'd rather spend her afternoon with the handsome stranger, Jasen.

Books by Rochelle Bradley

THE FORTUNA, TEXAS SERIES
The Double D Ranch
Plumb Twisted
More Than a Fantasy
Municipal Liaisons
Here We Go Again
The Playboy's Pretend Fiancée
Cole's New Song

THE FORTUNA DARE SOCIETY
Brad

BOOKS by Rochelle Bradley & CJ Warrant
Pandemonium in Peoria – Boba Book Babes Mysteries 1

BOOKS by Rochelle K. Bradley
Dragonfly Wishes - Dragons of Ellehcor 1
Dragunzel -Dragons of Ellehcor 2
Descended - Secrets of the Fallen 1

ABOUT THE AUTHOR

Rochelle puts an artistic spin on everything she does but there are two things she fails at miserably:

1. Cooking (seriously, she can burn water)
2. Sewing (buttons immediately fall back off)

But she loves baking and makes a mean BTS (Better than Sex) cake. When in observation mode she is quiet, however, her mouth is usually open with an encouraging glass-is-half-full pun or, quite possibly, her foot.

She is a Bearcat, a Buckeye, an interior decorator, and fluent in sarcasm.

In 2008, she decided to get the stories out of her head. Midway through her first novel, hurricane Ike (yes, a hurricane in Ohio) rendered the laptop useless with a nine-day power outage. She didn't give up but continued to pursue her dream.

Rochelle shares her home with a big black cat, an itty-bitty orange tiger kitty, her daughter, her son, and her Prince.

She loves to connect with readers. You can find her on Facebook (search Author Rochelle Bradley), Twitter, Pinterest, and Instagram.

Visit Rochelle's website to sign up for her newsletter to keep up to date about future novels and book signings (RochelleBradley.com).

www.ingramcontent.com/pod-product-compliance
Lightning Source LLC
Chambersburg PA
CBHW011348010726
47493CB00011B/3011